The Karm

Meet George Jackson

George was admittedly beautiful – long blonde hair, sparkling blue eyes and legs that went right up to her neck. At 33, George was single. This, on George's part, was not a conscious choice but merely the result of every once-perfect relationship gone wrong. You see, although George was bright and an aspiring marketing consultant for a fashion house, 'God' had missed out one seemingly vital ingredient: common sense! Worse still, disaster did seem to track George down and strike at the worst possible time.

7.00 a.m. and the Monday morning routine was in full swing. The stereo pumped out Franz Ferdinand – 'well do ya, do ya do ya wanna' – and the smells of soap, perfume and body spray lingered around the clean, but badly unkempt, room. All the mirrors had steamed over from the hot running shower and George resisted the urge to write a childish message with her finger right in the middle of the bathroom unit, the thought bringing back feelings of nostalgia and scribbling 'clean me' on dirty work vans as a child.

'Shit.' The shower had started to leak through the roof again and a puddle of water was forming at the bottom of the stairs. George knew that at some point fixing the damn thing would have to move up her list of priorities, but for today, Karl Jones was going to be in the office and he was priority number one. Ahhhhhhhhhhh... Immediately, thoughts of beaches, sex and scandal ran through her overly creative mind. Karl's muscular shoulders, his sensuous mouth...

CRASH. Letters spilled unceremoniously through the front door, landing chaotically on the hall mat. Immediate frustration flashed in George's eyes as she realised that Postman Jarvis the Zit-Faced Pratt would be knocking at any moment. Slowly, she counted in her mind '1, 2, 3' and without further delay hurdled the stairs gazelle-like and flung open the front door, mild annoyance etched across her face.

'Good morning, Jarvis, and which envelope couldn't you fit through the letter box this morning?' Jarvis was 20 and bore a strong resemblance to an active volcano; his pimpled, flared skin, red hair and bony body did little to build his street credentials. Jarvis licked his lips as his eyes rolled from George's feet up to her chest, where he paused before shifting his gaze towards her face.

'I thought this might be important, Ms Jackson – I didn't want to crease it.' Jarvis was fingering a small white envelope. She grimaced at the thought of taking the letter from him – their hands might touch. Her mind shifted a gear. What if this was Pervy Jarvis's wanking hand? He probably hasn't even washed it... eeeeeeeeeeeew! George quickly snatched the envelope with precise coordination in order to avoid skin contact.

'Look, Jarvis, it's a bill. SEE,' she said, thrusting the envelope inches from Jarvis's face, hissing 'SEE' like a venomous snake.

George lived in a well-maintained detached house in a little close. On occasion, she had heard rumours of wife-swapping and feuding neighbours and so had decided to be friendly but distant. Life was hard enough without adding fucked up neighbours to the list. However, the street was kind of cosy, and once moved in, George instantly felt at home.

Glancing at her phone she noticed the time. 8.10. 'Fuck, SHIT, fuck!' Hastily she snatched up her car keys from a small decorative bowl in the hall along with her work bag and headed for the front door. On the drive stood the trusty grey Ford Escort, a bit of a banger which had definitely seen better days, what with its beaten door panels and flecks of paint missing towards the rear of the car.

'I must change this car,' she muttered and mentally added the car to the long list of things that needed to be dealt with. Thrusting the key in the ignition, the engine quickly roared to life and with it came a screeching noise not unlike the sound one's mum might make when extremely outraged. 'It's the belts,' her father had told her earlier that week. *Fucking belts*, George had thought. *I didn't realise my car had any bloody belts*. Today the noise was unbelievably loud and George's cheeks flushed with embarrassment, the screeching continuing for longer than usual; she knew that upgrading the car would have to come sooner than she had originally planned, and in addition to this, she was sure she was breaking some sort of noise pollution law.

Fiddling with the knobs on her radio, she hiked up the volume and selected a song that best suited her mood: 'I'm Every Woman' by Whitney Houston. Karl Jones had found his way back into George's mind, and an involuntary 'mmmmm' escaped her lips. With an imagination like hers, she was sure she could write for Black Lace. The traffic lights ahead were red and she slowly pulled the car to a halt. Singing loudly now, George lowered her window a little to let in some air, tapping the steering wheel and moving her feet, face contorting to the lyrics of the song. Reaching a key note, George really went for it, visualising her many adorning fans cheering her on, belting out the tune, not holding anything back. Roaring laughter broke out to the left of George, startling her, breaking through the daydream. Her mind often took little holidays from reality. She could just see to the side of her a scruffy old builders' van full of middle-aged men howling as if what they had just witnessed was the funniest thing they had ever seen. She prayed that they had not yet embraced mobile phone technology for fear of appearing in her own YouTube video. Looking directly ahead to avoid making eye contact George acted as if she had no idea what they were laughing and jeering about. The lights eventually returned to green and George was relieved to be on her way. Hugely embarrassing start to the day… *nailed*.

Now in the car park, George showcased how she had become a creature of habit, choosing to park in the same spot every day.

A previous disaster had forced her hand. Whilst on a shopping spree at Marks & Spencer, George had managed to lose her car for 45 minutes. Now, this may not seem like a long time, but when you are stalking a car park, sweating and swearing, people do tend to throw some odd glances your way.

With the car safely parked, George made her way to the front entrance of the elegant office, carved stone adorned the outside, an old building and a remarkable piece of architecture. Whilst the outside maintained all its original features, the inside, by stark contrast, was extremely modern. Through the glass, she could already make out the portly security guard munching on some food. *Jesus, what a fucking waster. How the hell would that man be able to help in a real security situation?* A quizzical expression appeared on her face as she seriously considered the probability of some sort of security threat. No, she couldn't think of why anybody would want to storm the office. Comforted by this thought, she swiped her security card against the electronic reader to gain access through the doors. Her security card picture was hilarious since they had managed to take it with too much light in the background. George, on the day of the picture, had her hair swept back in a bun and the effect of the light made George appear bald.

Exchanging a rushed 'good morning' with the security guard, she sauntered down the hallway towards the department where she worked. Surprisingly, she clocked Karl Jones already sitting waiting for her *at her desk*, flicking through *her* to-do list. *SHIT. Oh God... Would it look bad if I walked back outside and dashed into the loo to make sure that I'm looking my best...? Probably, considering he's just seen me...!*

'Hiya, George.' Karl's eyes twinkled as the corner of his lips curled to form a sexy smile. 'So is it the bikini wax or the fashion shoot that's top priority?' he enquired, eyebrows raised mockingly. At first, George wondered what the fuck Karl was talking about, but then it dawned on her: occasionally, George would add items to her to-do lists which were not work-related. Her reasoning was that if she read the list often enough, at some point, surely she would actually remember to do them. You know – like gurus who practise positive affirmations.

Karl's smile was hypnotising and George could feel herself drawn to the movements of his mouth. Outrageously handsome, he had a classic Italian look with a toned upper body and great thighs. His black hair had just started to get flecks of grey, and at 38, this man was actually improving with age.

'Hi, Karl – the shoot tomorrow morning. We're all ready to go here.' She nodded politely and smiled in his direction, then suddenly, as if by magic, her mind went totally blank. For a very odd moment, George kind of just stood there without being able to say a word. (AWKWARD.) Karl rose, muscles pressed tightly against the fabric of his shirt.

'Well then, if you have it all under control, I'll leave you to it.' And with that, he immediately turned his back to George, coolly dismissing her in favour of chatting up one of the beautiful receptionists.

Her heart sank just a little and she fumed. *What kind of Muppet am I?* she thought, acknowledging that she had built herself up all morning for this encounter and had managed to blow it in less than two minutes. Okay, she hadn't been counting on him just being sat there at her desk the minute she walked in, but to resort to the antics of a goldfish for one of those minutes was simply inexcusable.

Disappointed with her lack of flirting skills, she turned on her PC and began to make her way through her emails. *I'm not going to work too hard today*, she thought. In all fairness, for the past two weeks, she had worked flat out to get ready for the shoot.

'Urghh.' A large lady cleared her throat and made her way towards the front of the office in an attempt to capture George's attention. On hearing the throat clearing sound, George looked up, and sure enough, her mind started rambling. By nature, George was not a bitch and her mind rambled about the most beautiful of people. *Wow, this lady is really big, size 24, no, maybe 26 – wow, look at her ankles, all puffy, I wonder how old she is... where does she buy her clothes? That tunic is huge – I wonder whether big tits with huge nipples make you a better milk carrier and a more effective mother – suppose the government did a study and proved it to be true, then we would all need to have super-size titties on the NHS... fucking break through, I wonder if there is a government website for suggestions...*

'Urghh.' The lady looked, frustrated, at George. 'What do you think, then?' Her cheeks joggled as she spoke, and it was at this point that George realised her mind had rambled on shamelessly while she had been asked a direct question. Fuck. What was the question?

George, not wanting to look a total flake in front of a complete stranger that she just so happened to work in the same office with, responded confidently in an even tone with 'I think you should do what you think is best. I'm sure you're right.' (Textbook answer from all managers that haven't got a clue what the right answer actually is.)

The woman's face lit up like a pinball machine. 'Thanks for the opportunity – I was hoping you would agree!' As she smiled, the fat from her cheeks heaved up the sides of her face, causing her eyes to all but disappear. George didn't really take notice of her response and was just pleased to have the lady moving away, her presence now a reminder of the fact that George was not always as tuned in as she should be.

The office was a large open-plan room with numerous cubicles weaved up and down, each representing a different area of the business with about nine colleagues appointed to the adjoining booths. George really enjoyed the atmosphere, which was friendly and very fast paced. There was something about fashion and designers that had everyone energetically buzzing around, talking loud and proud. The culture was great and having fun at work was rule number one. It always surprised George when people that hated their jobs would bitch, moan and whine but never really do anything to change their situation – a truly sad daily waste of the 86,400 seconds entrusted to each individual.

With the exception of Karl Jones, the only downside to George's place of work was a distinct lack of eligible bachelors. All the great guys were already taken, the handsome ones were gay and the funny guys still lived with their mums (a very bad sign when it came to selecting a forever partner).

It meant a lot to George to work with such a tight-knit team, the kind that pranks one another and has each other's backs, ensuring that the establishment never truly has control. Her current project meant that she had spent longer than she had liked working alone, so she attributed her mental tardiness demonstrated earlier with the larger lady to her recent lack of human contact. Working with numbers was both isolating and depressing as well as a task that George vowed she would never indulge in quite so much in the future.

Working at speed meant that routines like eating lunch and having a break were surplus to her requirements but great for her waist. Daily project update calls kept her on track and, if anything, needing more time to meet the deadlines. Today was different in that all of her hard work had paid off. Everything was ready to go for the new designer campaign tomorrow and she intended to milk the day for all its worth. Flicking to the internet, it was time to shop, view all her mate's houses via

Google Maps (including her own) and take continuous breaks whilst consuming large cappuccinos and copious amounts of chocolate.

Texts started to arrive from her team to thank her for the small gifts she had eagerly chosen. Each gift had been carefully selected to delight. It was important to George that she look out for her people, and for this recent campaign, they had really pulled it out of the bag. She could never really work out if this was a selfish gesture, as it made her feel really good inside, but the smiles from her team suggested that the thoughtfulness went a long way.

It was 5.00 p.m. and George had achieved very little; it was a relief to finally be clocking off. Being idle was more than just dull – it was completely soul sucking. She swore to never repeat the experience again, not that the pace of her work afforded her many breaks ordinarily.

Portfolio in one hand? Check. Handbag and car keys in the other? Check. George was on her 28th credit card and was shockingly good at losing her most important possessions. Dusting off the crumbs from her blouse, evidence of her earlier gorging, she hit reception, adjusting her handbag strap when it pinched the top of her shoulder. A familiar voice sounded from the direction of the stairs. It was Karl, waving his arms high in the air as he called her name. George's heart began to race. She hadn't banked on seeing Karl again today, her appearance now less than flattering, eight cappuccinos and five chocolate bars in. Without thinking, she pulled in her tummy; Karl would not want to shag a jelly baby.

'I was wondering, George, if you could do me a huge favour and drop me off at the Hill Crest.' Karl was slightly out of breath, holding his chest as he spoke.

'Yes, that's okay,' she quickly replied. Considering that the spit had all but dried up in her mouth, she had coped quite well, albeit with chocolate caked around the corners of her mouth. 'I'm just over there.' She pointed to her Ford Escort. Karl leaned over to take the portfolio case from her left hand, his proximity intoxicating.

'Nice picture,' he remarked dryly as George swiped her security pass to exit the building. George gave a cynical shrug and swiftly lost the photo ID to the depths of her handbag. 'Bad hair day. Bastards wouldn't do a re-print due to cost.' Massive lie because, in fact, they had done *several* reprints. However, if you look awful on a picture, then, in general, a reprint will do you no favours. To escape the hysterical laughter from the security guards, George, in the end, had decided that enough was enough and that she would accept her photo ID as it was.

She opened the car door cautiously, doing her best to move the old McDonalds wrappers and drink cartons beneath the seat, aware now of a stale pong lingering in the air. The interior represented an unloved space, both cluttered and drab, something she currently wished she'd taken more pride in. Karl didn't seem to notice efficiently buckling himself in, giving George the nod to start the car. On igniting, the notorious deafening screech from the belts, a sound that offended without discrimination, defiantly sprung to life.

Startled, Karl brought up his left hand to partly cover his face and his ear as his elbow rested on the side of the car door. *Fuck me*, thought George. *Please stop. Please stop.* She could already feel the droplets of sweat forming under her armpits. Cheeks flushed rosy red, she kept her arms wide on the steering wheel for fear of blotting the dampness onto her blouse, already feeling more Alabama chic than avant-garde. Covertly, she peeked over at Karl – he looked as though she had just taken a giant shit on his face. *Embarrassment* didn't even come close to adequately describing what George felt as she glanced at his pained expression.

Steering the Ford into the Hill Crest car park, the screeching noise had all but stopped and a feeling of cool relief washed over her. She imagined she would now be known as 'The sweaty mess with a crap car' at work. She tentatively turned to face Karl, knowing she would have to politely wish him a good evening or something, words escaping her once again. She was nervous to see what his reaction would be to the noise from the belts. She wasn't wrong to be apprehensive – his face was contorted with disgust. Panic stricken, he was trying to free himself from the seatbelt and gain as much distance as he could between him and the Ford Escort. She didn't think he was going to say anything as he dramatically scrambled to get out of the car but he suddenly paused, holding the door ajar, waited a few moments to collect his thoughts, then mumbled a weak 'thank you' to George, adding 'You really should get that looked into' before turning on his heel and walking away.

'No shit, Sherlock.' George was left with a reality check. What man in his right mind would want to be with her when she screwed up even the most basic of formalities? Why had she said yes to giving Karl a lift? She knew her car was in bad shape and wouldn't ever have considered openly offering to take anybody anywhere, understanding the risk of alienating them forever... *WTF... I need a drink.*

Quick Scoop

Carmen lit a cigarette, puffed for a while, then exhaled triumphantly in George's face.

'You mean to say, G, you let that man in your car? What were you thinking!? He's never going to want to shag you now.'

Carmen was an extremely good-looking woman – tall, slim, with shoulder-length brown hair. Her taste in clothes was exquisite and tonight's getup was no exception – a long golden vest with accessories to match and tailored shorts which perfectly clasped her hips. Carmen and George had been friends since nursery, sharing secrets, jokes and on the odd occasion a boyfriend or two. What she truly loved about Carmen was her thoughtfulness, her elegant calm in all situations and the fact that she was always there for her, day or night.

Carmen could have practically any man she wanted. Wherever they went, blokes would busily swarm around her, offering her drinks and chattering eagerly, doing their best to impress. This noise appeared to irritate Carmen, who just wanted to be with her friends. Her looks were not lost on her but it would take a wonderful man on the inside to win her heart, not some shallow but good-looking chancer with a fake tan.

'Oh, come on, G, plenty more fish and all that.'

Carmen's slim fingers moved along the length of the cigarette before she began to stub it repeatedly in the table ashtray. The trendy wine bar was starting to fill; the volume of chatter had risen considerably, businessmen popping in for a swift one and local girls dolled up to the nines catching up on the latest gossip.

'Look, it's your birthday this weekend. I'm sure we'll have a ball and there's bound to be some totty knocking about in town.' Carmen was gesturing in the air with her hand, palm upward, trying to promote the glass-half-full theory. (Even if the glass did feel half-empty to George, if she was being totally honest – she had spent the previous nine long months dreaming about Karl Jones.)

It was 7.30 p.m. and, eyeing the time cautiously, George made some lame excuse about work and left Carmen to seek refuge at home. Carmen was meeting up with a few of the others and without a doubt would be knee-deep in men in no time… bitch.

After a long, hot soak in the tub, George fought off the urge to indulge with her vibrator, the Deluxe Rabbit, all-singing, all-dancing! Her thought was that it was better to avoid mechanical sex and so she would, by default, work harder at getting the superior, more authentic, kind… so far, this hadn't worked. LOL.

Draping a towel around her wet hair and gathering a robe around her, George set about making a list of essential beauty treatments before her big birthday night out:

1) Self-tan
2) Eyebrow wax & eyelash tint
3) Bikini wax (you never know)
4) Haircut and blow dry

Searching the address book on her mobile phone, George began to make appointments with the relevant parties. However, George wanted to feel like a total DIVA, so she had decided not to opt for her usual St. Tropez tan, which smelled revolting and left her looking like a bog rat with a skin disease. She wanted the more natural booth spray-tan which boasted on its leaflets that it would leave her instantly glowing!

To feel the full benefits, the leaflet advised, the recipient should get the tan two days prior to the big 'day – or night – out'. George dried herself off and got ready for bed. *This weekend is going to be epic*, she thought, smiling to herself. *Karl Jones will be sorry he never snapped me up!*

George's Big Day at Work

7.00 a.m. 'Arghhh!' The alarm quickly woke George from her slumber; half-awake, she jumped across the bed to switch off the offending noise from the alarm. Still a little dazed, she suddenly jolted upright: today was the big day.

Feeling totally proud of herself, George set the volume on the stereo to maximum, and KT Tunstall filled the room. With a skip in her step and a total feeling of power, George got ready for work. Today, she selected a sexier outfit – a black fitted top that emphasised her breasts and tailored low-rise pants – to oversee the shoot. She wanted to feel her absolute best, what with the models hanging around everywhere. With a quickened pace this morning, George was ahead of schedule. Anticipating the leaky shower, she gathered some toilet paper and left it at the foot of the stairs to soak up the expected wet patch. Pleased with her proactive actions, she was ready to leave. She swung the front door open and could see that Jarvis was next door, busy posting away.

Good start to the day. Congratulating herself on missing pervy Jarvis, George set off to get an early start at work.

The shoot was taking place in an old factory building just four blocks from where George worked. The clothes were designed by Jacques Vintage, and this was a rare opportunity for her to get up close and personal with some of the most expensive dresses on the market. The clothes were very glam and the designer house wanted something a bit more unusual this year. They didn't just want to see girls wearing outfits – they were looking for an edge, something that would inspire women all over the world. George hadn't meant for her idea to come out so loud when their usual 4 p.m. flash meeting had turned into a discussion about this year's billboard and magazine strategy.

It was a simple but brilliant idea. The women who were going to wear these clothes would have to be stinking rich, either by marriage or their own accord. Although women have been climbing the corporate ladder, it was clear that men were still dominating the top-paid jobs and that it would continue to be this way for some time yet. George thought that by showing independent women in what were largely thought of as men's roles, she could capture the imagination of women worldwide and there would be endless possibilities. The first action shot of the day would be of a model wearing a blue satin gown with 6-inch stilettoes, holding a fire hose. Other shots would include women chairing board meetings and giving a team talk to some football lads. All the necessary props had been brought in a few weeks earlier. There were 7 different sets within the factory and each had everything installed, down to the last detail. The football changing room had the benches, hooks, lockers, towels… Christ, it even *smelled* like a real changing room.

George had been shocked by the others' reactions to her idea. Surprised that nobody had laughed out loud, she was taken aback by the agreeing nodding of heads. The vote was unanimous! Secretly she was absolutely thrilled and gave out more hours to work than ever before, her passion fuelling her drive.

She could just make out the building coming up on the left. The factory car park was littered with weeds and small potholes, and the white lines which should have indicated the spaces were only just visible. Arriving early meant she could pretty much leave her car wherever she wanted, and without much thought, she turned off the engine and gathered her personal effects. She knew that the entrance was at the side of the building, a big red metal door, battered, with graffiti sprayed all over it. It was heavy so she pushed with all of her strength, an awful scratching sound escaping as she did so.

One might expect to see this building in some B-grade slasher horror flick. The first floor was filled with old machines which had been abandoned to decay, ropes, chains and what can only be described as roadkill. Unimpressed with the factory's inhabitants, George quickly pressed on to take the spiral stairs. The second floor had been cleared of the old factory equipment to make way for the impressive sets. Charles Cunningham, one of the photographers, was already setting up his equipment; a very expensive photographer to book but a true professional and worth every penny. Charles was in his early forties, with very chiselled features, brown eyes, dark brown hair and a masculine frame; an attractive man with impeccable taste in clothes, he likely started off as a model before taking an interest in photography. Sensing her presence in the room, he threw George a smile and gestured with a wave. George responded but continued on towards the end of the room where a makeshift office had been assembled. In the corner of the room, two portable toilets had been positioned – unfortunately, the factory toilets had been closed, as the floor panelling was unstable and deemed unsafe to use. Portable toilets reminded George of festivals, which she loved, so using them was not an issue for her. However, visions of over-demanding models pouting in horror over the toilets flashed through her mind and she could see the toilets creating tension later on.

The makeshift office had a black leather spinny chair which was soft and reclined as her body made contact. Squealing with delight, she spun 360 degrees, a mischievous grin on her face. She also liked to swing on the back of trolleys when she was shopping, something she never saw other grown-ups partaking in. She found this strange, as she embraced her inner child at every opportunity. Her laptop sounded like an aeroplane getting ready to take off. A swirly icon indicated that it was still thinking about the password she'd just entered. She needed today's itinerary before everyone arrived and just hoped that today wouldn't be the day her laptop would give up the ghost. Voices could be heard entering the far side of the room and George knew that within the next 20 minutes the large room would be full of people, the majority with egos the size of the universe. (No, actually, bigger – is anything bigger?)

There were six models attending the shoot, so it was important to get the right look, and Charles did like to change his mind at the last minute. Prop men and company officials buzzed around the room and George could see Karl talking to Hilary Bloom, one of the models, by the football locker set. Hilary was laughing flirtatiously, slowly closing the distance between her and Karl, inching herself into a position where she could whisper into his ear, lips very close to his skin. Before moving away, she gave him a wink and that look which said 'later, baby'. George could not help but feel totally outclassed and jealous.

Hilary was new to the circuit but was quickly becoming a favourite amongst photographers for her ease in front of the camera. Her fresh-faced good looks and long wavy brown hair would have her on the cover of *Vogue* in no time. George looked on as Hilary and Karl exchanged numbers, chatting excitedly amongst themselves. She wished she possessed just an ounce of Hilary's confidence.

Not wanting to let this ruin her big day, George did her Eleanor Rigby and emerged from her desk, smiling, confident and in control. (You know, Eleanor, who paints her face – the Beatles song? ...Never mind.) Sliding over to set one, George commanded everyone into their correct places and Charles Cunningham began to work his photographic magic. Two of the models were bickering and pointing in the direction of the portable toilets. George raised her hand to cover her mouth, a snide cackle brewing in the pit of her stomach. She laughed inwardly, as catty as she knew this made her. It was always the stupidest of things that made her smile.

'George!' Karl barked from behind her, face taught and serious. 'Did you tell Mamma Cass that she could be in this shoot?' He was waving his arm and pointing towards the entrance. George's eyes narrowed as she examined the lady standing just to the side of the door. *Oh my God*, she thought. *It's the woman who was at my desk yesterday.* George desperately tried to recall their conversation to determine what she could have been doing here. Whilst George was thinking, her facial expression must have given her away.

'Oh, for fuck's sake, George, this is for the premier designer house, not bloody Weight Watchers!'

George had never seen Karl so angry before. He was really shouting. Some of the models were giggling and George was concerned that the larger lady could hear what was going on.

'Sod it, George, get her the fuck out of here! Now!'

On that note, Karl started for the far side of the room, taking long strides, barking at some other poor soul on his mobile phone. She could feel what was meant to be the best moment of her career now spiralling out of control simply because she couldn't hold her concentration. Charles Cunningham was making his way towards her. *What now?* Charles leaned over and spoke quietly so just the two of them could hear the conversation. George was amazed by what he was proposing but also relieved and actually quite touched that he would come to her aid like this. Charles wanted to spare the larger lady's feelings and suggested to George that she come back once the major shots had been wrapped up. Jacque's Vintage had some great fabrics in this range and Charles was sure he could pull off something tasteful.

In a very apologetic manner, George explained to Laverne that the photographer was not ready for her yet and rather than have her hang around all day it would be best if she came back at 5.30. *Thank the Lord for security badges*, George thought. The fact that she could say the lady's name when telling her the situation made it all the more feasible. Considering Karl's outburst, Laverne made no mention of it and thankfully was happy to leave and return later. The beautiful Karl Jones was an arrogant pig. She replayed the scene in her mind but could find no justification for his despicable manner. Hilary Bloom was welcome to him, and this was definitely closure for George. The intensity of the episode had caused George to perspire quite significantly and she instinctively knew that it was time for a visit to the little girls' room.

Entering one of the portable toilets, George snatched a piece of tissue paper from the roll and furiously dabbed at her face to remove the excess moisture. The toilets were very basic, with no mirrors, a small bar of soap (which smelled of fish) chained to the wall and that darn tracing paper tissue that your wee just rolls off of; obviously, the inexpensive kind. Straightening herself up, she sighed deeply and left the toilet to go and grab herself some coffee. Walking the length of the room, George could feel everyone's eyes boring through her. Karl had made quite a scene, but was this kind of attention really necessary?

'George,' sang Hilary, 'come here, darling.' Hilary was holding out her compact, smiling smugly like a Cheshire cat. Accepting the tiny mirror, she caught sight of her face – inarticulate pieces of ugly white tissue paper were cemented to her forehead. *Oh my God.* If ever there was a time when George wanted the ground to open up and swallow her whole, this was it. Knocking the tissue away with her hand, George thrust the compact back into Hilary's hand.

'Thanks,' she managed to squeeze out through gritted teeth, and, totally devastated, she turned to seek refuge at the coffee machine. Feeling the models' eyes following her, she wished them all unfortunate cosmetic accidents, faces like Sylvester Stallone's mum and Jacko.

Hilary took great pleasure revelling in George's misfortune, her eyes dark, full of detest, she squeezed George's mishap for all it was worth. Repeating the story to her colleagues, exaggerating the scene whilst pointing at George and laughing. Hilary was self-absorbed and didn't care much for people she didn't think could progress her career and George Jackson clearly fell into that bucket. She would make her life a misery just because she could. She hated people like George, caring, smiley, weak and pathetic – everything Hilary despised, characteristics of 'losers'. She sighed impatiently. The group had lost interest in the gossip and had begun to disperse back towards the sets.

Hilary eyed George resentfully, anger bubbling, feeling somewhat dismissed by her fellow models. She hadn't finished taking the piss out of George just yet. *What was it that vexed her so about this woman who practically fell apart anytime Karl was within inches of her?* She felt a tinge of jealousy and disregarded the thought immediately. She wasn't jealous of George. The woman made an ass out of herself all the time. So what if everyone liked her? That wasn't the way to get ahead in the world. One thing she did know for certain? George Jackson should stay out of her way.

The day had not gone quite as George had planned, on a personal level, and it appeared that the harder she tried to pull off finesse, the worse she ended up coming off. It was a small mercy that there were no other dramas during the shoot – her already bruised self-confidence was not entirely sure it would be able to cope.

At 5.00 p.m., everything was finished. The volume of noise in the room had slowly faded until the only people left were George and Charles.

'Have you ever considered being a model?' Charles enquired, looking directly at George. This was more than she could take.

While she had a sense of humour, being the butt of everyone's jokes for the day had worn her patience dangerously thin.

'Look, Charles, I've had a really shit day. I appreciate what you are doing for me here but I can do without the sarcasm.'

Charles looked baffled, but before he had chance to speak, Laverne was upon them, who also looked confused.

'Where is everyone?' Laverne enquired, concern in her eyes.

George was trying to think fast and was nearly about to spit out the truth when Charles cut in.

'We wanted this to be a special shoot, without any distractions.' His even tone was persuasive and confident. Laverne smiled and was pleased to be getting Charles Cunningham's special attention. By about 6.30, Charles was happy with what he had captured and thanked Laverne for her time. He could tell that something was off with George but judging by the look on her face she didn't want to talk about it. Sensing her discomfort, he smiled and reassured her that she could go home.

'I couldn't – it wouldn't be right to leave you here,' she defended.

'Look, George, a couple of the prop guys are on their way back to pick up my equipment. You should go home, we can take care of this.'

Not needing to be further coerced, George collected her things and mournfully dragged herself to the exit.

Swinging open the side entrance door of the old factory building, George took in a deep breath of fresh air and was grateful for the day to be finally drawing to a close. She scanned the car park through squinted eyes, looking for the familiar Ford

Escort. *Damn. Should've made a mental note of where I parked.* It dawned on her that there was a car right at the bottom of the car park, the same colour and make, but she knew she hadn't parked there. *Curious...* Then a look of disbelief slowly started to impress across George's face. It *was* her car, and to get to the bottom of the car park, it must've rolled, and if it rolled, that meant she must have left her hand brake off (#blondes#can't#drive)! Walking quickly towards the car, George could now make out the four bricks which had been placed in front of each of the car's wheels. Still puzzled, her walk now turned into a slow jog... This couldn't really be happening.

Once at the car, George could see a white piece of paper tucked neatly behind one of the windscreen wipers. Extracting the paper, she began to read the message that had been scrawled in black ink: 'You left your hand brake off and your car has gone into the back of mine. Ring me. Joe'. Looking in the Ford Escort, she could see that the handbrake wasn't on. Making a 360-degree sweeping surveillance of her surroundings to check that the coast was clear, she let out a huge cat screeching scream, kicking the Ford Escort with all her might, uttering a flabbergasted 'FFS!'

Wowzers

The alarm clattered but George was not so eager to get ready for work this morning; she felt like a deflated balloon. Defiantly, she pulled herself out of bed and made her way to the shower. Yesterday's events began to flash through her mind and she wondered if Karl would be plotting with the senior directors to sack her, or, worse still, demote her. Could they actually do that?

Focusing on Karl in her mind, the humiliation began to lift, and in its place, anger started to rise like a volcanic eruption. *Let him try and sack me!* George slammed down the sweet smelling shampoo bottle and left the shower. Scraping her blonde locks back into a bun, she climbed into her tight jeans and a shirt. Dress code was not on George's mind this morning. Instead, she began to rehearse what she would say to that arrogant pig should he try and do anything to jeopardise her career.

Flinging open the front door, Jarvis was teetering on the step and it was all he could manage to do to stop himself collapsing into a heap on the floor. She looked up and noticed how swollen the ceiling had become, and the leaky wet patch on the floor this morning resembled more of a river than just a patch. She didn't have time for this today.

'Jarvis, move,' she barked angrily, jumping into the Ford Escort and starting the engine. Jarvis covered his ears as the screech from the belts cut through the morning's tranquillity. He couldn't understand why anyone would drive a car like that, especially a woman as fine as George.

In what seemed like record time, she pulled into the car park, and she broke one of her rules by not selecting the car spot she usually parked in. Her walk was more of a jog, and on entering the building, the security guard informed George that Ms King, the director of the company, had been down earlier looking for her, raising his eyebrows with a *what the hell have you done* type of look. He told George that Ms King was waiting for her. Not wanting to appear a coward or the least bit out of control, George managed a *WHATEVER* facial expression in return and shrugged, and instead of walking towards her department, made her way up the stairs to the third floor, where Ms King had a corner office. Knocking once and completely ignoring Ms King's PA, George did not wait for a response before she calmly strode into the room. After all, at this moment, George felt like she had nothing left to lose, and if she was going to go down, she was going to do it in her own way (#StubbornAquariusStreak).

Ms King looked surprised and quickly brought the conversation on her mobile phone to an end.

'Drink, George?' Ms King looked disapprovingly at her jeans and added, 'Dress down day for charity?' Before George had a chance to answer either question, Ms King was talking again.

George had never met Ms King before (way above her pay grade!) and took a moment to take in her appearance. She was in her late forties, quite a large lady but dressed very elegantly in a black tailored suit.

'I got the shots through first thing this morning, and I have to congratulate you on a marvellous job.' Ms King was on her feet and walking around the room whilst she spoke. 'I think it was a gamble to use a larger model in some of the shots, but it has really paid off. You see, the company has always produced the same kind of material, skinny girls, wonderful clothes and, for the most part, it has worked; however, we have been slated recently in some of the tabloids about our use of more slender models, given the average size of women these days.' There was a slight pause as if Ms King was drawing attention to her point, in that she, herself, was a larger lady. 'I think this will endeavour to win some points for us. I wanted to personally thank you, and I can see you are going to do well here. You obviously have your finger on the pulse, and these days, that is very refreshing.'

George stood rooted to the spot, amazed, confused and totally chuffed. How had Ms King got hold of the pictures so quickly? Jesus. She owed Charles Cunningham – BIG time.

'George, I do need to get on.' With slight amusement on her lips, Ms King was ushering George towards the door.

'Of course.' She bowed her head and quickly left the room. *Shit, she's not the bloody Queen.* George felt a bit stupid for bowing but nothing today would be able to break her newfound feeling of total euphoria.

Skipping back down the steps like Hayley Mills in *The Wizard of Oz*, George could see Karl Jones talking to one of the sales assistants, and for the first time ever, she really didn't care. *Bring it on, Karl*, she thought smugly, but on seeing George, his reaction was one of triumph and he flashed his sexy grin.

'Why, you little minx,' Karl teased, playing with his words. 'I didn't think you had it in you. Maybe there's a bit more to George Jackson than I originally thought.' He circled George, looking her up and down in an approving manner. 'Of course, I told Ms King that I signed off the idea of using a larger model, so perhaps when I get back from my trip we could grab a celebratory drink together.'

Men like Karl Jones didn't have to wait for a response; they were so used to getting what they wanted. Unfortunately for George, caught completely off guard, the earlier rehearsals had gone completely out of her mind, and Karl had already started up the stairs before she could string any words together. *Damn, damn, damn!* But the smile would not be easily wiped from George's lips, and she continued to beam as she made her way past reception. The assistant Karl had been talking to earlier was greeting a client. Unfamiliar with her, George began to wonder which section she belonged to. *Wow, great calves, bet she works out – I wonder what gym class she attends to get that kind of shape – good bum, too, bet she looks great in beachwear; I wonder if I asked her... no, no, no that wouldn't do, probably think I'm a lesbian or something, but yeah truly great shape.* The sales assistant was now ushering clients towards one of the board rooms. George, aware of her mind's rambling, quickly averted her gaze, hoping no one had witnessed her little mind blurb and accompanying intrusive stare.

The whole episode had worked out fantastically. George would not even have to lie to Laverne, as some of her shots were going to be used. *Laverne is going to be a huge freaking star.* The journey back to her department was most pleasurable, greeting her colleagues like an excitable puppy, doing the Michael Jackson moonwalk, she was coming off a little crazy. George was bursting with energy, sitting down at her desk taking an unusual amount of focus, limbs twitching like electricity lines. Idly she flicked through her emails, and to her surprise, there was one from her mother, who was currently in Greece and a technophobe by right!

Hello Dear

Could you get me my shopping, terrible to fly home to an empty fridge you no darling?

Dad has burnt his bottom dear, very embarrassing, the man can't sit down without fidgeting and complaining.

1) Tiramisu
2) Flora Butter
3) Milk
4) French Bread
5) Fat free yoghurt – plain
6) Apples/oranges/pears
7) Figs
8) Avocado
9) Wine – couple bottles of red
10) Quiche
11) Salad,
12) Eggs
13) Bacon
14) Sausages
15) Ham
16) Cheese
17) Packet of conference pears

And could you pick Bruno up from Olga's darling before I get back, I always like to have him there first thing when I get home.

Oh, and Mrs Egerton is dead, frightful woman, lips were always purple, I did wonder about her health.

Must dash sun to catch

Mum & Dad

X

Jesus, I hate shopping. 'Conference pears'... WTF is a conference pear? George printed off the list and popped it into her handbag. Her mother was like a channel for the dead. She never missed an opportunity to pass on the unhappy news. It would be hard to sit at her desk all day accepting praise from her colleagues over the success of the shoot, but she was sure she could manage it. It was also a good opportunity to congratulate each member of her team to ensure that they knew just how much she valued their efforts. Developing colleagues was something George loved best about her work, giving people the platform to shine and supporting them to be the best they could be.

Retrieving the piece of paper she had found attached to her windscreen wiper the day before, she decided that there would be no better time than now to call Joe. Dialling the number carefully, George cleared her throat. The stereotypes surrounding blonde women drivers were making her nervous, and she was hoping that Joe would settle for her insurance details over the phone. Unfortunately, the phone diverted to voicemail, and she was pushed into leaving her details. *Ball's in your court*, she thought dryly, considering what Joe might look like. She was such a fantasist. Feeling a little ashamed of her desperate imagination, she decided to put her dreams on hold so she could pursue the real thing. This weekend was her birthday and if ever there was an opportunity to score then this was it!

Bruno was her mother's pet Chihuahua – cute fluffy ginger thing that liked to take a dump wherever it wanted. Any time her mother visited, George would have to be on maximum alert to monitor Bruno's swift rounds, cocking his leg over anything and everything in the house. To top it off, the very thought of dog poo, never mind the smell, made George retch, and them temperamental little poo bag things were equally awkward and disgusting. Though, having handled Karl the egotistical pig the day before, George decided that Bruno the Chihuahua would be a breeze. In any case, there were a few more days before the deed needed to be done. All thoughts of dogs and their poo were pushed to the back of George's mind. *Trouble for another day*, she conceded.

What was meant to be an utterly crap day had turned out to be joyous, so thanking Charles Cunningham had completely escaped George's mind, which, for George, was completely out of character, but good things just didn't happen to her that often. Was it so bad for her to indulge in something so positive and successful just this once?

The Booth

The tanning shop was on Brindley High Street and boasted an elegant exterior. Gold letters on the glass advertised the salon's opening hours and telephone number. Pushing the door set off a small beeping noise which attracted the attention of the salon staff to their incoming customer. George always felt a bit ragged in places like this. The girls wore matching white uniforms, their makeup was immaculate and the receptionist's eyebrows had been savagely plucked, with pencil added to emphasise the shape.

'Do you have an appointment?' the young receptionist asked, lips glossed and pouty.

'Eeerm, yes, 7.00 p.m. for the tanning booth,' replied George gingerly, trying to make eye contact.

'Have you been before?' The assistant was gesturing with her hand for George to follow her to the tanning rooms. Before she could respond, the assistant thrust a dog-eared guide towards her chest and started to recite each line verbatim; George could tell she had made this speech many times before... Was it the dullness in her tone or her expressionless face that betrayed her? The assistant started to demonstrate the manoeuvres, which made her look rather like a pensioner body popping. George fought off the urge to laugh and nodded an 'I understand' type of nod. The assistant continued to throw shapes with her arms, pointing at the guide and yawning. George wasn't sure what she found funnier – the body popping or the assistant's sheer disinterest in the presentation. They both sighed with relief as the demonstration came to an end. George bolted behind the booth door as fast she could, letting out a series of chuckles. *Jesus!*

Removing her clothes she pushed the red tan-stained start button and started imitating the positions she had been shown earlier by the glamorous assistant, chuckling inwardly. The spray wasn't unpleasant smelling but did feel slightly unusual as it made contact with her skin, goose pimples forming on her naked flesh. She considered how far beauty had come over the ages, remembering the women with their white painted faces in the old fashioned history programmes her mother had made her watch as a child.

A spluttering noise sounded from the nozzle and a few more gurgling sounds indicated that the spray tan was coming to an end. George cautiously opened one eye, then the other. A smile curled across her lips. *That wasn't half-bad*, she thought. She quickly dressed and was about to unbolt the door when she captured a glimpse of herself in the small silver mirror attached to the back of the door. Along George's eyebrow line, a deeper tone of colour to the rest of her face had set in. She began to rub it furiously, hoping that it might not have yet taken hold, but it was too late. *SHIT, I look like I belong to a tribe! Perhaps Bruce Parry will want to come and live with me.* George had already paid with a voucher, so if she could just get to her car without anyone seeing her, she might be able to use some emergency facial scrub once she got home. Detaching the latch from the door, George walked hastily, head purposefully turned away from the assistants with the hope that they wouldn't see the mess she'd made of her face. She had almost succeeded when the assistant with the large inflatable glossy lips called out to her.

'Ms Jackson, Ms Jackson, are you okay?'

George slowly turned, embarrassed beyond belief, holding her arm towards her brow. 'Fine,' she managed in a not-too-convincing tone. The assistant looked bemused but it was nearly time for her to clock off and the effort of chasing her client who was partially hiding her face like a weirdo was clearly not in her job description. The glam assistant shrugged and turned to her co-worker, tutting loudly. George rolled her eyes and darted through the door, the little bell ringing as she made her escape.

The Bathroom

George studied her tan in the full-length mirror. Legs fine, arms fine, stomach fine, face... AWFUL. The dark line across her brow was now an angry red rash from rubbing and George could no longer tell if the tan had lifted or gotten worse. In need of reassurance, George dialled Carmen, one eye still on the mirror, the other glancing at the keypad on her iPhone.

'Hello?' a sultry Carmen answered, almost singing the words. Carmen was always relaxed and confident which at this point was almost irritating to George.

'Carmen, I'm having a fucking crisis.' George's high-pitched shriek drilled through Carmen's ear.

Carmen quickly told her to calm the fuck down.

'Carmen, it's okay for you! It's my birthday weekend tomorrow and my tan boothy thing has just gone horribly wrong!' George's fingers traced the red line across her brow as she studied her face in the mirror.

'George, how can it be that bad? If you have streaky arms, wear a long top. If it's your legs, wear pants. I'm sure there is a fashion antidote.'

'It's my face,' she replied dryly. 'What do you suggest, Carmen, a fucking balaclava?' There was a moment of silence on the line and then Carmen could be heard in fits of laughter.

'Ha ha I'm sorry George but only you could manage something like this. Is your face streaky?' Carmen managed to ask between giggles.

'No, Carmen, I just have this one line across my brow. I did all the body popping malarkey... Was I meant to raise my brows as well? Jesus!'

A louder shriek of laughter could be heard on the line and George's cheeks flushed as she began to fume.

'What's so funny, Carmen? You *are* meant to be helping me?' Enraged, she pushed the End button, disconnecting the call, as she felt humiliated enough without her best friend's lack of empathy. The phone jingled to life as Carmen quickly phoned her back. *BITCH*, George sourly pouted as she picked up the phone.

'I'm sorry, G, but it does say on the pamphlet to put Vaseline across your eyebrows to stop it resting too heavily there.' Carmen's voice was sincere and she would genuinely want to help because this weekend's piss-up was going to be phenomenal. It wouldn't bode well if the birthday girl didn't turn up. 'I will call round tomorrow see if I can't work a little magic on you.' Carmen lifted her eyes and waited for George's response.

'Okay. I'm sorry for being such a bitch, Carmen, but I was really looking forward to tomorrow. Is 12.00 okay with you?' George was still looking intently in the mirror.

'Fine, G. See you at yours,' Carmen offered reassuringly. They both hung up. George decided that climbing into her duvet would be her only means of escaping the dark tan lines this evening. She was now convinced that she would never marry, never bear any children or even be trusted to have a pet dog. She pictured a lonely funeral with one or two direct family members in attendance and the local church attendees looking on knowingly with expressions that said *She should've avoided the tan boothy thing.*

Big Night Out

A group of 'rescue' friends had gathered at George's house, each offering fresh advice on how best to disguise the killer brows. It was only 2.30 in the afternoon but already a few bottles of wine had been opened 'for inspiration'. Debbie insisted that they come up with a cunning plan. Debbie was in her mid-thirties, a little on the larger side with humour to die for. Debbie was one of those people who didn't mind laughing at herself and was always up for a good time. The last time they had all been out together, Debbie had very nearly got nicked by the police, which had made for a great tale down at the pub over the last few weeks. Carmen was busy fussing with George's hair, framing it around her face, which made it almost impossible for George to see but in doing so had done a good job of covering her brow.

'That's it, Jackson.' Shaz offered a thumbs up to Carmen and George to show her approval. George wasn't sure, but the wine had started to swill around her head, and her body and mind were no longer putting up so much of a fight.

'It'll do,' George managed, a twinkle in her eye. The room filled with a round of applause as Shaz lead the celebration dance, shoulders shimmying from side to side.

Shaz wasn't slim or fat, just had great proportions for her frame. Her short, uncontrollable frizzy red hair highlighted her cheekbones which were dotted evenly with freckles. She lived in a world where everything was wonderful. There was always something positive to be gleaned from a situation. The air always felt lighter when Shaz was around. Somehow, she always defused any tension. Occasionally on nights out, lads would call out 'Ricky' to Shaz, insinuating that she resembled Bianca from *EastEnders*, which, of course, all the girls denied (even though she really did look a bit like Bianca). *Carpe diem* was one of her favourite sayings, and her house was littered with uplifting, inspiring quotes. Her favourite was tattooed across the top of her left thigh in blue ink.

A trademark of Shaz's was to call her friends by their surnames, like a colonel demanding the attention of his troops. It was clearly a sign of affection because only those within their friendship group were awarded this honour. All outsiders were respectfully called by their first names.

Like most women in their thirties, Shaz had her fair share of facial hair. At the corners of her mouth, a very lengthy ginger moustache resided which she would play with, twisting the strands between her finger and thumb. The girls would look on and giggle, but Shaz didn't care. She was way beyond trying to impress people.

The music on the stereo was hiked up a couple of notches as the girls' inhibitions mellowed and spirits began to rise.

'Let's get this fucking party started,' bellowed Debs with a huge grin and a mischievous look on her face.

'Don't leave me alone with her later,' George whispered into Carmen's ear. Debs was renowned for getting people rather pissed and, nine times out of ten, in some kind of bother. Debbie never planned any of this – she was just totally bonkers.

'Let's call a cab,' Carmen suggested dutifully, and all the girls rose to their feet without a glimmer of hesitation. More wine was swiftly poured into each glass and Debs ensured no waste by emptying the last couple of drops from the bottle directly into her mouth. 'Rock on!' she cried, arms raised in the air as if they were about to go into battle. The rest of the girls echoed a drunken 'Wahoo' as they stumbled towards the door – this day/night was going to be incredibly messy.

It was 4.30 p.m. when they reached Tony's Wine Bar and Debbie was already barking orders at the attendant to line up Sambuca shots at the bar.

'Jesus, Carmen, we will be fucking legless before the others even arrive.' George spoke nervously under her breath to avoid being detected by Debs. Any hint of them 'pussying out' in front of Debbie would only make her more determined to get them wasted. The glasses clanged together in the air as a 'happy birthday' toast was chanted and the group knocked back sambuca, all but Debbie straining their faces as if they had just licked a cat's arse.

A second round of more bearable drinks was ordered and Shaz picked out a table where their afternoon session of drinking and debauchery could begin. Retrieving her phone from her bag, Shaz passed round some rather distasteful pictures of women in some rather peculiar positions which she had gotten from some guy at work. Who knew how the conversation had come about? The phone was turned in all different angles as the group laughed and tried to work out was going on. 'Have you seen this one, Jackson?' Shaz pushed the phone into George's face, who instinctively pulled her head back from the image of tangled bodies partaking in some form of sexual orgy.

Anyone entering the bar that afternoon rather wished they hadn't as the girls continued to party hard, talking loudly and drinking far too much, way too quickly, which most men were finding highly intimidating.

Debbie had recently quit her job as a telesales representative at Barclays and was studying to become a teaching assistant for children with special needs. To fund this new lifestyle, Debbie had taken a cleaning job at one of the local supermarkets, working out of hours for minimum wage. Debbie started to tell her story of the three differently coloured cleaning rags: a red rag for the toilets, blue for the counters on the shop floor and green to be used anywhere near consumer food. Management had told Debbie that if she made it to three weeks, she would earn herself a big purple work fleece and a chewing gum scraper! Debbie laughed out loud and the girls joined in, tickled by her facial expressions and sarcastic tone.

Debs scoffed: '"Housekeeping to aisle 23!" That bloody Tannoy. And it's always the wet food aisles! Smashed Dolmio jars and shit. Have to get down on my hands and knees and use my arms to pull the shrapnel from under the shelves. Not a brush. My arm.' She was enraged and mimicked a screechy, high-pitched voice through gritted teeth. '"Housekeeping to the toilets!" Some bloody big fat dude walks out of the toilet and says to me "I don't fancy your chances, love, with what I've just left in there…" Dirty BASTARD!' Lucy did her best not to spit out her drink, giggling as she imagined Debbie's face confronting an enormous turd.

'A young kid was sick the other day and with the red rag being in the toilets, I could use it on the toilet seats and the mirrors and sinks as well. Now, I'm no chief cleaning officer but that's just rank. The sooner I qualify, the better.' Debbie downed another drink and was off to the bar, the girls laughing loudly behind her.

By 7 p.m., Tony's Wine Bar had lost its sparkle, so it was time for the girls to find a new establishment which could offer more than just cheap booze. George's cell phone tinkled to life as 'Club Foot' by Kasabian charged into full swing.

'Who is it, Jackson?' Shaz slurred.

'SSSHH.' George pressed her finger to her lips as she tried to identify the caller amongst the noise. 'It's our Bell,' George announced triumphantly. 'She's going to meet us at the Vic in half an hour.' The girls let out another drunken 'WAHOO'.

'Bell' was short for 'Bella', who was George's sister. George could only assume that her mother must've consumed a large amount of vodka while watching *Beauty and the Beast* before instantaneously going into labour, and then, caught off-guard holding a baby girl, could only come up with 'Bella' as an excuse for a name. (For the entire pregnancy, their mum had assumed the baby was a boy.)

Bella was a nurse and worked in the local hospital looking after children with eating disorders and other debilitating mental illnesses. Once, one of the children had devised a kill list and named Bella as her number two to be bumped off should she get the chance. *A kill list... WTAF.* George admired her sister's patience and ease of conversation with just about anybody. She just wished she'd let her hair down more, stop worrying about her weight, whether her arms looked fat in the top she was wearing or if she was showing a little too much tit. Bella's prudish, serious nature meant that she gravitated towards the motherly role of the group, always pointing out the potential consequences and pitfalls of their plans.

Take today, for instance. Bella hadn't come to her house earlier on because she didn't want to get too drunk. She said that she would come later and make sure everyone got home safely and some other boring bollocks. Not that the safety of her friends was bollocks.

George's mind started rambling again, and in her semi-conscious state, Debs had dragged her from her seat and was heading towards the door. Outside, the weather had taken a turn for the worst, which had escaped the group's attention until now.

'SHIT,' wailed Carmen. 'I haven't got a brolly. My hair is going to be a bloody mess.' Carmen didn't do messy. She was always the vision of demur elegance.

Without warning, Debbie tugged at the canopy hung outside the wine bar's door, which had been sheltering them from the rain above. A large surge of cold water tumbled onto the girls.

Debs shrugged. 'We're all wet now, so let's get a fuckin' move on to the Vic.' She trudged on, unconcerned with the rain and puddles which had started forming on the pavement.

'Debbie!' shouted Carmen. 'I'm gonna kill you!' Rain dripping from her long hair, she took a drag on her cigarette in an effort to instil calm.

Debbie could be heard laughing loudly and knew that with her build, the only one doing any killing would be her!

'Shit.' George clasped her arms around herself, trying to keep out the cold.

The Vic was an older pub; the furnishings were worn but that only added to its charm. The atmosphere was electric and generally the clientele were a good sort. Debbie barged her way through all the waif like wags at the bar. Small tuts could be heard through pursed lips and orange glowing faces. One snarl from Debbie and the girls at the bar were all smiles and niceties – no one was going to mess with her. It was at times like these that George was always glad to have Debbie around. The shots were being racked up at the bar; a sticky pink liquid filled the glasses and the group clinked and drank before any of them had time to think about what they were doing and what exactly it was that they were drinking. George's head was feeling rather hazy and she was sure she wouldn't be able to last much longer. She desperately needed a wee, and as she turned to make for the ladies' room, George caught sight of Charles Cunningham sat at a small table in the corner of the pub with a couple of his photography buddies. She couldn't be sure just how long she had been staring when Charles turned to meet her gaze. Her cheeks flushed scarlet and she hurried forward to the ladies' room. *Why am I embarrassed?* thought George. *Why didn't I just wave and say hi like a normal person? But then, I am really pissed, aren't I?* On entering the stall, George hiked her blue playsuit to the side, not wanting to unbutton the full garment and rather needing to have a wee quite badly. With one hand holding the stall door shut, George tried to balance above the toilet as elegantly as she could manage, but a massive shove on the door made George reach out with both hands to try and protect her modesty, which meant failing to keep her thong out of the flow of pee!

'SHIT.' George fumbled to quickly remove her playsuit in full and her sodden G string. 'Oh my god, how do I explain this?' George crumpled her knickers in her hand and quickly deposited them into the sanitary bin. She climbed back into her playsuit, surprised at just how good it felt not to be wearing any knickers; it was actually quite liberating. She wafted the playsuit back and forth to get a feel for the air passing up her leg onto her bare flesh and private bits, crisp cool air enveloping the folds of her most intimate parts. The lady waiting outside the toilet was beginning to get restless and started to bang on the door again, shouting for George to hurry the fuck up in a much deeper voice than expected. She pulled the chain on the toilet, fixed on her most confident smile and exited the stall with the kind of look that said 'I haven't just pissed myself in the toilet, you know'. The larger lady, adorning what can only be described as an 8 o'clock shadow, heaved her weight against the door, moving into the stall, threadbare tights already close to being around her ankles.

'Thank god you're here,' shrieked Jenny, all out of breath, crimson in the face with her more-than-generous bust bouncing up and down to the rhythm of her breathing. 'I've trapped my flap in those spanky knickers! Will you have a look, G?' In a flash, before George could respond, Jenny was hitching up her dress to fully expose the now-swollen purple vagina lip, which looked rather like a bollock from the angle it was being exposed at.

George immediately burst out laughing and pulled down Jenny's dress, telling her that the spanky knickers probably needed to go if she was ever going to get blood circulating in that area of her vagina again. Jenny frowned and seemed to weigh her options before she burst into the toilet, announcing to the lady with the beard that it was a dire emergency and that if the circulation to her flap cut off then she would be holding her solely responsible. I tell you: this stuff, you just couldn't make it up.

Jenny was in her early thirties, pretty, with a brown bob. She'd married a guy called Mark earlier in the year and they'd just had their first child. Her weight had become an obsession since giving birth and she'd tried every fad diet, tonic and pill along with every mad bit of clothing that claimed it would suck in her fat. It was a shame, really. She spent entirely too much time focused on what she didn't like about herself when she had so much going for her. Jen's broad Northern accent was unmistakable. Every text she sent, you could almost hear her speaking the words in your head. She was like the female Liam Gallagher.

George openly chuckled to herself leaving the toilets as she thought of her lack of knickers, the bearded lady and Jenny's left bollock. Poor Jenny. George had done her best to reassure her and build up her confidence. To her right, George could hear Charles chatting away. He was ordering drinks at the bar. The doe-eyed waitress was hanging on his every word; she could have been only about 22. Pretty little thing but almost too eager to please. Charles wasn't biting.

'Can't take your eyes off me tonight, eh, George?' Charles had suddenly turned, catching George off guard. He looked great as usual but tonight, for the first time, George appreciated just how handsome Charles was and couldn't quite work out why she had never noticed this before. In an attempt to reply coolly, George took a step closer to Charles – and stumbled in her 4-inch heels, just managing to cling onto a table for balance and feeling for the first time this evening just a little bit vulnerable if not a little stupid.

'Sorry, Charles, I've been out all day. You know how it is.'

George was clinging to the table as if it was a mountain she was climbing without a safety rope. Her eyes darted wildly around the room. She was more than a little afraid that if their eyes met then somehow hers would give her away. She wasn't attracted to Charles... was she? Surely not. Her type was more, well, egotistical. They were rude go-getters. I guess, like other women, she had been attracted to bad men, yet here was Charles, handsome, successful and had actually never been anything but nice to her.

'George, are you getting pissed or what?' Debbie shouted over. The WAGs could be seen rolling their eyes but their efforts of displeasure were wasted on Debbie, who really couldn't've cared less. George couldn't be sure if the interruption was welcome, but it provided her with the opportunity to escape and gather her thoughts, given that her inner voice was probably now intoxicated with sambuca. The whole Charles attraction thing was probably just the drink.

'Duty calls.' George pointed over to the girls at the bar. Jenny had just returned, winking and giving her a thumbs up (*a sign of the spanky knickers having been removed*, George duly noted).

'Thanks for helping me with the shoot. I never got the chance... erm, to, er, phone you, because the time and the, erm——'

Charles swiftly cut in, sensing the unease in her voice. His tone was kind and reassuring,

'George, its fine. We're friends, and friends help one another out, don't they?'

She nodded with an unconvincing smile and, letting go of the table ('mountain' when drunk), counted her steps towards the girls, concentrating on every move as she teetered slowly away from Charles. *Please don't let me fall, please don't let me fall.*

'Well he's a bit of alright,' Lucy mused wickedly. 'I thought you were shagging that Karl bloke?'

Lucy flicked her tongue up and down provocatively.

George wasn't ready to share how she felt... she didn't actually know, herself. She decided to turn the attention elsewhere, deflection always being the best tactic in a time of crisis.

'Look, Lucy, just because you can manage to shag every handyman that comes to your gaff doesn't mean we are all doing it. I've never touched Karl, and anyway, I'm soooo over him.' George exaggerated the 'so' for effect.

Lucy had managed to sleep with the guy that cuts her grass, the electrician, the plumber and the man that came to clean her carpets! Shagging was definitely her thing.

'Well, George, if you don't want that Charles, I will just have to go over there and shag him for you.' Lucy laughed, eyeing up Charles in the corner like a big cat eyes up its prey.

'I met this bloke last week online. He came around mine and we ended up having sex *four* times.' Lucy enthusiastically emphasised the *four*. 'Weren't even quick shags either – bloody marathons. Was walking like John Wayne for a week.'

They both laughed. George hadn't had sex in months, but here was Lucy having enough sex for all of them.

Lucy was about 5'2" and loved watching Keep Fit DVDs but almost never joined in – she would sit on the couch, get comfy, armed with a full fat can of Coke and some snacks. Exercise was something that she wanted to do, but it just never seemed to be the right time. When she had accompanied George and Shaz to the gym, she would often sneak outside, quickly followed by the male instructor. (Perhaps that was her game – let's face it, she hadn't shagged one of them yet.) Lucy was clearly in denial about her body size and clung onto the fantasy of being a size 8. Earlier in the week she had been shopping with her mother, looking to buy a dress for today's events, and ended up being cut out of a very tight size 8 by a very nice shop assistant who could clearly see just how deep the disillusion of size ran with Lucy. She quickly comforted her by saying that the label sizes must've got mixed up. The shame!

George was beat. Faces were merging into one and her sense of time was becoming all squiffy. People were talking in slow motion and a sinking sickly feeling swept over her, draining all colour from her cheeks. Hand over mouth, eyes wide, brows raised in alarm, George bolted for the door. She would never live down the streaky tan plus being sick in the Vic – she had to get home. Carmen and Shaz were right behind her, both looking a little worse for wear themselves. The nearest cab was hailed, and before Debbie had chance to assess what was going on, the three of them had escaped her clutches for the night.

Debbie was never one to get hung up on anything for a prolonged period of time and within a few seconds had reframed the whole scenario, soon dragging what was left of the birthday party crowd to the Yummy Hut where she would demand hairy chicken wing legs to eat in the queue while waiting for her food. Totally disgusting, but even the out-of-hours food crew wouldn't mess with Debbie.

'Give me SAUSAGES!' Debs would shout, eyes bulging like a woman possessed.

In the taxi, George began inhaling big gulps of air with the hope that it would steady her churning stomach and still the tumbling Waltzer ride her mind had been engaged in. Carmen carefully nudged her way over the sticky plastic back seat of the taxi to George, recognising the signs all too well that George was in trouble.

'Put your head down,' ordered Carmen. 'You know, brace. Brace, like the aeroplane instructions.'

Right, the aeroplane instructions meant to help whilst crashing a 100-tonne plane at 300 miles an hour – George knew better.

'Stop the car,' she managed feebly, makeup smeared across her face. Shaz had started to stroke George's back and was echoing the instructions for the cabbie to stop unless he wanted to spend the next two hours of his life cleaning up vomit.

The cab pulled to a halt and George bolted like a bull released from its restraints, hand planted firmly over mouth. Shaz followed honourably behind, scraping George's hair into a makeshift bun, understanding only too well the horrors of having one's own vomit laced in one's hair. George stooped over, head hung low, hand against the wall for support, and began to spill the contents of her stomach onto the pavement. Shaz took a step back as the liquid splashed over her Calvin Klein shoes. 'Watch out, Jackson, my shoes!' George's hair was quickly released, free to be coated in the putrid liquid that continued to erupt from a gasping, horrified George. The smell was overwhelming, and Shaz, who up until this point had felt rather dandy, suddenly experienced the mouth-watering sensation that often arrives just before the crucial moment of throwing up. Shaz reluctantly ambled forwards, grasping the wall for support, and almost immediately joined George in what can only be described as a chorus of vomit. Carmen looked on from the cab, laughing quietly to herself. This truly was a memory she needed to capture forever. Reaching into her handbag, she retrieved her iPhone and busily began to snap photos of the girls from different angles whilst thinking of a witty caption to serve up on their WhatsApp group later. The cab driver, clearly unamused by the behaviour of the girls, pointed out to Carmen that the meter was still running and that any-so called accidents in the taxi would be costly for the girls. Carmen flashed the cabbie her award-winning smile and reassured him that there wouldn't be any further problems. Now here was a girl that did everything well, even while drunk!

Hurt Locker

George groaned, feet curled inward towards her stomach, one hand cradling her throbbing head. Immediate feelings of embarrassment and regret flooded her brain at 100 miles an hour as memories of the previous night's events came rushing back. George had grown used to this ritual of self-loathing and swearing that she'd never drink again. Give it a day or two and she would be busily preparing for the next alcohol-fuelled debacle – she would never learn.

George smelt bad, her hair was tacky with large chunks of food welded to the strands, her clothes were scattered randomly around the room and adorned light shades amongst other pieces of furniture and the faint but pungent smell of vomit lingered in her nostrils. Writing off the day was definitely not out of the question, but never one to be beaten, George decided that a shower was badly needed. For once, she was happy not to be in a relationship. George imagined the shame of waking up next to her soulmate covered in her own sick and was about to dismiss the thought when a large grin formed on her face and a soft chuckle echoed around the bathroom.

Debbie had once told her about this guy she was dating who had woke her up in the middle of the night as she was retching. He had been scared that she might choke on her sick as she lay on her back. In waking up Debbie, however, the poor guy invited her to be sick on his face. He apparently screamed in pain, as the vomit had directly entered his eye, burning the soft tissue. Don't think the relationship continued after that messy night.

The shower sprang to life. The water jets pounded the shower tray, deafening George, whose fragile state was rapidly deteriorating by the minute. Slouched over, George took a deep breath, steeling herself for the shower ritual she likened to hiking away from base camp to climb a mountain. Gripping the wall, she slowly lifted herself into the shower, head hung low, the sick feeling bubbling deep in the pit of her stomach. Pacing herself was the key to getting through this. This sort of experience was something George had in spades.

This stooped position ('the hurt locker') had been mastered over the years. George kept her body hung over low, which eased the spinning sensation in her head and prevented the nausea from becoming more than just a feeling. Without much focus, George emptied the contents of one shiny bottle from the shower tray onto her hand and began massaging the sweet-smelling liquid into her hair... God, she hoped this was shampoo.

Different bottles were pulled in turn from the shelf and added to her hair or body and then flung mercilessly to the bottom of the shower tray. *Job for another day*, she thought numbly. Half leaning on the wall for support, George heard water pounding the floor. Although she was acutely aware of being in the shower, the sound was different and appeared to be coming from somewhere else. Eyes still closed and body hanging over, limp, George could not decide if the decision to have a shower was a good one, as she still felt closely related to the living dead. Thoughts of what to do next were whirling around her mind, and just before the intention to get out of the shower could actually be put into action, an almighty crunching sound and the sudden movement of the shower basin immediately had George fully alert.

There was a further snapping and creaking as the floor under the shower tray began to give way. Years of the leaky shower dripping onto the floorboards and plaster below had finally taken its toll. The shower tray groaned as the last of the plaster gave way, hurtling the tray – and George along with it – through the ceiling and onto the landing floor in precisely the spot where she so often lay pieces of tissue to soak up the leaked water.

Somewhat shaken but, miraculously, not injured, George straightened herself, raising her gaze to the front door, which was somehow wide open. Through the matted hair that covered her face, George could make out the frame of a man slowly coming into focus. As she strained to see, she felt even sicker: *Jarvis*. Of course it was Jarvis. The name in her head was like an alarm going off, and with the quickened pace of an Olympian, George sprung from the remnants of the shower tray and slammed the front door. She also let out a shriek, as the crash landing had obviously hurt her more than she had first realised.

Through the door, Jarvis called, 'Nice to see ya, Ms Jackson.' She heard him quietly add, 'Real nice to see all of ya,' his perverted grin audible in his voice.

A cold shiver ran down George's spine. Of all of the detestable men in the world to see her at her lowest – naked, having just fallen through the ceiling – of course it had to be Jarvis.

She felt truly ashamed. She had been so drunk that she hadn't even locked her front door. A new all-time low, even for George.

High on adrenalin, George raced up the stairs to her bedroom, where she began pulling wildly at sweaters in her drawer. She needed to get dry and get dressed. There was so much mess everywhere that she needed to find a way to take back control. Her fingers trembled as she wrestled with the items of clothing, blueish purple blotches starting to seep through George's skin, revealing the full extent of the accident. The last ten minutes had seen George awaken from a stooped, slobbering mess to a wide-eyed junkie equivalent; hard to say which state was worse. The sicky feeling had been replaced with one of dread. There was a hole in the ceiling of her house and the pervy postman had copped an eyeful – this really was the hangover from hell.

There were not many occasions in George's life where she felt the support of her mother might just be the remedy needed, but her inner child was craving a hug and for someone to come and make everything okay again. Plus, her mother who would be fresh from having been on holiday had a great relationship with Tod, the builder – perhaps she would even be able to wangle a discount.

George began frantically searching the room for her clutch bag. She needed her phone and it would be nice not to have to cancel her Switch card given that she was on her 28th issue. As desperation started to kick in, George got on her hands and knees, trawling the length of her room, throwing everything she came into contact with onto her bed until, finally, there it was: her clutch bag, nestled under some clothes and strewn makeup brushes. She pondered for a moment just how she was able to function when she was so drunk. How did things get to be everywhere? On second thought, it was probably best that she didn't know. An inner shudder of dread took hold but George pressed on. There was so much to do.

In her clutch, she found thirty quid in pound coins. This was such an obvious trademark of George's, who couldn't quite bring herself to pay for drinks with coins. It had to be notes. Her Switch card was safely tucked away in the zip pocket. *Thank God*, she thought. *First Direct should be feeling relieved right about now!* Also in her purse: some random pieces of chewing gum, tampons (hundreds of them?), tissue and, right at the bottom, her iPhone.

George retrieved her phone swiftly and thought about what she might say to her mother when she answered. How about, 'Hi mum, I've fallen through the ceiling'? No, no, she would be frantic with worry. What about, 'Mum, are you busy today? I could really do with your help'. *Fuck it, get on with it, George.* Scrolling through her list of contacts, George selected her mother's number. She inhaled deeply and pressed dial. Her mother answered promptly, dominating the conversation from the outset. After about two minutes of constant, meaningless chatter, she paused, sensing that something wasn't quite right.

'George, darling, are you okay? You've barely said a word.'

There was a short pause and George, unable to contain her emotion any longer, spit it out.

'I'm not okay, mum, I've just fell through the ceiling.'

Mum to the Rescue

George's mother was a formidable woman: large frame, wideset shoulders, purple quiff. The name *Beryl* didn't quite do her justice. Pacing back and forth in her new spandex jodhpurs (horrific on anyone, but terrifying on anyone over 60 – it should be illegal), Beryl tutted and puffed, shaking her head whilst assessing the large hole in George's ceiling.

'How did you let it get like this, George? Pfffftttt, you must have known it was leaking.'

George stood in the opening to her kitchen, hands clasping a hot cup of coffee. Mimicking her mother's words behind her back, she felt 12 again.

'Mum could you please just call Tod and ask him to come and take a look?'

Turning on her heel, George started to focus her attention on the mess that was her kitchen. Empty wine bottles, vodka and glasses everywhere, Beryl followed closely behind, shaking her head disapprovingly.

'Not good for you, you know, George – all this alcohol, it will give you memory loss, you mark my words. Remember Edna from the estate? Well, she's as mad as a bag of frogs, that one, and she was always on it.' Beryl was imitating a wino using one of the empty bottles as prop.

'Mum, Edna was about 87, and I daresay it had more to do with her age than the wine. Anyway, the wine didn't make my ceiling fall through, so can we just get on and phone Tod?' A sharp coolness was wrapped in George's tone, which Beryl did not appreciate.

'Don't you get cross with me, young lady. Right, give me that phone, I'll phone him from the back garden and give Bruno a chance to stretch his legs. Bruno, come on, sweetie, let's go outside.'

George could never quite work out why people spoke to dogs like babies. Bruno looked up defiantly at George and began sniffing heartily at the rim of her bin before cocking his leg up, never taking his beady eyes off her for the entire wee. It was like he knew that what he was doing was wrong but he wanted to see what she was going to do about it. George took a step closer to Bruno, gritting her teeth. Like a bullet out of a gun, Bruno shot outside to the safety of Beryl. The kitchen was starting to feel a little tidier, and the fresh breeze blowing in from the back door was just what George needed to blow away the cobwebs... that, and her mother to actually do something helpful given the crisis at hand. Beryl could be heard yelping outside and already George was regretting the decision to involve her mother. Leaning forward impulsively, intrigued by the noise coming from Beryl, she stepped closer to the doorway.

'Oh my lord, oh my lord, get it off me, George, get it off!' Beryl's eyes were tightly closed, causing her to bump from one cupboard in the kitchen to another. George put out a hand to stop Beryl and, in pulling her to a standstill, could for the first time make out what the noise was all about.

Like most mothers, Beryl liked to interfere with everything from George's washing ('Washing blacks with whites – who does that?') to emptying all her handbags out, and today, when she should have been outside on the phone to Tod, she had decided to strim the border in George's garden. Little did she know that her gorgeous Bruno had taken a dump amongst the grass and long weeds, allowing the motion of the strimmer to cascade leafy green poo shards all over her face and clothes. George suppressed the urge to laugh out loud and began the process of wiping the faecal particles from her mother's face. Beryl gagged, totally enraged by the experience, pinning the blame on the state George had left her back garden in and how she had felt compelled to intervene. What with there being a hole in the ceiling as well, Beryl was just looking out for her daughter's best interests. George didn't retaliate – an inner victory had been won. She would never forget this moment for as long as she might live, her mother crying like a baby, covered in poo from that little shit of a dog Bruno. And there it was: karma. So it did exist!

Telling the Friends

'Ha ha ha that's fucking hilarious, George – I can't believe you fell through the ceiling.'

Carmen was suitably amused, laughing and patting George's hand rhythmically.

'Bitch,' hissed George, taking a sip of her tea.

'I bet you made that Jarvis fella's day. Probably never seen a woman naked until now; you've done that guy a good service there, George.' Carmen relaxed back into the soft leather couch. They always came to this café. Lovely staff and super comfortable seats.

'Why does nothing like this ever happen to you?' complained George, face sullen, pouting like a child.

'Because, darling, I always take great care of my things. I fix the things in my home and in my car and I never, ever, get shitfaced drunk – or get shit on my face, like your mother.' She raised her eyebrows and gave George a knowing look. George launched a serviette at Carmen. She knew she was right. She needed to sort out her life. The car was a disaster, her house was a bomb site and her sex life was, at present, non-existent.

Carmen's phone jingled loudly and she instinctively reached for it.

'Hi, Debs. Hilarious isn't it? I'm with her now.'

George could only make out one side of the conversation but she knew it was about her. She wondered how long this story would be told and pondered if it would be worth hibernating until someone else did something completely crazy so the world could forget that George was a total fuck-up.

Carmen slung her phone back onto the table, bursting to update George with what Debs had gotten up to after the three of them had made their exit the night before.

'Well, George, if you think you should be embarrassed, listen to this: After we left, Debs and a few others carried on.'

George was only half-listening. She was busy staring at some old guy to her left who was pulling food from his beard. *I wonder how old this guys is – late fifties, sixties, hard to tell with all that hair matted around his face. I wonder if men with beards shampoo them.* Carmen gently slapped George's thigh, demanding that attention be paid to the story she was telling.

'Well, you know what Debbie's like. She went to the chicken house for some food, where she picked up some random bloke.' Carmen was already laughing between talking, which sparked George's interest. 'When they got back to her place, the bloke sat on the floor to eat his chips and Debs got on the couch with her legs up, feet propped on the back of this fella's shoulders.' Carmen was now talking as quickly as she could in an attempt to get the rest of the story out. 'The guy Debs picked up starts to complain of this bad smell, and you know Debs, she's shrugging it off, tucking into her food. Anyway, he turns to his right, where Debs' feet are propped up, and she's got dog muck all on the bottom of her shoes!' The pair were both laughing hysterically imagining the scene. 'Anyway, Debs said he started to gag, calling her a mucky bitch, so she threw him out and chucked her shoes at him as he left.' Carmen approvingly smiled at George. An energy existed between them like that of sisterhood, and George already felt that a weight had lifted from her shoulders.

'Anyway, George, there is a silver lining to your story. Whatever it was that you used in the shower this morning – before you fell through the ceiling, that is – well, it's got rid of that streaky tan line on your face.'

The pair fell about in a fit of laughter. *The world could be a shitty, horrible place*, thought George, *but with great friends, you could survive*.

Carmen could always be relied upon to be there for her at the drop of a hat. It's not even like George's "emergencies" were real emergencies. They were always just some stupid stuff. But that made Carmen's willingness to pick her up after a fall an even sweeter gesture.

The Car

George dialled the number on the piece of paper she'd found on her car, afraid that she might lose her courage. This month was turning out to be an expensive one, what with the huge hole in her ceiling and having crashed into a stranger's car within days of one another. George was determined to get back on track and so had decided to face all her issues head on: both the house and her car. She thought the message she had left the previous day on his voicemail would've done the trick, but so far, no joy. A male voice, high-pitched and sing-songy, greeted George at the end of the phone, immediately dashing the rugged images she had impressed on her brain. Joe, the guy whose car she had crashed into the day of the shoot, was gay, and a very out-there gay from the sounds of it. He had a friendly manner, talking casually about where he'd been the day of the little crash and how that had sent him to the garage, where he'd met the love of his life. George crossed her fingers, praying that Joe wouldn't want to take the incident any further, having practically set up the guy with the man of his dreams.

'So, George, do you want to go through insurance or do you want to just give me a couple hundred? Alfredo said it wouldn't cost a lot to fix and he's going to give me a discount. I'm not lying to you, it really is a good deal, *and* Alfredo is *so* handsome.' Joe sounded as if he was on cloud nine. His tone exuded an excitement and a hunger that fresh new love was known to bring. George felt an ache in the pit of her stomach, a loneliness that no great job or great friends could mend. Joe repeated the question.

'George, so do you want to pay Alfredo or go through the insurance?'

She felt bad for thinking of herself when Joe was so obviously in love and by all accounts letting her bony arse off the hook.

'Joe, paying Alfredo sounds great. I'm so pleased that you met someone you really like, and I just want to thank you for not getting all mad about it… I know how you men love your cars.' At that, Joe scoffed.

'Not me, darling. Not a car man, not one bit.' They both laughed, and for once George was happy to be tackling her 'issues' list head-on. Maybe this was just beginner's luck, but boy, it felt good to be making progress.

George hung up and saw that there was a text from her mother waiting for her: 'I've just found out that Mrs Arnold has died who lived at number 72, terrible you know, she had a lovely camel skin coat'.

Her mother's dark obsession with spreading word of those who've died would need to be tackled at some point. Who texts about death *all the time*? Beryl certainly was a complicated woman, though, so perhaps later in life, death becomes one of the major topics of conversation. George prayed that she would never find out. *For fuck's sake.* She hit the mobile phone's delete button with brutal force.

Work – Everyone Loves a PowerPoint

George grabbed a chair at the weekly flash meeting, sinking as far as the battered back support would let her. This meeting generally took George all week to prepare for, and no, we're not talking prepping the meeting's content. We're talking clothes prep, hair prep, makeup prep, all in an attempt to catch Karl's eye. Today, however, was different – she hadn't thought about her looks in any way. In fact, she couldn't give two hoots about her appearance. Karl was an egotistical pig and, frankly, given the recent run of events, she couldn't afford for any more bad stuff to happen.

Karl sauntered into the room. He was wearing a beautiful blue Armani suit, hair flicked casually, grinning like a cat that had gotten the cream. George hoped that she had bracketed and not actually rolled her eyes at him whilst sneakily inhaling his masculine fragrance... *Yikes,* she thought. *He smells good.* Karl gave George a wink, flashing his sexy smile, teeth perfect and white. George pretended not to notice, and instead fixed her gaze on the administrator, who had just opened up a death-by-PowerPoint slideshow.

Her mind ramblings kicked in.

Why is Karl so perfect, why did he have to look so great, smell so great? How did God get off by dishing out way more to this guy than he deserved when other blokes looked like they'd hit just about every branch of the ugly tree on the way down but were actually decent guys? Why was life so unfair?

'George, the estimates?' Hugh, the slightly overweight administrator with the annoying 1950s moustache, was looking over his glasses at George, eyes wide and probing.

Shit. She'd been asked a question, but as per usual, her mind was off in la-la land, thinking about a completely unimportant and unrelated topic. Annoyed that the unrelated and unimportant topic just so happened to be Karl, she decided to be honest.

'Sorry, Hugh, I missed that. What do you need again?'

Hugh the administrator cleared his throat and took the slide deck back a few slides. There was a low groan in the room and George swore that she could see the energy fields from some of her colleagues physically disintegrate.

The meeting continued for about an hour or so. Hugh had the inspirational zest of a rock, and a *dead* rock at that, and it was evident from the faces of her colleagues around the room that no one was listening. Karl saw his opportunity to bolt.

'Hugh, dear fellow, you couldn't summarise where we've got to, could you? Only some of us have a 2 o'clock with Miranda and I'm starving.' Karl was half-smiling, creating a few chuckles around the room and comments of support. Hugh shifted uncomfortably, stuttering something about the need to prepare some draft storyboards, but already people were on their feet, chairs scraping along the floor as a stampede to exit the room began. George waited patiently. She was never one for queues and hated waiting in line like you do at buffet bars – what a waste of time. Hugh looked crushed and began to power down his equipment. George felt a little bad for the guy but equally prayed that he would inherit a personality or read some self-help books, as trying not to doze off in his company was absolute torture.

George made her way out of the briefing room, making a conscious effort to smile and inhaling deep breaths, trying to free herself from the doom cloud Hugh had unwittingly unleashed. She had decided to follow the herd towards the canteen, not really one for lunch but needing some light relief following the PowerPoint experience. Passing the chief production team's office, she heard a familiar voice and stopped inquisitively to peer through the blinds. Charles Cunningham and Pete from the production team were talking about dates for the next launch. George stood, fixated on Charles, stomach knotting, butterflies she hadn't felt in years emerging with the stark realisation of just how much she admired and quite possibly fancied this man.

'Hey there, sexy.' Karl's arm hooked around George's waist, breaking her thoughts and spinning her close towards his muscular frame. 'I was thinking 7 o'clock Saturday at that new bar in town. Meant to be kicking.'

George looked up; Karl's face was within inches of her own. Oh, how many times she had dreamt of this moment, his sexy smile, arms holding her firmly... but this wasn't what she wanted anymore. Before she could protest, Karl's mouth was on hers, gently teasing her lips apart. Her body tingled, relishing his gentle but skilful touch. Karl took a step back, flinging his suit jacket over his shoulder, and winked at George.

'7 o'clock, then, babe.' As usual, without waiting for a reply, Karl was on his way. George was completely stunned. Oh, why couldn't she have slapped him or something? Why did she just stand there and let him kiss her? Balling her fists, she turned to go back towards the canteen. She found that Charles was no longer in the production team's office but was stood behind her, eyes cold and disapproving. The atmosphere was tense and silent. Charles was looking deep into George's eyes and she wondered just how much he'd seen and what he was thinking.

'You still here, Charles?' Pete the production manager was leaving for lunch, oblivious to the scene playing out in front of him.

'I was just saying hi to George but I'm off now. Take care, Pete.' Charles broke his gaze from George's, marching briskly towards the exit. George panicked, frantically thinking of something to say, and in the absence of a bulletproof plan settled for calling out Charles's name. He didn't look back. Maybe he couldn't hear her, but she knew deep down that he probably could. Men like Charles didn't waste time with women like her – women who needed attention from men like Karl.

Walking Bruno

It was Saturday morning and the phone hadn't stopped ringing since 7 a.m. so George was still half-asleep and somewhat grumpy. Saturdays were the only lie-in she ever got, and here was some inconsiderate idiot phoning her. Pouncing on the handset, ready to give someone a piece of her mind, the ringing abruptly stopped, instead clicking to voicemail.

'George, darling, I feel terrible. I've been trying to call you for ages. Where are you? Bruno is desperate for his walk, Dad's out and I can't manage it, darling – can you ring me back, please, as soon as you get this? Where are you?'

George crumpled her face in dismay. She knew she'd have to go around to her mother's, so better to eat the ugly frog than wait and receive even more begging phone calls. The bathroom was still a complete bomb site so George decided that she would pack a few things for her mother's and take a leisurely bath there, utilising her mother's expensive spa soaps once she got back from her walk with Bruno.

The car started without any noise. *What bliss*, thought George, managing a smile and turning on the car radio. 'Positive thoughts' is what Carmen always recommended to her. *Blah blah blah*, thought George. *Easy to say when your life flows so easily and every man wants to fall at your feet and declare his undying love.* But she needed the unfortunate events in her life to stop unfolding and was prepared to try just about anything to change the cards fate had dealt her... *Positive thoughts.* It was at these moments that she used to fantasise over Karl, but with him out of the picture, perhaps she could think of Charles. Did she want to think of Charles? A small ripple in the pit of her stomach was an indication that she did, but he'd seen her at her worst so many times that he couldn't possibly want her in that way, could he? But blowing off the date tonight with Karl would be the first step in the right direction.

George reached her mother's townhouse, which was white brick with beautiful decorative artwork above the windows and doors. George had always loved it here as child and it still held a special place in her heart.

Beryl opened the door, nose like a beacon, forcing out a dry cough and sniffing heavily.

'Okay, mum, you can stop the amateur dramatics, I'm here now. Where's the dog?' George pressed past her mother and looked for the little mutt Bruno, whom she knew was born from the bowels of hell and reported directly to Satan on a daily basis.

'George, darling, no need to rush. Anyway, I've bought a new coffee machine and I wanted you to taste "mocha". I've made you a cup.'

Beryl was handing George a long and slender glass, encouraging George to drink. Having missed her morning brew to instead help out her mother, George took the glass and greedily guzzled a mouthful, which she immediately regretted.

'Mother, what the hell is this meant to be?' George was fuming. The mocha tasted like milk-infused hot water. George spat angrily into the kitchen sink, outraged that the first thing to pass her lips this morning was this shit.

'But, darling, it's my new Tassimo. See, you put in this carton and press the button.'

George examined first the Tassimo, then the packaging of the mocha, and then rolled her eyes.

'Mother, you have to put in the mocha capsule first and *then* you put in the milk capsule. What did you just give me?'

Beryl stepped away, aware that only one capsule had gone into the machine, meaning that George had sipped hot water with a hint of milk.

'Well, I'm not quite myself, darling, you can hardly blame an old woman who's not very well for getting things mixed up. Anyway, I'm upset, as Mr Gregson died last night.'

Beryl waved her hanky in the air and retreated into the living room to look for Bruno. George bit her lip, resisting the urge to respond. Fighting with her mother was futile, especially when she was playing the victim, which she did so brilliantly. How her dad had coped for all these years, she would never know.

George focused on the task at hand.

'Bruno, come on, dipshit. Walkies, Bruno. BRUNO.' Each time George yelled, she would raise the volume of her a voice a notch. She was well-aware that this irritated her mother, which is why the action was so satisfying. Just as George was about to start shouting again, Bruno bounded into the back of the kitchen wearing a tartan jacket. George rolled her eyes, realising that it was the second time she'd done so since entering her mother's house. She released the lead from the tiny hook and connected it to the little loop in Bruno's collar. He rolled over, revealing his belly while panting heavily, the odours of fish and pedigree chum on his breath.

'Nasty,' George muttered, motioning for Bruno to get up so they could go for a walk.

'Don't forget the poo bags,' Beryl sang from the living room. All signs of the flu had evaporated. George went to roll her eyes for the third time and froze her eyelids mid-motion, instead pursing her lips. Her mother was not going to lead her back into negative thinking. She needed to be positive. As Carmen had said, good thoughts lead to good things, and she seriously needed some good things.

Walking Bruno was painfully slow. He sniffed hard, nose-deep into every nook and cranny, and, well, fair play if he was hunting for truffles, but the dog was just sniffing for girl dog piss. *Really?* thought George. *What a deeply disgusting thing to do.* Every couple of blocks, Bruno would receive appreciative looks from passers-by: 'Aww, isn't he cute?' One old lady bent down and patted him softly on the head. Bruno must've picked up a scent, as he turned his attention to the old girl's hands, sniffing and licking away as if his life depended on it. Old lady hands were like doggy heroin. George's stomach churned at the thought of what the smell could be and yanked hard at Bruno's chain so they could get on with their walk.

As they approached the end of the lane, Bruno started to back up onto the grass verge. Face all strained, Bruno squatted, pushing out his rabbit-shaped shit balls, George had rolled her eyes even before she realised she was doing it. Separating the poo bags in her pocket, she slowly bent down, hovering over the shit balls with exact precision. Getting poo on her hand was not part of today's agenda, no sirree.

Spreading the poop bag wide over the offending matter, George began to grab the contents, breathing out in an attempt to block out the smell for fear of gagging. Her fingers could feel the warm balls of poo slipping into the bag… and then a cold poo merged with the contents in the bag. George retched, because now she was picking up shit balls that didn't even belong to Bruno.

'For fuck's sake.' George muttered this phrase under her breath at least thirty times a day. Carmen's positive affirmations didn't quite seem fitting for such an occasion. While George was distracted, thinking too long and too hard, as she usually did, Bruno decided to go in for the kill. He repeatedly kicked his back legs in her direction, flicking mud and grass and, yes, you guessed it, more poo into George's face.

Had it not been for the passers-by, George would've gladly flung Bruno into the street to see how he fared with the fast cars and motorbikes, but as it happened, she had quite enough on her plate without adding animal abuse charges to it. She forced a half-smile at the old man walking a rather handsome greyhound. He nodded in response, but the quizzical look on his face said it all. Desperately she fumbled around in the pockets of her grey mac for a tissue to wipe her face with but had no luck. Her rescue would have to come in the form of an empty Skittles wrapper. George started to slide the inner packaging across her face to remove the patches of shit-stained mud.

'For fuck's sake.' There was that phrase again. 'You get what you ask for.' She could hear Carmen's voice mockingly echoing around her head. George prayed that the Skittles packet had done the trick and decided that she would run back to her mother's lest she dared to be seen with a streaky poo face.

Once again, George reacted with Olympian focus. Her feet were moving so quickly that she was sure some of her steps were not even connecting with the ground. (Where was this Hussain Bolt power when she needed to show off?) Turning quickly, she scanned behind her for Bruno, tugging the long lead harshly, a faint waft of Skittles and poo filling her nostrils. She gagged, covering her mouth with her hand, which was more of an automatic reflex than a decision given where her hands had been not two minutes earlier. Bruno's tongue lolled around the sides of his mouth, eyes bulging with desperation and fear, paws padding as fast as he could manage. George felt an awkward pang of guilt but with her mother's house in sight she couldn't slow down now. A flashy black Mercedes Benz honked its horn. *Oh God.* It was Hilary Bloom. George dismissed the noise and focused on the job at hand. Stopping abruptly, she tucked Bruno securely under her arm, deciding that the little fellow didn't look like he could make the last ten yards.

George crashed through the front door, deposited the poo bag on the stairs and ran as fast as she could into the bathroom, locking the door.

'George, darling, is that you?' Beryl was on her feet, walking towards the door, eyeing the suspicious-looking bag on the stairs and dabbing her nose with a hanky.

'George, darling, now listen, you can't run in here like a whirlwind. I'm not a well woman, you know, and what's this on the stairs? Don't tell me it's... a little Bruno parcel... it *is* a little Bruno parcel! Well! That's just not on.'

Beryl swiped up the bag ferociously, marched it to the outside bin and deposited it there with great care. In the kitchen, Bruno was on his bed, panting heavily, body limp, drool dripping from the sides of his mouth.

'Bruno, what's the matter, my handsome little man? What has she done to you?'

George turned on the silver taps of her mother's grand porcelain bath. It truly was a thing of beauty, something George would aspire to have once she'd sorted out her list of things to do (including fixing the hole in her ceiling, as it had been a week since the dreaded incident). Steam rose into the air, and out of spite, George rummaged amongst her mother's most luxurious and expensive bath treats, a wicked smile setting across her face. A soft lavender scent filled the room. George exhaled loudly, relaxing her shoulders and slipping out of her clothes. Up until this point, George had taken great care not to look in the mirror – she didn't need confirmation that she was a little bit useless. She needed to feel strong and powerful.

'I won't be looking at my face. Surely the incident today won't be able to scar me if I don't look at my face? Perhaps Hilary wasn't waving at me, and if she was, she was probably too far away to see that I had a bit of a mucky face?' George began frantically pulling at the face wipes, scrubbing her face up and down, taking great care not to cover her lips for fear of tasting the offending matter. Bloody Hilary Bloom. Of all the people to see her at her worst, it had to be her. She prayed that Hilary hadn't got a good look at her face.

There was a knock at the door. 'George, darling, what is going on with you? Why can't you be more like Kara's daughter? She has a lovely house, a lovely fiancé and they are looking to get married this year in Venice, you know.'

George didn't respond. She stepped into the bath and sunk quickly and quietly beneath the bubbles... Anything to escape the incessant wittering of her mother.

'Did you hear me, George? Venice.' Beryl tapped on the door again. 'Venice! Oohhhh, you've not changed since you were a little girl. And I'm not well, you know!' Beryl huffed, recognising that George wasn't in the mood to bite. Shaking her head, she slowly started to retreat back down the stairs, muttering quietly to herself, 'What did I do to deserve a daughter that just wants to go drinking with those friends of hers? Never looks after anything! She will *never* learn!'

Unfortunately for George, Hilary had captured quite the photographic gem and aptly created a message saying 'George Jackson, is that really shit on your face?' Pulling over to the curb, Hilary briefly paused before hitting send on her iPhone, then fired off the message to everyone she knew at the fashion house. George would never live this day down. A momentary pang of guilt was swiftly replaced with a fierce loathing. She detested how George fussed around her people; subordinates were meant to do what YOU said, surely that was the point? Otherwise it was like having a dog and barking yourself. Mean-spirited and not one for taking others' feelings into consideration, Hilary judged her appearance in the rear view mirror, applied a liberal layer of lipstick and smoothed her sleek hair behind her ears. With one last look at the photo, she cackled before pulling her car back into the traffic. She couldn't wait for the message to get some replies. Today was going to be memorable.

Night Aerobics

A deafening beep from outside the house brought George swiftly back into reality. The girls had decided to trial a new night aerobics class tonight, one with glow sticks where they would be bouncing about to old school rave tunes. It actually looked pretty fantastic on the leaflet. George had managed to rescue some old black spandex from her drawer and thoroughly checked the mirror from all angles in search of an unsightly camel toe. She tugged at her crotch, hoping that there would be much worse sights in the class, or, better still, *no* sights at all in the dark.

Diligently locking the front door behind her, mentally noting how she had left it open after that drunken night out, she piled into Debbie's yellow two-door Beetle. This car made George feel slightly more appreciative of the noisy thing she had on the drive.

'Yay, get this on yer, girl!' Debbie flung an oversized purple t-shirt in George's direction. Lucy and Jenny were already modelling the same top and smiling mockingly. She knew it would be useless to put up a fight.

'Er, thanks... I think.' George pulled the t-shirt over her vest top. It was a little stiff but really long so at least her hideous spandex crotch would be camouflaged.

Jen was wearing some sort of fat corset to pull in her blub. Sat bolt upright in the back of the car, it looked like she might burst at any moment, her expression pained and serious. How she would physically move in that thing was yet to be seen.

'You okay, George? Managed to get shagged yet?' Lucy didn't waste any time getting down to the nitty gritty. Holding an imaginary penis in her right hand, she pumped it like a deprived sex fiend, tongue flickering around a makeshift rim. Jen shifted uncomfortably in her seat as Lucy notched the sex show up a gear by pretending to spit polish the shaft.

'Shut up, you disgusting pig.' George rolled her eyes, flipping Lucy the bird, and tried her best not to chuckle.

'Sshhh Lucy, we are not talking about George's sex life tonight. In fact, girls, you are in for a treat. I've checked the website tonight and they've got "Touch Me in the Morning". George, how good! We're gonna get fit and rave our tits off! This is gravy.' Debbie was laughing hard. Lucy had the coordination of a blind sloth; whatever they were going to be doing tonight, it wasn't going to look pretty.

The class was taking place in an old tennis gym and already groups of girls were huddled around the outer edges of the room, chatting idly. One girl whose hair was scraped into a severe bun was stretching and exhaling loudly for effect. She was obviously the class pro, looking for gold stars with thighs like Fatima Whitbread. George urged Debbie to keep walking towards the back of the class. She didn't fancy dancing next to Fatima – there was way too much wrongness going on there. The room was cold and a damp caravan-like smell hung in the air. Lucy held her nose in disgust, her brow furrowed. This was definitely going to be an interesting hour.

Around the room, girls were eyeing up the purple t-shirt crew, glancing from head to toe, nudging one another, taking care to laugh as discreetly as they could manage.

'That's it, girls, take a good look. Debbie's here to rave her tits off and none of you scrawny fuckers better get in my way.' As usual, Debbie was bold and firm like a mountain – drawing attention was actually part of her plan. George was dying a little inside, and she prayed that the other girls would find something more interesting to study and/or belittle. Girls were such bitches, but on this occasion, George could honestly see things from the other girls' points of view: Why were they dressed in oversized, itchy, stiff, matching purple t-shirts? Utter TWATS!

Robin, the class instructor, glided gracefully into the room. Fatima went straight over. *Told you*, thought George. *Class brown-nose!* Gesturing with big arm movements and laughing just a little too hard, Robin clapped her hands twice, loudly asking that everyone come and grab two glow sticks from a box at the front of the room. Debbie's eyes lit up. She was smiling from ear to ear and before any of them could speak, she was off, jostling to collect her sticks. Linking arms with Jen and Lucy, George decided there was safety in numbers, although the three of them looked particularly ridiculous in the oversized purple t-shirts.

'Come on, girls, let's get our sticks.' George forced an enthusiastic grin. Lucy let go of her nose, hesitantly shaking her head in disapproval of the gym's tatty attire. But she accepted that she was there, so she might as well get on with it.

There was a loud giddy scream as the lights went out. George fought the urge to say *for fuck's sake* under her breath and tried instead to adopt a positive attitude towards this new experience. The music quickly followed and once again shrills of excitement filled the room. *It's really not all that*, thought George, *but who knows what these ladies get up to in their lives? I bet none of them have fallen through* their *ceilings recently.*

Debbie was in the zone, knocking out moves like a machine. The girls to her left and right were getting a right pounding as she moved in time to the music, hips gyrating back and forth, arms high in the air, twisting her glow sticks, face contorted and fierce. Lucy ambled about like a limp donkey, completely clueless, lacking any and all hand–eye coordination; she was always three steps behind and moving in the opposite direction to everyone else. George laughed out loud. This was exactly what she needed. It didn't even matter if the class was doing her any good – she was pretty sure that all the laughing was giving her stomach a good workout.

The room quickly warmed up. Debbie's cheeks were bright red and beads of sweat adorned her brow and upper back. Lucy smiled energetically, oblivious of her lack of timing and coordination. Robin announced the last song and suggested that everyone put in everything they've got for the last five minutes. Once again, a little cheer went up in the room, and

Fatima was right at the front, doing her best to impress Robin, lunging wildly into the turns.

All too quickly, the class was over, the lights were back on and all the ladies were clapping and patting one another on the back. George was starting to enjoy the camaraderie and found herself clapping without even realising it. Debbie was wafting her t-shirt, trying to let in some air, having worked up quite a sweat during the routines. Whilst George clapped, she noticed that her hands had a light purple hue to them, and for a moment was a little baffled. Debbie mopped her upper lip with the bottom of her t-shirt and very quickly things came into focus.

Debbie had started to resemble a rather unusual Oompa Loompa. Purple dye covered her face and the sweat patches around her neck and back were also leaking dye onto her skin. All the girls started to inspect their tops: Lucy had purple armpits and a band of purple going right around her stomach, George had managed to get off the lightest, with dye only on her hands and lower back. Debbie, on the other hand, was completely covered – there really wasn't anywhere that she hadn't managed to sweat, and the purple t-shirt had transferred most of its colour to her upper body.

'What the actual fuck, Debbie! What is going on with these skanky tops?!' Lucy had lost her earlier lightness and was outraged by her purple skin, especially with the funky smell well and truly back in the air combined with the snobby glaring looks from others who were clearly beyond amused with the girls' antics.

'Chill your beans, dude.' Debbie gestured to the exit with a sidewise nod of the head. They walked tall and proud, or at least Debbie did, purple stains like battle scars from the ultimate rave.

'Debbie, just out of interest, why did you get us these t-shirts?' Jenny ventured in her best non-critical voice as a way to break the tension. Lucy continued to mutter profanities under her breath, braying like a donkey, and George broke eye contact with the world. If she didn't look, they couldn't see her, right? This was a strategy she had gotten used to adopting, but it was also one she knew didn't actually work.

'Girls, one of the lads at work owed me a favour. I wanted us to feel like a team, you know? What's wrong with that? It was a fuckin' great idea.' The words came crashing out of Debbie's mouth like a twister unleashing its wrath on the earth.

'Good enough for me!' exclaimed George, choking back the urge to laugh, knowing that messing with Debbie at this point would be sheer insanity.

'And me,' offered Jen sheepishly, unaware that the purple dye had started to drip down her leg. A nasty sight indeed – where was she, in fact, sweating from now? Her corset was probably to blame.

To make matters worse, Debbie insisted on a team selfie before she would unlock the car doors. She ushered the girls closer, Lucy pinned to her side under protest, teeth gritted beaver-tight. The Facebook message was aptly named 'The Purple Warriors' and once again George wondered what type of man she would inevitably attract based on the company she kept and the general inappropriateness of her life.

'You coming this weekend, George?' Debbie asked, sliding into the driver's seat of the car, face almost unrecognisable from the dye.

'What, the mini festival thingy?' George wasn't even curious. Her hands were purple/black for most of the winter, so camping and anything even slightly tent- or camper-related left her feeling drained and somewhat weak.

'Yes, G, the bloody festival. It's going to be a belter and we've got actual beds and a heater.' She was now blinking frantically to emphasise the heat part, knowing this was all the encouragement that George actually needed to become a willing participant. A few seconds passed and George, not known for her ability to stay away from mad weekend benders, nodded in agreement.

'Count me in, Debs.'

The tunes were turned up on the radio and the windows lowered. It was obvious that Debbie wanted to celebrate or show off her purple hue. Either way, they weren't going to leave the gym unnoticed.

Mini Festival

Glastonsocial was 40 miles north of George's hometown, and with Bella driving, the 40-minute trip would feel like a dash to the ASDA. She was a very scary driver, indeed. George always insisted on sitting in the back to avoid adopting the Mrs Bucket persona of the car, pointing out other vehicles on the road and the odd cow in the field. Bella would get so mad when any of the others commented on her style of driving, flushing red in the cheeks, eyes bulging and red... not a pretty picture. However, the added bonus of not driving meant that the other girls could get rotten shitfaced drunk without panicking about leading the journey back the next day (silver lining and all that).

The girls were going to be staying in an old horsebox that Tracey, who was Sharon's sister-in-law, had kitted out over the years, driven by her love of horse riding. The living quarters had a sink, stove and a table and chairs area, which converted into a bed. The rest of the girls would be slumming it in the back where the horses would normally sleep.

Five of them would travel in Bella's skanky grey 7-seater Skoda, with Tracey driving the horsebox alongside her rather annoying posh other half Derek, who was amazingly horsy to look at, and Lucy, who would tag along because she lived closer to Tracey than she did any of the other girls. The plan was for everyone to be picked up by 5 p.m. Bella would start with George and then work her way around until every girl had been collected. Debbie added her things to the boot: a sleeping bag tied with some woollen yarn, a giant bag of alcoholic beverages and some rather unusual looking cakes.

'I'm sitting in the front, girls. Ain't getting no fat cramp in the back.' Debbie was unscrewing the top of a large bottle of rosé, and the girls took that as a signal that the day was about to step up a couple of gears.

Outside Shaz's house, Bella honked her horn impatiently. Debbie started to pass round the bottle of rosé, insisting that everyone take at least a three-second swig, which is rather difficult if wine makes you gag. On taking her phone out from her pocket, George started to text Shaz just in case she was in the far side of the house or her music was too loud to hear them. Bella honked again, winding down her window, fingers drumming on the side of the car.

'Come on, Shaz, I want to get a good parking spot so it's easy to do one in the morning.'

There was no movement in the house. Shaz wasn't running to the door in her usual excitable fashion, asking for them to hold on, smiling feverishly. George's phone abruptly vibrated. It was a message from Shaz.

'Can't come Jackson, I'm detoxing'. George read the words again slowly, somewhat in disbelief, and decided that she better break the unwelcome news.

'Er, girls, Shaz says she isn't coming because she's detoxing.' George said the words quickly, edging backwards for fear of Debbie's reaction, whose head was now spinning like the kid's from *The Exorcist*.

'Fucking detoxing. Is she having a laugh? Right, girls, we are kidnapping the bitch.'

Debbie leapt from the car and placed the bottle of rosé securely on the ground. Debbie rarely parted with alcohol, so this meant that some serious shit was about to go down.

'Come on, then, wankers, get out of the car and help me.'

The Skoda's grey roof sounded like it would cave in as Debbie knocked down hard, signalling that all the girls needed to get out of the car and be ready for action.

Bella groaned, one eye on her watch. 'Should we just leave her? If she doesn't want to come, well, we can't just force her, can we?' Bella was once again assuming the stiff adult role of the group.

There were no words needed for Debs' face in reaction to Bella's outburst. Like ninja warriors, the girls tiptoed around to the back entrance of the house, ensuring that they ducked whenever they came close to a window. All curtains were drawn, so there wasn't much chance of discovery; all the same, Debbie was taking no chances. On reaching the back door, Debs raised her finger to her lips, signalling for quiet. She slowly reached out for the back door's handle and the lever was steadily pulled down. The door clicked open. Debbie screwed up her face in delight, half smiling, knowing that an unwitting Sharon would be calmly relaxing inside.

Crawling awkwardly along the kitchen floor, Debbie turned every few seconds to offer either a slow or a fast gesture, using her hands as silence signals, arse high in the air, rubbing her knees and pulling her leggings out of her crotch (nice). Bella fought the urge to laugh out loud but, at size 18, she was quite a large lady herself and the army-like manoeuvres were starting to take their toll, her pants wedging uncomfortably up her crack.

In the distance, the girls could make out Shaz lazily drinking tea, laying on her couch, stroking her Golden Labrador Molly Moo and watching *Annie*, FFS. Debbie shook her head angrily and sounded the charge.

'Let's get her!'

All three girls swiftly got to their feet and ran at the couch, where an ashen-faced Shaz, who looked like she'd just seen a ghost, eyes staring in disbelief, could do no more than wait for the full force of the girls to come crashing down upon her.

'Arghhhhh!'

Legs, arms, arses, faces everywhere, it was messy for sure. Shaz was sandwiched at the bottom of her friends, gasping for breath, trying to speak but only muffled sounds escaping from under all the tangled bodies. Debbie stood up, arms folded, urging George and Bella to do the same so that they could circle their friend, who, instead of travelling to Glastonsocial for a top night of bands, was, instead, staying in to detox. The teacup Shaz had been drinking from earlier was placed on the side table, a china teacup decorated with exotic birds and wild flowers. Debbie angrily picked it up and sniffed at the contents.

'What the fuck is this shit, Shaz?'

There was a moment of silence.

'Sat there in your dog pants, watching *Annie*, drinking shit tea… what the actual fuck?'

Shaz looked down at her pants. She couldn't really argue. They were her slouch pants, covered in dog hair and stains from various meals over the years, pants that really should've been binned decades ago but were soft, with something homely and satisfying about them.

Debbie decided to make her move.

'You girls grab her arms and I'll get her legs.'

Shaz started to scream like a high school girl in protest, but it was too late – her friends were wrestling her up from the ground and dragging her towards the front door. The inevitable began to dawn on the startled Shaz. Whether she liked it or not, she was definitely going to Glastonsocial.

'Can I at least change my dog pants?' shouted Shaz, her wavy ginger hair dragging along the floor.

'No, you can't, Shaz, and you know *why* you can't – because I don't trust you. I know you have a lock in that there bedroom, so I'll tell you what's going to happen: We are going to strap you into the car and G will come back inside to grab some of your things and lock up. I'm even gonna squash my fat arse into the back of the car to watch over you.' Debbie was looking Shaz squarely in the eyes knowing that she would eventually get the message. Debbie couldn't quite believe that Shaz thought she could bin them off for green tea and detoxing so easily – surely she knew her better than that by now?

Flying around the bedroom, George grabbed various garments from different drawers, ramming them into a bag she found by the side of the bed. Going through Shaz's underwear drawer made George feel deeply uncomfortable so she decided to quickly grab the top layer of everything and stash it in the depths of the carrier bag.

Meanwhile, in the back of the car, Shaz had a face like a smacked arse. She was pouting with her brow furrowed, unable to believe that she had just been kidnapped from her own living room by her friends while she was wearing nothing more than dog pants, a flowered PJ top and no bra!

Flinging the bag over her shoulder as she left the house, George began the process of locking Shaz's doors. Items of clothing spilled out as she pushed her weight behind the hefty lock. Shaz looked like she could just about burst any minute.

'For fuck's sake, Jackson, a blind man could have done a better job with the packing! Shoot me now, why don't you?!'

In an attempt to relive the tension, Debbie pushed the large bottle of rosé under Shaz's nose and insisted that she have a drink. Shaz shrugged her head defiantly but Debbie was not one to be beaten and knew that eventually Shaz would cave. You would need some serious face to be seen out in the state that Shaz was currently in.

Climbing into the grey Skoda's passenger seat, George flung the carrier bag aimlessly into the back. She was going to have to deal with Bella's driving from the front, cautiously peeking through half-open eyes. The bag was quickly scooped up by a crazed Shaz, who closely regarded the contents. One by one, items were pulled out and she stared in both horror and amazement at the lack of matching garments. Hastily she snatched the bottle of rosé from Debbie's grasp and began to drink large, unadulterated gulps. Debbie smiled a smile of achievement and patted Shaz on the back like a small child being congratulated for winning a race. Debs was clearly proud of this moment and was happy for everything to be back on track again. Next stop was Jenny's, and everyone, including Debs, was hoping that she would be coming without a fuss.

The Skoda was back on track. Bella turned the keys in the ignition and the engine roared to life. Bass and drum music filled the car, and the bottle of rosé began its rounds once again. By the time they reached Jen's house, Shaz had cheered up considerably, knocking out her favoured feed-the-chicken and climb-the-ladder moves. Time was ticking. Bella honked her horn loudly, keeping the car engine revving, and glancing restlessly at her watch. Her motherly itinerary was being blown all out of kilter. Almost immediately, Jen appeared and a huge cheer went up in the car. Jen was ecstatic at such a welcome, unaware of the troubles they'd had some moments earlier at the Morphett residence.

As a way of initiation to both the car and the road trip, Jen was handed the bottle of rosé, absolutely no convincing needed. Big smile on her face, she chugged back the wine. In fact, she already looked half-cut, which was generally Jen's style, usually down to the lack of food and mad diet powders or perhaps simply from getting away from Mark and that child of hers. The girls let out another cheer. Debbie admired Jen's enthusiasm for the trip. A kindred spirit, indeed, which meant there was a lot of fun to be had this day – Jen was a willing pawn just waiting to be played with.

As they reached the large signs for the festival, traffic started to slow down and queue. The girls were extremely wired. They eyed up the passengers in other vehicles, knowing that they would all soon be partying and having fun together. Bella apologised, and just as George was about to enquire what Bella was apologising for, the most stomach-churning, foul smell filled the car. Windows were rolled down as quickly as was physically possible (no electric windows – skanky grey Skoda, remember). The girls held onto their noses tightly whilst heaving and gagging in unison.

'It's not that bad,' protested Bella innocently.

'Not that bad, are you fucking kidding, Bella? They could use your arse for toxic warfare. You could kill an entire village! Smells like something has died up there,' Debbie raged, now very drunk and needing to leave the car. Bella chuckled to herself. *Amazing what folk are proud of themselves for these days*, George thought. George leaned over and dug Bella sharply in the ribs.

'Bella, pack it in, you bloody stink.' She couldn't help but smile, and a full-on belly laugh followed. They had grown up together and during many family occasions, Bella was encouraged to let off one of her unforgettable farts just to cause a scene or to let them go home and play.

The car was 100 feet from the entrance and the girls could make out security guards and sniffer dogs checking tickets and rummaging through luggage, removing any alcohol in glass bottles. Bins on either side of the entrance were mounted high with various alcoholic beverages: vodka, whisky, gin... you name it, it was in there. (*Sacrilege!*) Debbie caught sight of the carnage ahead.

'No fucking way.' Her face was furious and you could see the cogs of her mind turning, wondering how she could work out a way to rescue her booze.

'Stop the car, Bella,' Debs roared.

Bella was about to protest but knew better. She pulled to the left of the queue and did as instructed. She pushed the button on her dashboard to activate her hazards, indicating that they were having a little bit of a problem.

Debbie pounced from the car like a panther. There it was again, that majestic stealth, a power that appeared only at random moments. She ran around to the boot and began removing the alcohol. She passed it to the girls at the front of the car.

'What do you want me to do with this?' Jen asked quizzically.

'Stick it up your bloody arse, Jen. I don't know; hide it!' Debs was getting a bit of a sweat on, moving from the back of the car to the front, handing over the contraband.

'Eat these cakes, girls,' urged Debbie, impatiently ramming ugly brown dome cakes into the faces of each of her friends. They smelt weird, a bit earthy and not at all appetising.

'I'm not sure I like the look of this, Debbie,' Bella offered politely.

'I didn't ask whether you liked the look of it, Bella, just get it down your grid.'

The atmosphere was tense and the cars passing them in the queue were rubber-necking to try to work out what the girls were up to.

Debbie lunged back into the car, big wet patches under her armpits from the sudden exertion.

'All the beer hidden, ladies?' Debbie eagerly looked over each of her friends to see if she could spot the booze. 'Good job, girls. Bella, get us back in the queue. We are fucking ready.'

Bella started to nudge her way back into the queue for the entrance. Lucky for them, the festival-goers were quite laid back and sociable, so it was easy enough to get back on course.

The car was third in the queue. Bella gulped, a little anxious that they may get found with the glass bottles and have their tickets taken from them. The rest of the girls were pretty relaxed and casual; the large bottle of rosé had softened the edges and they were inclined to believe that they weren't doing anything wrong. On approaching the security station, Bella rolled down her window and presented the group's tickets, smiling broadly, unaware of the brown cake stuck between her teeth. The skinny man with a face full of piercings, greasy pores and elaborate tattoos up his arms examined the tickets closely, eyeing Bella suspiciously, whose grin was not entirely genuine. He motioned with his arm for his colleague with the sniffer dog to go around to the back of the car and open the boot to check for glass bottles and have a quick rummage through the girls' things.

'You don't have any alcohol in glass bottles, do you, ladies?' He had a thick Scottish accent with an unhealthy dose of gob rot. He began peering through the window of the car but the girls had done an amazing job of hiding the contraband. The sniffer dog at the back of the car had hold of the tray that the cakes had been on earlier, growling and pushing his nose up hard against the tray and the remaining crumbs. The guard round the rear yanked at the dog's chain. They marched back round to Bella and held out the offending tray.

'Is this yours, miss?' he asked rather sternly, poker-straight face unamused at Bella's toothy grin full of cake.

'Er, erm, yes, that's what we had our birthday cake on earlier. We are really sorry we didn't leave any for your dog.' She sounded meek and quite pathetic; she knew those cakes were a bit wrong and had her suspicions about the main ingredient.

Her mouth was like a sand pit. All moisture had evaporated, causing her lips to almost stick to her gums as she spoke. The security guard frowned and forced the tray onto Bella's lap, whose heart was pounding uncontrollably fast.

'On your way, girls.' The Scottish guard was already moving onto the car behind them and Bella was relieved for the security checks to be over. Once again, she started up the car and sluggishly creeped away from the entrance for fear of the glass bottles clanging together somewhere in the back. She sighed heavily, looked for the parking signs and followed the signals being given by the guys in florescent jackets. Her heart rate was just about back to normal. Debbie cheered and the rest of the girls joined in – they'd made it past Checkpoint Charlie. They had their own beer, which meant they weren't going to have to spend their hard-earned cash on diluted piss sold at inflated prices.

They had the luxury of parking in the camper-van entrance since they were staying in the horsebox. The toilets were always so much cleaner than the rest of the camping sites full of shit heaving over the sides of the loo. George liked to think that if she was slumming it, at least she was doing it in style. The girls piled eagerly out of the grey Skoda. The air was stale and humid as though it had been trapped in a plastic bottle with one of Bella's farts.

'Thank God that's over,' exclaimed Bella. 'It's alright for you shitfaced lot... Did you hear my heart beating? Did you?'

Adrenalin soared through Bella's body, making her giddy. She grinned at the girls, pleased with herself for getting them through the barricade of confiscated booze. George immediately laughed when she spotted the cake lodged around Bella's front teeth. What must those security guards have thought?

'What's up, G? What're you laughing at?' Bella's giddy high was formally over and she demanded an explanation from her friends, who were almost pissing themselves just looking in her direction. George offered Bella her iPhone and turned the picture-taking gadget around so that Bella could see herself in the reflection.

'What the fuck, girls.'

They laughed even harder now as Bella used her fingernail to frantically scrape at the cake firmly lodged around her front tooth and upper gums.

'Oh my God, the shame,' she wailed, thinking how stupid she must've looked when using her winning smile to charm the security guards.

'Three cheers for Bella,' cried Debbie. The girls whooped and patted Bella on the back, thanking her for driving and for getting them through the entrance.

'Always said you had a lovely smile, our Bell.' George couldn't help herself teasing her sister.

Bella shrugged, beaten by the joke that no doubt would make their entire weekend. The girls dumped the alcohol bottles into a pile on the floor. Jenny had managed to neatly balance a litre bottle of vodka across her tits, her corset coming in handy for more than just redistributing her fat for once, and Debs was massively impressed. Shaz looked down at her top, where both tits were pointing south. She shook her head, half-pissed, and pulled a yellow bra from the bag George had packed.

'For fuck's sake, Jackson!' Shaz was digging out some leggings and a grey Stone Roses t-shirt, discarding the dog pants whilst hopping about on one leg, desperately hoping that no one was watching. They collected their things from the boot of the car and began the long walk up the trail towards the camper vans to find their home for the night, along with their much-loved friend Tracey.

The Bands

Having finished off the large pile of booze Debbie had brought, they were now forced to drink expensive pints of watered-down Carling. The cakes they had eaten earlier had been made with pot and they found themselves laughing at everyone and everything; Bella in particular was off her face. Ironic, really. Normally she would be the one assuming the moral high ground.

They found a great spot near the front of the field where the bands were playing. Glastonsocial was a mini festival so consisted of only one main stage, a rave tent and a curious circus canopy that they'd never ventured into before, as the film *It* had ended their love of clowns many years ago. There were lots of food and drink stalls scattered around the grounds and George asked Jen if she fancied getting something to eat before the next band came on, taking advantage of Jen's semi-pissed state, as she would now be lacking the will power to put up a fight for her diet. A delicious smell of cooked pork and apple drew them in to the nearest hog roast. There was a full pig turning on a skewer in the back of the hut with tubs of crackling laid out along the counter. Whilst they stood in the queue, George fumbled in her pocket for her blue joke sweets and popped one into her mouth. Using her tongue, she sucked hard on the sugar capsule, ensuring that she coated her teeth and lips with a generous layer of the blue chalky film, and turned towards Jen. Grinning wildly, she asked, 'Have I got something on my teeth, Jen?' mimicking Bella's voice. The gag from earlier continued and Jen roared with laughter. A little bit of blue spit dribbled down George's chin, who laughed a little too loudly with her friend.

She was about to turn around to read the menu boards when something caught her attention – rather, some*one* caught her attention. George recognised a face in the queue quite near to the back.

It was Charles.

Her stomach knotted. He didn't look vaguely amused. George quickly wiped the spit from her chin with the sleeve of her coat. She was drunk enough to think she might just go over there and start a conversation, looking over confidently, never taking her eyes from his. She stepped forward, trying not to overthink it, heart hammering in her ears, eyes blurry from the booze. Then, there she was, a beautiful, tall brunette who had waltzed up to Charles and kissed him tenderly on the cheek, arm placed casually around his waist, talking excitedly. Her heart almost stopped and she turned, swiftly lodging herself proficiently back into the queue, a dull anguish throbbing where the laughter had been. Jen noticed a sudden change in the atmosphere.

'You okay, George?' she asked sweetly. George nodded and was glad that it was her turn to be served. She quickly pointed at the boards to what she and Jen would be having and paid the guy, offering a small tip. She liked to think that the universe would offer some positivity back into her life in return... not that she felt like it was doing anything of the kind at this precise moment.

Scooping up their food, embarrassed by her blue teeth performance, George gripped Jen's arm tightly. She chatted cheerfully and steered her friend away from where Charles was standing with his lady friend so they wouldn't have to pass by him. Once clear of the food queues, feeling somewhat dejected, George unlinked from Jen's arm. The corners of her mouth curled down, abandoning her previous faked, happy-go-lucky demeanour. Jen, thankfully, was now walking just slightly in front, so George had just a few moments to get her shit together before they were back with the rest of the group.

'Here they are. How's the hog roast?' Debs was over to see if any food was on offer and began picking at the pork lumped at the side of Jen's tray, dipping it in the apple sauce.

'Mmmmmmmm. Tasty, girlies. Good choice,' Debs chuckled. The band made its way onto the stage and the crowd applauded in appreciation; you'd have thought U2 was playing or something. The band was aptly named The Cats. Some scrawny-looking dude up front was howling like he was in severe pain. The music wasn't actually that bad and George decided that, from this distance, at least, the drummer actually looked pretty darn hot.

Bella danced around like a crazed spirit, her thin blonde hair covered with a hair hanky to stop the sun from burning her scalp. It looked like she was performing some kind of Indian ritual, legs spread wide, jumping on the spot whilst rotating, arms spread out like eagle wings. A guy with dreadlocks joined in, thrusting about, trying to copy Bella's moves. It was all the encouragement she needed.

'I'm going up front,' she wailed, yanking dreadlock dude by the arm, and started barging her way through the crowd towards the stage.

The girls looked on and laughed. It wasn't often that Bella let herself go to such an extent, so it was good to see her having so much fun.

'What the fuck is she doing?' Debs started to dance about like a lunatic, shaking her arms wildly in the air, kissing each of the girls in turn. Now was as good a time as any to ramp up the delirium and so George retrieved a small bottle of shots she had managed to stash at the bottom of her bag, covered in tampons and pads, since men never looked farther than these items at bag searches. Usually their hand would touch a tampon and they would recoil as if bitten by a snake, a look of disgust on their faces. It never ceased to amaze George just how easy it was to get away with it.

George unscrewed the lid and took a big swig of the pear-infused shot. Debbie went next and handed it to Jen, who retched repeatedly after swallowing. If any of them were to part with their stomachs, they would then incur a forfeit from Debbie, so it was far better to keep the shots down than to let that happen. The girls had taken their eyes off Bella for literally a few minutes, but when you're off your face, it only takes a few minutes. As they turned their attention to the front of the stage, they could see Bella climbing over the small partitioned fence that kept the crowd from the band. On making it over the barrier, Bella was heading for the steps to the left of the stage. George swore that this was the fastest she'd ever seen Bella move, except for at the all-you-can-eat buffet bars, where she was a woman on a mission.

'What the actual fuck is she doing, G?' Debbie was the only one brave enough to put her astonishment into words. None of them were running to the front of the stage to help – they were all kind of glued to the spot, watching in horror as the scene unfolded in movie-like slow motion.

Bella was running at the lead singer of The Cats, sheer determination on her face. If it had been a film and the scene was paused right at this moment, you would think that she intended to rugby tackle the scrawny singer to the ground. In actual fact, she stopped within a few inches of him, abruptly turned towards the crowd and offered them a show of her Indian dance moves. The crowd cheered loudly, whistling and chanting 'Dance! Dance!' Bella twisted and writhed about, pushing the lead singer of The Cats behind her so she could be centre stage for her adoring fans.

Security is never great at these types of gigs but it took this bunch of idiots at least 2 minutes to recognise that there was even an issue before getting onto the stage. If Bella had intended to harm somebody, security would've been far too late. It kind of reminded George of the portly security guard at her office. Men now entered from the wings at both sides of the stage and Bella's arms were pulled firmly behind her back. The crowd booed as Bella's Indian jig was brought to a halt. The singer for The Cats attempted a comeback but the crowd continued to boo. He threw his microphone to the ground in a dramatic strop and sulked off.

They decided to go and see what security would do with their Bella. They were all far too drunk to be driving home this evening. George prayed that Bella wouldn't be handed over to the police; spending a night in the cells was not something that Bella's self-righteous conscience would be able to endure and besides she hated enclosed spaces. Luckily, the security team comprised of volunteers from local farms who didn't really know what to do with Bella once they'd captured her. They were more than happy to hand her over to her willing friends.

'Did you see me, G? Did you see me?' Bella was pulling at George's coat, eyes bright, looking for a well done, a bit like Fatima at the aerobics class, except with Bella, it was adorable.

'I did see you, Bella. You were hilarious.'

The scene reminded George of all of the fun they used to have listening to their record collection as kids, singing along with the words. Bella always used to screw up. On one Kula Shaker song, she would screech at the top of her lungs 'I'm just a stupid dickhead', as if those were the actual words. Funny thing was, she had convinced herself that they were. George chuckled to herself. Bella would be devastated when the girls played back what she'd been up to tomorrow morning.

The crowd parted as the girls walked through with their Indian dancer. Randomers were leaning in and kissing Bella and patting her on the back as they walked towards the beer tent. Bella was loving her new celebrity status and George wondered if she would ever come down from the damn chocolate cake Debs had force-fed her more than six hours ago.

It had been a really great evening but it was a relief when they eventually decided to call it a night. 'The Temple of Boom', which was a barn with hay and rave music, had managed to finish the girls off. The horsebox was close now so the girls stopped at the next set of toilets, hoping that this would be the last wee any of them would need for the rest of the night. Tracey and horsy Derek were fast asleep in the converted bed, Tracey snoring like a pneumatic drill. Jen fought the urge to laugh. The girls began the arduous task of unravelling their sleeping bags and arranging their pillows around the outer edges of the horsebox. George had a caterpillar-shaped bag that she'd bought in town the day before. It was a decent make and on offer, so she was really pleased with herself. The reality of her purchase, though, was about to become clear. She climbed into the bag, and when her feet touched the bottom, she realised she couldn't pull the back part of the bag up any further. At first, she thought it was stuck. Then she firmly understood that the bag only came up to her waist. The hooded part that she was meant to snuggle into was never going to make it anywhere near her head. George had been sold a sleeping bag for either a dwarf or else it was, in fact, a junior's. *FFS.* It was a good job she was drunk enough to fall asleep. She cradled down on the floor, hoping it wouldn't be too cold in the night. #campingsucks

A loud noise woke George from her sleep. Her mouth was as dry as a desert and her head pounded. For a moment, she struggled to focus and was sure she could see her own forehead from the corner of her eyes. What sounded like a camel pissing outside turned out to be their Bella, who'd accidentally allowed the horsebox door to spring shut. Bella shuffled back inside, hunched over, looking dreadful. All the guys adopted this stance when feeling utterly wounded and actually gave it a name: The Hurt Locker. George groaned. There was no way she was going to get back to sleep with cotton mouth. She needed to find a drink, and fast. Using her iPhone for light, George was able to find a bottle of Coke near Jen's bag and began to pray that there wasn't any alcohol inside for fear of projectile vomiting. She unscrewed the lid and sniffed cautiously. It did smell like Coke, so she went in for the kill, swigging greedily and drinking so fast that her stomach hurt. Recoiling back into the foetal position, forehead still very visible, she hoped she would drift off before Bella started to snore. She was a little worried about either her distorted vision or her distorted face.

Horse Face

Waking up in the horsebox was no fun at all. The five girls had created a toxic fog from their alcohol-infused breath, which was stifling and deadly. Debbie looked like a resident smackhead, pale with big dark circles bulging under her eyes, new spots forming along her chin. She proceeded to make herself a concoction of tonics: paracetamol mixed with Berocca, caffeine tablets and an anti-sickness pill. Bella's jowls flapped together as she continued to grunt, animal-style, not quite in the land of the living yet.

'Fuck, it stinks in here,' muttered George, deciding that she needed to get out and try to shake off the hangover by getting some fresh air into her lungs. She kicked off the kid-sized caterpillar sleeping bag and clambered ungracefully to her feet with a wide yawn, arms stretched skywards. Debbie, who was halfway through her pint of rescue remedy, paused to check out her friend's profile. It wasn't unusual after a night like they'd had for them to be looking somewhat dishevelled and rough, but there was something about George's face that wasn't quite right.

George turned to meet Debbie's enquiring gaze, aware that something was troubling her friend.

'You feel alright, George?' asked Debbie, still staring.

'A bit shit, to be honest. My head is pounding.' This statement appeared to further trouble Debbie.

'Pounding normal, like on other nights, or worse?' Debs sounded panicked and had lost all enthusiasm for her rescue remedy. She placed it on the floor so she could pull herself up to stand. George wasn't entirely sure what Debs was getting at or why she was so interested in the severity of her hangover. She stepped awkwardly backwards as Debs walked towards her.

'I don't know how to say this, George, but you look a little bit like Rocky Dennis.'

Whilst the statement was clearly unflattering, it was obvious that Debs was attempting to be sincere, offering George a small compact mirror to check it out for herself.

'Jesus Christ!' exclaimed George so loudly that all the girls were now awake and protesting the sudden outburst.

'I look like bloody Horsey Derek. What the actual fuck, Debbie?!'

George was now full-on panicking. Her forehead and nose were swollen and bulbous. It was then that she remembered waking earlier in the night and thinking that something might be amiss.

'What do I do? What's happening?' George could feel the tears welling up in her eyes. She was really scared about what was happening to her. She'd seen programmes on the TV where people had been bitten by mosquitos and ended up with elephantiasis and had deformed, swollen legs for their rest of their lives.

All the girls were on their feet, packing quickly and agreeing that they best leave and get George to a hospital. Lucy threw George a towel.

'What's this for?' asked George.

'I thought you could wrap it around your head. Stop, er, you know, everyone looking as we walk back to the car.'

Lucy, God bless, was trying her best to help but instead was putting her foot in it big time.

'Good one, Lucy, make her feel better, why don't you?' Debbie flung an arm around George's shoulders. 'Stick with me, kid. I'll get you sorted.'

The group huddled together as they walked back down the muddy path towards the car. Debbie scowled at anyone that even glanced in their direction, hissing like a wild cobra. George had her hoody up, head down, holding onto the back of Bella's arm for guidance. It was hard for George not to think about the worst-case scenario. Not only was she the stupid girl with blue teeth to Charles, she now had a deformed face that may never go back. They'd have to sack her from work under some law that nobody's ever heard of and pack her off to some sort of leper camp like you see in the Jesus films shown at Eastertime. Her mind ramblings were in full swing. She could sue the bastards if they let her go just for being a bulbous-headed freak. A tear rolled down the side of her cheek and she wiped it away quickly before any of the others could see. She didn't want to add *crybaby* to the list of less-than-endearing nicknames she'd earned that weekend.

The girls dumped their stuff into the boot of the car and piled in, trying to look anywhere but directly at George, who was obviously panic-stricken.

'How do I look? Come on, Jen, how's it looking? It feels like it's gone down a bit.'

A tumbleweed moment followed. Jen turned to her friends for guidance on what to say. George waited, wide-eyed and scared, for someone to give her an update.

'It's, erm... er... it could be going down. I wouldn't want to say it has but there definitely could've been a change.'

The offering from Jen was pitiful and George sank back down in her seat, tearfully strapping herself in.

'Come on, Bella. Get me the fuck out of here.'

The car had moved literally less than 100 yards before the back wheels became firmly lodged in some colossal mud pit adjacent to the camper-van's toilet block. Bella had obviously been paying little attention to the state of the track and had ploughed on regardless, trying to get them on their way as hastily as possible, keen for George to be given a diagnosis, praying that the condition was not contagious. (Selfish bitch!)

The constant revving of the engine and the foul outbursts soon drew quite a large crowd. George brought her hand up to cover the top half of her face, quietly mumbling 'For fuck's sake', hoody gripped ever tighter. Bella got out of the car and began to enthusiastically round up volunteers to help push them out of the pit. Everyone but George was on their feet to assist, having developed a newfound energy and eagerness to set the car free. A couple of the volunteers were trying to work out what was wrong with the girl in the passenger seat, getting up close to the Skoda's windows to peer through, but promptly decided she must simply be a smashed-up mess like the rest of them. Maybe just a little further along, like the paraplegic stage from *The Wolf of Wall Street*.

'JEE-eez, mate! Have you checked out that girl's gizzard?' one volunteer with long, dreadlocked hair said to his skinny mate, who'd already lost interest and was puffing away on a fat joint. Bella got back in as one of the handy helpers instructed her to try the engine again whilst the supporters pushed. On a count of three, Bella turned the key in the ignition, and within a few seconds the car had been pushed free of the mud pit. Bella was ecstatic, beaming proudly. The volunteers, on the other hand, were somewhat less impressed, as the wheels had spun free large amounts of mud and blue loo liquid, which had sprayed them from head to toe.

Debbie shouted every single profanity under the sun as she got back in the car, wiping her face on the sleeve of her jumper. Turning cautiously, Bella wanted to see what all the fuss was about, the smell reaching her nostrils almost instantly.

'Smells like shit, this, Bella. Better not *be* fucking shit, this. I am fuming. You pull into any more of that shit' – she pointed wildly at the offensive matter just outside the toilets – 'and I'm gonna *feed* it to ya.' Debbie closed her eyes, praying for calm. Her head was completely gone. She felt like shit and, by all accounts, now smelt like shit as well.

The Drive Home

Halfway home, in the back of the car, Debs leaned on Lucy's chest, fast asleep and snoring aggressively. Bella was fighting off the urge to be sick and congratulated herself on every mile that passed. How anyone could sleep in that putrid smell was beyond her. The car shook furiously and alarmed everyone. Bella diligently checked the gauges and saw that the temperature dial was all the way over. She looked at George sympathetically and knew that this was going to add yet another delay to their journey. At this point, she felt more for George than for whatever it might cost to fix her car.

The car dials flashed and Bella, now frightened of a fire, pulled the Skoda onto the hard shoulder. Smoke bustled from under the bonnet in thick grey plumes. Unconsciously, George pulled her hoody tighter around her swollen horse face for fear of anyone seeing her, like the Hunchback of Notre Dame lurking in the shadows. Panicking, Bella searched the contacts on her phone for someone that could quickly rescue them from the situation; traffic police would be all they needed at this point.

'Stu!' she called out, beaming and clearly delighted with herself. 'I'll call Stu. He has a tow bar.'

Debs reached forward and patted George on the shoulder reassuringly.

'We'll soon be home, chick. Hang in there, G. That Stu will be here in no time.'

George had her eyes tightly closed in a desperate attempt to stop the little voice in her head from offering her any more advice. Her mind ramblings were in overdrive, spitting and hissing negativity. Lucy fumbled about in her neon backpack, elbows knocking Jen and Debs, and eventually retrieved half a dozen warm, squished cereal bars. Jen, never one to look a gift horse in the mouth, nasty smell in the car or not, snatched a bar. She tore at the wrapper, snapped off a large chunk of gooey crispies and popped it greedily into her mouth. Jen nodded her head in approval.

'You not on one of your fad diets, then, Jen?' Debs asked inquisitively. She was always on some stupid diet, touting bollocks about the benefits. One time she was trying to get them all to join in with the Palaeolithic diet, some caveman kind of approach to food. Jen's upper lip curled in disdain and she shot Debs a *drop-dead* type of glare. Debs immediately backed off. She wasn't trying to ruffle Jen's feathers, she was just so used to the diet pills, shakes, powders and weird antics in restaurants. Jen always created a scene because whatever diet she was on usually meant she could only combine certain sets of food groups.

Debs shrugged it off. She couldn't give a shit what people ate. Life was too short for that sort of nonsense. The thought of food made Debs' stomach rumble loudly but she wasn't eating no warm crispie bar, no way. She would be attacking a full cow with cheesy chips when she got home. *Show me the rump*, thought Debs, licking her lips.

'Mmmmm. Lovely, these, Lucy.' Jen dusted the crumbs off her legs, dismissing Debs' earlier comment, and casually looked to see if anyone else was going to take an interest in the food before she dived in for a second helping. Bella passed George some antihistamines, encouraging her to take a few, thinking she could be having some powerful allergic reaction to something or other... not that George had ever suffered from anything remotely like this until now.

A car beeped and pulled in close behind them on the hard shoulder, which caused the girls to all but jump out of their skin. They were extremely hungover, tired and a little worried that their friend might have something slightly on the contagious side. Stu swaggered over slowly. With his mop of blond hair, broad shoulders and sun-kissed skin, he was lovely to look at, but that's about as far as it went. He was as dull as dish water; a shame, really. Bella threw her arms around his neck and clasped his cheeks tightly between her podgy fingers. She repeatedly thanked him for being their knight in shining armour. *A little over the top*, thought George. Bella was clearly just up for a bit of a grope. The grey smoke had dissipated but a burning smell was distinctly present. Stu popped the hood and carefully eyed the frazzled parts, shaking his head. He decided that the best course of action would be to tow the car back to town, where he could take a better look. With swift precision, he pulled his car in front of Bella's so that he could attach the tow bar. He managed a perfect reverse park and the girls giddily clapped. George had to bite her tongue to prevent the *FFS* from escaping her lips. Patting the bonnet, Stu indicated that he'd secured the line, and shot George a quick nod of the head as a way of hello. George tried to politely nod back, hoody held securely around her face. Exchanging a few rushed words with Bella, Stu ensured that she understood what she needed to do, then raced off towards his car.

He held his arm out of the car window to alert Bella that the journey was about to begin. She gripped the steering wheel firmly and waited for the full force of the tug to kick in. The hookup was a triumph, and within minutes, they were back on the road, guided by Stu's skilful hand. There was a collective sigh from the girls, who were all beginning to tire of the endless catastrophes. It appeared that fortune had finally decided to shine in their direction as they navigated the rest of the motorway without incident. On approaching the centre of town, they were greeted by a number of road works with cones stretched out as far as the eye could see. Traffic was heavily congested, with some roads completely cornered off.

A temporary traffic light system was in play which allowed only a handful of cars to pass through at any one time, further fuelling the frustration amongst the disgruntled motorists. Stu carefully applied his brakes as the lights returned to red, and he waited patiently for the sequence to roll through, first cars from the left, then from the right, then from in front, until finally it was their turn.

The lights switched from red to green and Stu pulled forward, gently steering his car proficiently through the coned maze.

There was a loud thud and the grey Skoda jolted backwards as the unthinkable happened: the metal tow bar had come away from the back of Stu's car. The girls were left stranded across the lights.

Agitated drivers began to beep their horns repeatedly, furiously trying to fathom why the grey car in front was motionless and blocking the road. Bella was all red in the face and panic-stricken beads of sweat formed on her brow.

'Oh, shit, shit, what do I do, G?' She pushed the red triangle button on her dashboard to activate the hazards but the loud beeping continued. Some drivers had taken to offering abuse.

Bella covered her ears and closed her eyes as the pressure took its toll. She'd clearly never found herself in a predicament like this before. George, on the other hand, regularly found herself in situations like these and knew that she would have to take control, horse face or not. She couldn't bear to see their Bella in such a state. Muttering *for fuck's sake* under her breath for what had to be the ten millionth time that day, she opened the car door and stepped out. The girls gasped in admiration as George pulled down her hoody, holding up her hands to the cars behind.

'Okay! Okay. The car's broken down.' She tapped on the window and motioned for the girls to get out. 'Not you, Bella. I need you to steer.'

Bella hesitantly got back in the car and George began to clear away a number of cones so the car could be pushed free from the road and onto the construction site where materials were being stored.

The beeping abruptly stopped; George couldn't be sure if she had scared the motorists into silence with a glimpse of her horse face or if they were just happy to see someone taking action. Either way, it felt good to be assuming some authority, and once the car was off the road, George neatly stacked the cones back up in front so that the pathway would be clear for the other motorists. Stu had realised that he'd lost his cargo and had headed back up one of the connecting roads to see if he could get close enough to help. He approved of their quick-witted plan and whistled for the girls to come over, telling Bella that he would get one of the lads from the garage to pick the car up in the early hours of the morning when there would be less traffic to contend with.

The girls piled into Stu's car, with George settled in the front seat, hoody fully pulled down to expose her rather unusual profile. Stu caught a glimpse and turned awkwardly to face the road ahead. He'd learnt the hard way that women didn't appreciate the truth and he was pretty rubbish at lying. What was it that people said? 'You can roll a shit in glitter, but it's still a shit'? Well, this was one of those moments.

The car was deafeningly silent. Stu, true to character, didn't say a word and drove the girls safely to Debs' place, where he helped them unload their things. It was only as he turned to wave the girls goodbye that he noticed a strong smell of faeces and the girls' brown-stained clothes. He crumpled his nose and hastily retreated. These girls were barking mad, and he wasn't sure he wanted to find out what they'd been up to. Maybe it was safer not to know.

The Hospital

The accident and emergency administrator began noting George's details and quite unsympathetically asked for her exact symptoms, to which George rudely pointed at her face.

'Er, this. You see this?' The chubby woman remained unmoved and continued to make notes. She must see stuff like this all the time. The woman was in her late fifties and had short brown hair with grey roots plus stubble. (George checked her own face on a daily basis for any sprigs of unwanted hair; naturally, it's not that attractive to the opposite sex... or any sex, for that matter.) There was no evidence of a wedding band on her finger, and George concluded that the chubby lady probably wasn't married because she lacked empathy and was old and prickly. It wasn't like George to be having such negative thoughts towards another person. She generally found this kind of behaviour physically draining and avoided it at all costs. But today had been a very large bag of shite; she'd woken up looking like Rocky Dennis's twin, they'd broken down twice – well, sort of – and the sheer humiliation of the day was bordering on intolerable.

Beryl patted her daughter's knee as they took their seats in the waiting room. Other patients talked quietly amongst themselves, although it was more than obvious that a fair proportion of the conversations were centred around George's face. One patient who was sat directly in front of George shamelessly turned all the way around to get a good look.

'Take no notice, dear. It's not that bad. Couple of days and you will be as right as rain.' Beryl was doing her best to reassure her daughter that whatever had happened to her face was only temporary, and George was happy to have her there. So far, she was the only person to have offered a glimmer of hope into her condition since the nightmare had begun. Perhaps her enthusiasm was linked to her love of announcing the dead. Let's face it, if George carked it, the news would be public knowledge in no time.

After a painful 5-hour wait, George was eventually seen and some blood was taken. The doctors surmised that the swelling on George's face was down to an allergic reaction and guessed that since George recently stayed in a horsebox, the culprit could have been a horsefly. That was the final nail in the coffin, and George promised herself that she would never go camping again. She hated the cold, insects, and mud, and it appeared that the natural outdoors had an unrefined dislike for her, too.

A packet of strong antihistamine pills was subscribed and she was advised that the swelling may take as long as five days to go down. Hibernation and a sick note for work was what the situation called for, and George was ready to indulge. Usually she was rather judgemental about colleagues taking time off for what she often assumed was no good reason, but horse face, she believed, fell into the 'good reason' category and was not prepared to give the matter another thought.

Best Mate

George lay across the couch in her fluffy pink onesie, dark and heavy curtains fully drawn, eating salted popcorn and watching *The Proposal*, a staple romance story required for any girl feeling a bit low and unloved. The phone started to ring. George groaned, fretfully covering her ears. She couldn't bear to listen to her mother right now. She needed her Ryan Reynolds fix in great whopping doses. The answering machine faithfully clicked in.

'I know you are there, George!' shouted Carmen, a touch of mischief in her tone. 'Pick up, you bloody fool.' There was a sudden silence; George prayed that Carmen had found someone more important to torture.

'I will keep ringing, you know.' Then: 'I bet you are watching Ryan Reynolds.'

George leaped from the couch, somewhat upset for being so predictable, and lifted the handset.

'Hi, Carmen. I am NOT watching Ryan Reynolds.' George tried her best twinkly voice, but without success. It was true, what people said: You have to be laughing on the inside for it to shine through to the outside.

'I hear the festival was eventful.'

Carmen had obviously heard every last detail but was now here to get it straight from the horse's mouth – an apt expression given George's appearance for the better part of the week.

'I heard your B was a right old mess, crashing the stage with her Indian moves.' Carmen could be heard chuckling. 'And then the, er, horsefly bite, which you had a reaction to, and then, of course, the car breaking down.' The chuckle had rapidly evolved into a full-blown cackle. George listened without interrupting. This sort of stuff would never happen to Carmen; she was too cool. She would never go camping to then end up making a complete fool of herself. George scolded herself for having missed out on such an important life gene. Her mother Beryl, with her love of spandex and spreading the word of death, had a lot to answer for.

'Send me a picture, G. Go on, I bet it's not all that bad.'

George was half smiling. Here was her best friend in the whole world asking for a picture of her face, not handing out sympathy or offering suggestions, just plain old frankness. Good old Carmen.

'You can bugger off. Anyway, it's gone down now – I'm more donkey than horse.' The emphasis on her words had George in a spin, which caused her to accidentally sit on the TV remote and increase the volume substantially. Carmen seized the opportunity to strike.

'I *knew* you were watching Ryan Reynolds, you sad old goat!' George slammed down the phone, grinning to herself. There it was again: her unique ability for getting things wrong at crucial moments. Her timing for 'stupid' was perfect... Where was this audacious ability when it truly counted for achieving something agreeable or positive?

The phone rang again, and Carmen was braying into the answering machine like a donkey, laughing hysterically. George couldn't help but smile while walking back over to the couch, where she snuggled into the comfy cushions.

'Screw you, Carmen Parkes,' she hissed, and scooped large handfuls of popcorn into her mouth, completely content with her love for Ryan Reynolds.

Good Old Mum

It's funny how all the things we do to make ourselves feel better eventually start to make us feel worse. Take food, for instance – the happiness associated with scoffing down a cheesecake is remarkably short-lived, quickly followed by self-loathing and a critical assessment of one's waistline. George's sugar high had peaked and she found herself swiftly spiralling downwards. All serotonin drained from her body and her mind ramblings were back in full swing. Scathing reviews of her performance at the festival with her blue teeth whipped her into a sobbing frenzy.

'YOO HOO.'

Beryl had let herself in and was not wasting a minute to complain about the state of George's house.

'Why is it so dark in here? For heaven's sake, George, you're not a vampire. You will catch scurvy if you don't let some light in. Mr Jones died in a murky house like this.'

George had her head buried deep within the pillows, trying desperately to wipe away the tears but unable to stop the inward sob that caught in her throat.

The sound startled Beryl, who let go of the curtain she had been fighting with. A slight shade of pink became noticeable on her cheeks as she acknowledged that her pushy behaviour had driven her to focus on the house instead of her daughter. Rushing over to comfort George, she kneeled down beside the couch and reached out to gently stroke her hair.

'There, there, darling. Tell mum what the problem is.' Beryl's tone had softened. She was genuinely concerned and waited patiently for George to respond.

'It's just a mess, mum.' There was more sobbing. 'I'm just a mess. Everything is always going wrong.'

George was face-down on her couch, no longer trying to hold back the emotion but letting it surface in great big waves of tears and snot.

'I like this guy, mum, I really, really, really like him, and now it's too late.'

Beryl encouraged George to sit. She used her hanky to dab tears from under her eyes. She knew she was too critical of George but it was because she believed she had so much going for her, could achieve so much with her life. Her words were spoken out of love. It hurt to see her daughter like this. She recognised that instead of drawing her closer, she had been pushing her away.

'Darling… Any man would be lucky to have you.' Beryl looked George deep in the eyes and smiled tenderly. 'You are beautiful, caring and have a great career. I'm sure he will come to his senses.'

George blew her nose hard into her mother's hanky. Beryl tried desperately to hide her disappointment as green snot filled what was, an elegantly stitched lavender plant handkerchief, something she'd never intended on actually using.

As George cleaned up her face, Beryl was surprised by how much the swelling had gone down. She reached into her handbag for her gold-plated compact and eagerly held it out to George. There was a moment of hesitation, but Beryl nodded and again pushed the compact towards George. She had a big smile on her face and lifted up her right thumb to indicate that everything was fine and that she should take a look.

George swiftly opened the compact and brought it to within inches of her face. She eyed herself suspiciously whilst probing her forehead with her fingers. Her mother was right: the swelling had gone. She was no longer Rocky Dennis's twin or horsey Derek's ugly sister. She was back to being George again. Every sign of deformity was gone. All the tension in her shoulders immediately dissipated and the hopelessness that she had felt in the pit of her stomach was replaced with a new vitality for life.

George threw her arms around her mother's neck and planted a big kiss on the top of her head. She couldn't remember a time when she had felt so utterly grateful for things to work out. George momentarily contemplated how unfortunate people like Rocky Dennis would never be given a break. It would never work out for them. She cast these thoughts aside because she knew her time for wallowing in self-pity was over. She needed to stop apologising for who she was. No longer would she try to suppress the calamity that was her life. This was her, this was who she was: George Jackson.

It's funny how astonishingly irritating one can find their own mother, especially in times of great stress, but there is something to be said for the love that exists between a mother and daughter and how important it is to feel supported and loved, wholeheartedly and without judgement. George was so used to her mother picking away at her that she sometimes forgot how absolutely incredible Beryl was. Although affection between them was fleeting, she knew deep down that an unbreakable bond connected them and that she would always be fighting away in her corner... Be very afraid.

Sensing a new lightness in the air, Beryl decided to tell the tale of her best friend's son, Scott, who'd had a bit of an accident that weekend on a night out in Newcastle with the lads. She rather hoped it would be just the kind of humour that George would appreciate.

'Well, you know Scott, darling. Handsome devil. Well, he had rather... a weekend of it, you know. Turns out they'd been for a few drinks and got in a taxi to take them to a nightclub. Well, the cabbie, a grumpy old Scottish fellow by all accounts was yelling at the lads to put their seat belts on.'

George was busy looking around the room at the sorry mess she had to clear up. Beryl patted her gently on the hand, forcing her attention back to the story – a trend she recognised was happening all the more.

'Well, that cabbie, he did an emergency stop out of the blue, and poor Scott fell forward, hitting his face on the back of the chair. Both his two front teeth fell out, you know!' Beryl's arms were flailing in the air as she dramatically retold the story her friend Ivy had recounted only hours earlier. 'Poor thing was so drunk he put his teeth in his pocket and carried on partying with his friends at the nightclub. The silly fool only registered that something was wrong when he got back to the hotel and emptied his pockets on the 24-hour reception desk looking for his key card.'

George was fully bought in now. This was the type of story she liked – a blunder that belonged to someone else. Face alert and eager, she urged Beryl to continue.

'Well, the receptionist was screaming when she saw Scott's two front teeth on the desk and him stood there in front, mouth all gaping wide and horrible like a scene from that film *Saw*.'

George laughed out loud. How utterly terrible. Poor Scott. She couldn't believe he'd continue to drink with the lads after losing his two front teeth. What a piss can. Beryl was pleased with herself; George was laughing and walking towards the curtains to continue the job her mother had started on first arriving at the house. Beryl ran over to offer her expert assistance – old person moving at speed, watch out!

'It's okay, mum, I've got this.'

She squeezed George's shoulder lightly and gathered her belongings. She recognised that this was her cue to leave and let George get busy blowing away the cobwebs. Beryl felt a strong sense of pride, and a tear of joy welled in the corner of her eye. She loved her daughter dearly and sincerely hoped that the best was yet to come for George.

'Toodaloo, dear.'

Cooking

George was craving some proper food and although cooking was not a skill she had in spades, her face returning to normal size had instantly boosted her confidence levels. George opened the chest freezer and waded through the different bags and trays of meat, quite shocked that there was so much stuff in there. She'd been like a squirrel stashing away nuts for the winter; she sensed that she must carry out many tasks mindlessly if she did not know the contents of her own freezer. At the back of the second shelf was a chicken, and just the thought of it cooking had George's juices flowing. The Bisto advert sprang to mind, the one with the perfect family all sat and waiting for mum to bring in the gravy. 'Ah, Bisto'.

George fidgeted with the dials and buttons on her silver cooker – which looked like it had never been used because, in fact, it *hadn't* ever been used – George placed the chicken securely on a baking tray in the centre of the oven. She added a number of frozen sprouts to the outer edge and hoped that two hours would be long enough for it to cook. She wasn't sure she could wait any longer than that to feast.

A wave of satisfaction washed over her as more and more positive energy bubbled to the surface. With a click of a button, the old retro radio was given permission to entertain; Salt-N-Pepa's 'Push It' was on. George promptly picked up a hair brush and began to repeat the lyrics.

'Yo, yo, yo, yo, baby, pop, yeah, you come here, give me a kiss, better make it fast or else I'm gonna get pissed, can you hear the music pumping hard like I wish you would, now push it, push it real good.'

George was gyrating her hips back and forth – the only move the song really warranted.

Happy that the chicken could be left alone to get on with its roasting, George decided it was time to wash and get dressed, perhaps call Joe and get the car sorted. With a definite spring in her step, George waltzed up the stairs, and, for the first time, ignored the gaping hole in her ceiling. Energy spent thinking about the hole was negative and therefore wasted. George wanted her thoughts to be positively powerful – she needed more good things to happen.

Washing from the sink was rather awkward. Water dripped everywhere and the purple flannel would be dunked several times for George to thoroughly cleanse every part of her body, and she would still feel a little grubby. The experience made her consider what it was like for patients in hospitals to be given bed baths. She assumed that it must be the same for the poor folk that couldn't shower for themselves. Poor things.

She treated her teeth to an electronic tooth brushing extravaganza using four different types of toothpaste. George was happy to have progressed finally from the bulbous-headed smelly bitch stage to being altogether back on form.

It was now time to get back up to speed with work before she consumed her homemade feast. She turned on her laptop for the first time in over five days. It was amazing how many senseless emails one could accumulate in such a short period of time, so adopting a quick-fire delete strategy was not only helpful but entirely necessary if she ever wanted to have time for anything else.

Hugh's emails were the first to receive the bulk delete treatment. What a bore. There couldn't possibly be anything contained within those mails that would be uplifting or the slightest bit interesting… delete. The sales files quickly followed. George's inbox shrank by the second. She had a rule of keeping no more than 86 emails in her account at any one time (86 – go figure). If she had more than this number, a sense of panic would ensue. Each push of the delete button brought with it a feeling of euphoria and an underlying will to succeed. The 86 was in sight. Man, she loved hitting her own targets. Lurking amongst the scores of emails was one from Karl, and in a previous life she would've sorted her inbox by the letter K to ensure that his requests got immediate attention, but not anymore. Aggrieved at having been such a loser, George flipped her laptop shut. The scent of chicken reached her nostrils and she breathed heavily, a big smile on her face. Her chicken dinner was ready – the hole in the ceiling was actually coming in handy today. Aromas flowed freely around the house.

Rushing down the stairs, her mouth watering, George was truly excited to taste the toils of her labour. Using the oven glove her mother had bought her – for the first time, she believed – she proudly pulled the tray from the oven. The chicken looked glorious although the sprouts didn't look too healthy. She was sure this was the way her mother cooked them, though. Whisking some instant gravy together in a jug, George picked at the hot chicken, too famished to allow it the opportunity to cool down. She broke off a leg and sliced a generous number of portions, arranging the meat around her plate with the sprouts and poured thick lashings of chicken gravy over the top. Her taste buds were in a frenzy and she dived in, satisfied that her first attempt at cooking had been a complete triumph. The sprouts were still a little hard and she couldn't quite work out why they hadn't softened in time despite being in there for ages. Fuck it. She was eating it all regardless.

Night Shakes

George suddenly awoke with griping pains in her stomach and the unmistakable signs that a round of vomiting and diarrhoea were about to follow. Shit. She was back in work tomorrow; how had she managed to pick up a bug? She'd been at home all week recovering from horse face! George ran to the bathroom and crouched, her head draped over the rim of her toilet just in time. Large chunks of chicken and undigested sprout sprayed from her mouth and nostrils. She clung to the bottom of her toilet, throat burning and body shaking. Nervously, she began to consider the food she had made herself earlier... Those sprouts were definitely not cooked properly. Then a deeper and darker thought entered her head – could you actually cook a chicken from frozen, or did you have to defrost it first? She knew that turkeys had to be defrosted, but did chickens?

Another round of vomit had George gripping the bowl for dear life. Her stomach knotted in pain, and she spat angrily into the toilet, keen to empty her mouth of its returned contents. She knew that she'd done a very silly thing. Chicken, indeed, required defrosting... She had given herself bloody food poisoning.

Weak and stooped over in the hurt locker position, George guided her fragile body back to bed. Pulling the duvet tightly around her shoulders, George rocked back and forth, waiting for the next round of vomiting to arrive.

She wasn't left waiting for long.

Return to Work

George pulled her limp body out of bed. She looked dreadful. She was still retching but the only thing to come back was the water she kept making herself drink in an attempt to stay hydrated. Completely exhausted, George pulled on a blue suit she'd hung out the previous day. Lacking the energy to get down with the purple cloth, she rubbed at her face, but there was no disguising the misery she wore like a mask. She scraped back her hair and managed to pin a dishevelled bun in place. The hurt locker stoop was still in play and she wondered if she would ever be able to stand tall again. Sick or not, she'd already taken a week off work with horse face, so ringing in really wasn't an option.

She retched again. Her stomach was being given the workout of a lifetime. She hoped that maybe a six-pack might make an appearance at the end of the ordeal.

She climbed into her car and wondered again about her unique ability for 'stupid'. Cooking chicken from frozen... for fuck's sake, who does that? Driving at a slower speed than usual, George focused intently on the road ahead, face like boiled shite and bum cheeks squeezed tightly together.

George thought that she would keep this particularly pathetic story to herself. She was unsure she would ever live it down, especially as it directly followed the horse face theatrics.

Bugger, bum, shit, tits and wankers. Why do all the rottenest things happen to me?

She captured a glimpse of her face in the rear view mirror and shuddered. All she needed was a bell and she could imagine folk bringing out their dead to join her.

The car park was empty, and she gingerly pulled into her regular spot. She took the next few seconds to collect herself. She was fully engaged with the present, and a sickly sensation lurked in the pit of her stomach. Breathing in deeply, she considered how she could get through the next hour, never mind the impending day.

She opened the car door and a waft of cold air pushed past her face and invigorated her senses. She had to dig deep and find the strength to stand, although her posture still partially mimicked the hurt locker. Walking with as much dignity as she could muster, George headed for the entrance. A couple of colleagues walked by and offered a rushed 'hello', to which she just nodded, re-stooped and continued shuffling forward. At her desk, she pulled the bin closer. This would have to be her

Plan B if she couldn't make it to the toilets on time. The very thought horrified her.

Using every ounce of available energy, she half-heartedly switched on her laptop. She raised her hand to cover her mouth as her stomach continued to convulse. She retched involuntarily. Her body now apparently had a mind of its own.

Fuck it, I need to go home. Who am I kidding? George finally realised that she wouldn't be able to continue without creating a scene and further harming her reputation. At work, she liked to keep things just so. There were some really great people, but they were intentionally kept at arm's length for fear of getting too close and seeing the madness that was George's life. George stood, then wobbled ever so slightly. She was quickly overwhelmed with nausea, and she knew she needed to get to the bathroom – quick.

Karl had other plans for her. He marched over, face red with anger, Charles hot on his heels. George didn't have time to process what was happening. She needed to get to the bathroom. As their paths crossed, Karl tugged at George's arm, bringing her to a halt.

'Tell Charles here that Laverne was yours *and my* idea. He's only gone and told Kingy that it was all down to you.'

It was easy to detect from Karl's tone the sheer resentment.

'Go on, tell him.'

His request was now more of a command, and George knew she would say nothing of the sort, because it was completely untrue, which Charles knew just as well as she did.

Her face was pale and she was unable to hold in the inner torment of her stomach any longer. George lowered her hand from her mouth and showered the floor with a toxic blend of bile and water. Her calculated move efficiently splattered Karl's shoes and the bottoms of his pants with the putrid fluid.

'God damn it, George, these are two hundred and fifty pound shoes! What's wrong with you?'

Karl eyed George with sheer disgust. He shook his jacket and removed a hanky from the pocket, then wiped frantically at his suede shoes, uttering obscenities like a spoiled child.

Indifferent to what he'd just witnessed, Charles looped George by the arm and gently escorted her the rest of the way to the bathroom. Before she fully slipped through the door, he produced a card.

'I know my timing is really bad, but I'd really like it if we could go out some time. You know, get something to eat.'

George retched again and Charles immediately regretted his choice of words. He forced the card into her hand and she tried to smile at him but nature was in control today. With an apologetic look, she disappeared behind the restroom door, leaving Charles to scratch his head and wonder if he should've waited for a better time to ask her on a date.

Celebrating the Offer

No amount of food poisoning could dampen George's spirits now. On arriving home, she had managed to continually grin for some time, with only the odd involuntary stomach convulsion cutting in.

She knew she had to share the happy news with someone or else she might burst. She reached for her phone and texted her delightful friend, Carmen. Up until now, she had only ever shared her fantasies of Karl. This had been okay since George had only wanted to shag the arse off him and girls liked to talk about shagging. (Well, her friends did, anyway.) But this was different. Somehow, the feeling went deeper, which made the encounter all the more special and worth savouring.

George was rather bad at texting and was always in so much of a rush that she never stopped to read if what she'd typed was actually what she intended to say.

'Carms, I've got a date with Charles Cunningham XXX'.

George stared at her phone, waiting for a response. A vibration indicated that Carmen had replied. She enthusiastically opened the message, a mixture of butterflies and tension and a little bit of left-over food poisoning excitedly swirling around inside, a feeling she had almost forgotten existed.

'#WTF – you never mentioned Charles before, you sneaky cow X'.

'I know. Actually don't know why I've spent so much time chasing that pig Karl'.

'Well he is rather gorgeous but honey I am delighted for you. When are you going out? X'.

'I'm not sure yet, I text him earlier and he asked me where I wanted to go'.

'Ohhh somewhere posh I hope. What did you say X'.

'I think I said the Chinese on high street'.

'Well you better go to the beauticians, give yourself a spring clean. It's been a while……LOL'.

Bitch. George decided that Carmen was probably right, though, and a trip to the beauticians' for a little waxing and tinting was just the ticket... not that she intended to shag on a first date or anything.

Her mobile started jingling again and George wondered what witty comment her best friend had thought of now. She was smiling as she opened her messages. It wasn't Carmen, though – it was Charles. A fresh surge of excitement made her palms sweat, and she read his text with renewed fervour:

'Never liked dick that much myself but the Chinese on high street it is, I'll pick you up at 8 tomorrow night x'.

George's cheeks flushed red and her heart accelerated a healthy couple of notches as she read the message for a second and then a third time. She scrolled hastily through her text exchange with Charles, and there it was:

'The Chinese on high street, I love the dick there'.

Once again, on her iPhone, George had managed to mistype the letters I and U, texting *dick* instead of *duck*. An obvious mistake; however, she wished now that she'd scrutinised her wording *before* hitting send. George copied and pasted her mistyped message to Charles and sent it to Carmen, whom she knew would appreciate the humour of the situation. Her phone rang without delay.

'Hi, Carms.'

There was immediate chuckling. George was glad to bring so much fun to other people's lives. Perhaps she could take up the role of court jester. She was full of hopeless misfortune, which seemed to go down well with her mates.

'I know you haven't had a shag in ages, darling, but really? "I LOVE DICK"?' Carmen loudly belaboured the words to milk her friend's newfound dilemma.

'That's fucking hilarious, George. What did he say?' Persistent laughter spilled through the phone and George found herself laughing along.

'He said he doesn't like dick himself but we could go to the Chinese.'

Both girls were laughing hysterically and George wondered if her stomach could take much more, having already spent most of the day convulsing.

'Call round mine tomorrow, G, for a quick chat before you go.'

Carmen was probably after a bit more detail and she guessed she owed her that much, having not said a word about Charles until today.

'I'll catch you tomorrow, Carms, about 5. See you later. And don't tell anyone about the text!'

George knew she was wasting her breath – the text was probably all over their WhatsApp group by now in addition to the various other social sites their friends indulged in. Yet another misadventure for George to live down.

The Beauticians'

It was Thursday, and George's date was that night. She'd booked off Friday rather presumptuously, but to hell with it. George was throwing caution to the wind. It was okay for two older people to shag on the first date and she decided that if sex was on offer then she was definitely going to be taking it.

The two-week-old hole in the ceiling was, once again, only a small glitch in her life, and she danced ceremoniously around the room, fannying about with the purple face cloth, making a mental note that she would need to pop to her mother's for a shower before the big date.

The beauticians were inside the local rugby club grounds and Lynne, the head practitioner, had hired out one of the back rooms, successfully turning it into a treatment parlour with nail bar.

Lynne was not like other beauticians, who were often all smeared in makeup, with a caustic tongue, which George found highly intimidating. It's hard to muster up the courage to indulge in a treatment in the first place, so the last thing you need is some tarty young beautician telling you how badly you look after your skin… you're actually paying them, right? Lynne was of Spanish decent, with dark shoulder-length hair, big brown eyes and dark brows that framed her face beautifully. You felt totally at ease in her company. She never criticised your beauty regime or your looks, and when you required a bikini wax after months of neglect, Lynne was the type of person you felt comfortable enough with to unleash your bush.

'The usual?' Lynne asked, busily cleaning down the nail bar. George responded with a nod of the head, cruising on autopilot, a little uncertain of what 'the usual' actually was but feeling safe enough to press on. If it carried the label of 'the usual', it must be stuff she got done all the time, right?

The bikini wax was always first, and George prayed that she'd remembered to put on some half-decent knickers. These days, she wore some pretty unsightly numbers with cotton threads hanging from the gusset, as she had no real reason to upgrade. Pulling down her jeans, she groaned a little – the knickers weren't great, all yellow and bobbly. She wished that she wasn't so absentminded or that she could empty her head of all the mindless chatter so she could actually think things through. Lynne talked away, pleasantly sensing George's unease, and started to apply liberal amounts of wax to the overgrown topiary George had managed to cultivate in her knickers. Lynne yanked the wax strip with brute force – totally required in the sad case of George's bush tidy – and worked away, tugging the strips back and forth, unsightly pubic hair clinging to George's nether-regions for all its worth.

George yelped in pain.

'Christ!'

Then, having unintentionally verbalised her discomfort at a considerable volume, George quickly followed up with an apology for her outburst.

Several wax strips later, the bush was under control. George was extremely pleased with herself for having undergone the torturous experience and just hoped that her efforts would not be in vain. Lynne approached again with yet more wax, this time aiming for her face. George automatically pulled back, a look of uncertainty in her eyes.

'You keeping the tash and beard, missus?' Lynne gave George a playful nudge with her elbow. She was smiling intently while waiting in earnest for George's response. George instinctively moved closer to the counter and eyed up the offending facial hair in the mirror. She stroked the tips of her tash, then boldly replied:

'Get rid of the lot. I want to be as smooth as a baby's bum.'

Crazy Mum

It was funny how George continued to make decisions that she would later deeply regret.

Take today, for instance, with the whole waxing malarkey. Her face was red, raw and pulsating painfully, and while it did feel delicately smooth, an angry red rash mercilessly cloaked her cheeks and upper lip. The Desperate Dan look would definitely not do for this evening's events, so, like with most of the important things in her life, George would have to hope that praying would help.

Her first stop was her mother's. She needed to douse her face in the cold shower jets to tone down the redness and freshen up. The front door was ajar and she found her mother just standing there in the hallway, fixated on Bruno, who was humping the life out of one of her hand-stitched cushions. He struggled for breath, his limp tongue lolling out the side of his mouth.

'Mum... What are you doing? Why don't you stop him?'

You'd have thought this was happening in George's house, the reaction it provoked. Before her mother could respond, she was snatching the cushion from under Bruno, who was less than pleased to be stopped mid-thrust. Bruno shot George a look of disgust before he retreated, downtrodden, into the kitchen. Beryl shook her head thoughtfully.

'Never been the same since Poppin died.'

Poppin was her mother's budgerigar that had died not six months earlier.

'Poppin? Are you joking, mum?'

George couldn't believe what she was hearing.

'Bruno hated that bloody bird, chased it all round the house! You stopped letting him out of the cage in case he ate him!'

Beryl was infuriated at the suggestion.

'It's not because I thought he would eat him. It was to keep Poppin safe from the birds outside. You know they were all very jealous of my Poppin.'

That was it. That was her mother finally losing it, talking about the birds outside terrorising her pet budgie.

'Mum, where's dad?'

George just wanted to have a shower and get out of there. Wherever this mind-boggling conversation was going, she really didn't have time for it. George often wondered how her dad could bear such hysterical talk. One day, he enlightened her: The man was in his sixties and had been diagnosed as deaf when he was 42. Whenever he couldn't take any more of the incessant chatter, he would simply unclip his hearing aid and give the odd encouraging nod or wink to suggest that he was, indeed, listening. He quietly suspected that Beryl had contributed to him going deaf in the first place. Conversations with her mother were so one-sided that she never really noticed.

Ron (her dad) had been a good-looking chap in his youth, always tinkering with cars and bikes, so it was easy to see her mother's attraction to such a kind and laid-back man. This meant that the difference between her parents' personalities was enormous. They weren't just a little bit different – there was an entire gulf between them. George was always curious how love could bridge such an obvious gap but was happy, for her and her sister's sake, that this was one marriage that had worked out.

'Your dad's outside again, fiddling with the car.' Beryl nudged her head despondently in the direction of the yard.

George guessed that her mother was unimpressed at being second-best compared to her dad's old motor, the Ford Mustang.

'I'm going for a shower, mum – you know, hole in my ceiling. Still waiting on Tod to come and fix it.'

George's tone was uncharacteristically accusatory. After all, her mum had worked wonders getting Tod round and getting a discount. However, the hole was still very much there.

'Don't you blame me, young lady. Tod has done his best to fit you in. Don't you go blaming me.'

George preferred this side of her mother, the always-right, interfering old battle axe; the crazy Poppin side would have to wait. George had enough lunacy in her life without including a wacky mother with a sex-starved dog!

'George, darling... Why does your face look like a jar of pickled beetroot?' Beryl was genuinely puzzled, but she was more interested in how Bruno was feeling after his romp was cut short, as she scurried into the kitchen, unconcerned about receiving a reply.

Glad to be off the hook, George proceeded up the stairs to take a shower, somewhat agitated by the fact that her mother cared more about the filthy dog than about her. Glimpsing the time on her watch, she decided that now was not the time to ruminate over her mother. She needed to be at Carmen's for five. She turned on the shower and stripped, kicking her knickers to the side with the rest of her clothes. She was eager to feel the water jets on her face and stepped in without hesitation.

Moral Support

Carmen lived in a splendid house in the best part of town. Beautiful roses and lavender trees adorned the windows and the front of the house. The rooms were bright and cleverly furnished; select pieces of art and priceless ornaments were decoratively arranged around each room. Like everything else, Carmen did houses well. There was no hole in the ceiling of this house!

George used the large brass knocker to announce her arrival. She fixed a big grin on her face because she knew that Carmen would be eager to hear all about Charles and the date scheduled for later on. It wasn't long before the door was pulled open; the scent of fresh vanilla pods escaped from the luxurious rooms behind Carmen.

'What the actual fuck, G, your face looks like a baboon's arse.'

Carmen's expression said it all. The shower had managed to cool George's face but did nothing for the red rash, which was going nowhere. To be honest, this wasn't the greeting that George had been expecting but she knew that Carmen's outburst was because she had George's best interests at heart.

'Slight problem at the beauty parlour' was all that George could muster. She shrugged and screwed up her face in a humble *help me* kind of way.

'That's a bloody understatement, G.' Carmen ushered George into the house. She pushed her friend by the shoulders into the grand living room, where she had a bottle of wine waiting for them. Carmen expertly uncorked an expensive Rioja and poured George what could only be described as a very full glass of wine.

'Stay there, G, I'm going to get my makeup kit. Not entirely sure what we can do, but God knows we need to try.'

Carmen was quite serious and George found herself me-mowing her friend, as she did so often with her mother. She pondered where they got off with being so high and mighty. She thought, *I'm not* completely *inadequate...*

During the fleeting chatter in her mind, George caught sight of her face in the mirror hung above the rustic wood burner. Her face was still red, raw and, as her friend had accurately stated, looked rather like a baboon's arse. Fuck, she was in need of some counselling after all.

George groaned. Her shoulders dipped in defeat. Recovering the only way she knew how, she began gulping copious amounts of the red wine, unprepared for the bitter taste to hit her senses. George shook off the nasty kickback from the Rioja by twisting her head from side to side. She had absolutely no idea why she drank wine. Perhaps she thought it could make her look more cultured, but, in truth, George preferred the alcopop stuff that the kids drank. Her philosophy was that if you were going to get shitfaced, then at least enjoy the beverage that you would be tipping down your throat all night.

Carmen was back, emptying a trolley full of cosmetic products onto the thick cream-coloured carpet. George decided that the colour of one's carpet said a lot about them as a person. Seriously, who buys cream carpeting? George considered this question for a quick second and realised then that a cream carpet was perfect for Carmen, who, let's face it, wasn't far from perfect in everything she did. Grey-black was more George's colour, although right now she didn't want to think too deeply about why. She was already two steps away from a total nervous breakdown.

'What the bloody hell did you do, G? Looks like you've been slapped about the face a couple hundred times with a live trout.' At least Carmen had moved from anger to humour. The pair laughed and George swiftly emptied the contents of her glass into her mouth, tensing as the bitter aftertaste swished around her pallet.

'Face wax. You know, I thought, sort out the bush, my unibrow and...' Carmen laughed, and just a little bit of wine dribbled down her chin. She quickly wiped away the liquid to reassert herself, never one to look silly or out of control.

'I couldn't remember ever looking like Desperate Dan before, so I thought I'd really pull out all the stops for this date. You know, really put in some effort.'

Carmen appreciated just how badly George wanted the date to be successful and started to apply green and yellow concealers to George's cheeks, which kind of felt strange (green and yellow – WTF?). Happy to try any approach to fix the screw-up, George continued to chug merrily on the Rioja. She concluded that a little bit of a confidence boost was just what she needed.

The makeup intervention lasted twenty minutes and, several layers of product later, she could see that Carmen was finally satisfied with her handiwork. George looked at herself appreciatively in the mirror. The redness had definitely mellowed and a fog of anticipation had replaced the feeling of dread – perhaps tonight was going to work out.

The two chatted idly for a couple of hours, a strong, unbreakable bond between them. Never had two women been so different yet so drawn to one another. Each of them had something the other needed: George was Carmen's entertainment and Carmen was George's moral compass.

She was thrilled for George to be going on a date with a guy that wasn't an egotistical pig. She had learnt the hard way that interfering with her relationships or putting down these so-called men just encouraged George all the more. As always, these flights of fancy never lasted long and, as a good friend, Carmen always resisted the urge to throw in the controversial 'I told you so'.

George had pepped up tremendously after a large dose of Rioja. Her makeup, now thicker than plasterboard, combined with a good old chat had sorted her out a treat.

'Shit, is that the time?'

George shifted nervously in her chair. Time had passed quickly and she was left with only 25 minutes to add any finishing touches before the big date. George leaned forwards to embrace Carmen and then gave her a big sloppy kiss on the cheek.

'Carmen, as always, you've saved my life! THANK YOU, and fingers crossed for me.'

Carmen wiped the surplus spit from her cheek.

'You can't drive, G, you're half-bloody-baked now. I'll ring you a taxi.'

George worriedly bit her bottom lip.

'Nope, if it's delayed, I won't get home in time. It's only five minutes away – I'll run.' George was already pacing towards the door.

'You'll *walk* or you will be a sweaty puddle of piss,' insisted Carmen, kissing her friend swiftly on both cheeks. 'Go, go.' Carmen held open the front door and propelled George on her way, smiling to herself at just how mad her best friend was and at how much she loved her for it.

George, feeling more in control and less Desperate Dan – but also slightly pissed – decided to ignore the good advice from Carmen. She practically sprinted the entire way home and accidentally inhaled a bunch of flies. Amazing, the difference a couple of blocks could make. It was like she'd left the glamour of Chelsea and arrived in the ghetto. George quickly shrugged off the thought of mediocrity. She liked the place; it was good enough for her. She just wished they'd replace the bloody postman.

She began to undress the minute she opened the front door. The evidence she left behind might lead someone to believe that she'd been romantically seduced by some stud. In reality, she was just trying to save time. Old, reliable undies were replaced with more beautiful, yet less comfortable, counterparts, including a rather expensive plunge bra which perfectly complimented her breasts.

George finished off her look with her favourite black dress. She pinned her hair loosely to give the impression of sheik elegance, wanting to look good but not wanting to look like she'd tried too hard. She checked her watch and was impressed with how quickly she'd recovered the situation. Just enough time for a cheeky Jäger. Once a little drunk, George rarely considered the consequences of her actions, so, with the lightness of Mary Poppins, she danced down the stairs to pour herself a couple of well-earned shots.

'Who's gonna get a shag tonight?!'

The Date

Charles made his appearance bang on time. He knocked twice, and George could feel her heart in her throat. She paused to collect herself; she badly wanted to make a good impression. Smile fixed in place, George opened the door and, as expected, Charles looked amazing. He held out a fancy bouquet of roses and a bottle of Prosecco. She took the latter as a good sign... It did mean he wanted to come back to her place, right?

Charles stepped forward and placed the flowers and wine on her hall unit, apprehensively eyeing up the scattered clothes. George, embarrassed that he might see the hole in the ceiling, and spotting her bra strewn on the stairs, cut in with some polite conversation.

'Should we go? Table's booked for eight?'

Charles's lips curled into a smile.

'You really do like Chinese.' He laughed playfully and George shoved him in the arm, aware that he was teasing her about the 'dick' text.

'What was your favourite again?' Charles was seeing how far he could push her, but George appreciated a good sense of humour and laughed along, glad that Charles wasn't a stuck-up pig.

He opened the door of his slick grey Mercedes and, like a cat that had gotten the cream, she just drank him in, his beautiful skin, fabulous hair, toned body. What's not to like? George admired the exquisite leather interior and breathed in the new car smell, a million miles away from the toxic fumes and McDonalds' wrappers she inhaled in her car.

'You catch a bit of sun today?' Charles pointed at his own face, making a circular movement with his finger. She caught his meaning and turned away to survey her reflection in the side mirror. She was instantly discouraged by the face staring back at her. Being slightly pissed and jogging had worn away some of Carmen's plastering to unveil a little more red than George had wanted to reveal. She laughed nervously and nodded, scared that already she might have blown it with her genuinely ludicrous behaviour.

Charles, oblivious to the ramblings of George's mind, skilfully manoeuvred closer. He cupped her cheek in his hand and pressed his lips gently against her skin.

'You look beautiful.' His eyes were wide and admiring. It was obvious that either he was a great liar or he liked the pink baboon look.

Even though the kiss was fleeting, George could still feel the electric warmth of his touch on her face. She briefly considered suggesting they skip Chinese altogether and stay at hers for something else entirely more fulfilling (wanton hussy).

The restaurant was a bustle of clanging cutlery and happy chattering. A slim and surly Chinese man approached the concierge desk. He asked for the name of their booking in an authoritarian kind of way, decidedly aloof and full of self-importance. He tutted as he found the entry, then swiftly turned on his heel to indicate for the couple to follow. He impatiently walked to the far side of the elaborately designed room. The surly man was quickly replaced by a much fatter and altogether much jollier Chinese man who wished to attend to their drinks order. On hearing that another bottle of red was in store, George became most alarmed. However, she accepted that if she wanted to appear worldly, then sticking with the red was probably the best thing to do even though she hadn't fared so well the last time she'd drunk more than three glasses.

The waiter was off to the bar and back within seconds, expertly uncorking the bottle of red and pouring two very full glasses. 'I'm really glad you could make it.' Charles's blue eyes twinkled as he spoke, which caused George to gulp greedily on the wine, unsure of how to handle the sexual tension that was building between them.

'I thought for a minute you were with that Karl fellow.'

Charles appeared to regret the words as soon as they'd left his mouth. George stopped slurping her wine and tried her best to throw Charles a look of warranted disapproval.

'He's a pig,' George seethed, face burning and head feeling just a little bit foggy. 'He's fit, of course, there's no denying that. The man is very sexy. Very sexy. Great body. Very hot.'

George looked up, aware that her appreciative remarks for another man were not exactly laying a great foundation for a hot shag later on, but Charles had started the conversation. In need to regroup, George looked for an escape, but not before she necked the rest of her wine.

'I'm just nipping to the ladies' room; won't be long.'

She patted her mouth against the cotton serviette. She did not particularly wish to add clown lips from the wine to her already distinguishable monkey's ass look.

She steadied herself before she turned and mentally calculated the distance between her and the bathroom. Behind her, the waiter was delivering some snacks and lighting the four white decorative candles in the centre of the table. Oblivious to her surroundings, George discarded her cotton serviette without looking. It landed squarely on the open flames behind her. Considering every step as she walked away, she hoped that

Charles was getting a good look at her behind, purposefully throwing in the odd booty shake for good measure.

Charles, unsurprisingly, had other things on his mind. He was on his feet and anxiously dowsing the small serviette fire with his wine, smiling conservatively at the other guests, who had all turned to watch.

The toilets were tastefully laid out and George grabbed the cubicle walls for support. She was totally shit-faced. She had barely eaten all day because she had been so preoccupied with the Desperate Dan face and didn't want a bloated stomach just in case she bagged a shag. She'd forgotten to eat altogether, except for the Actimel consumed first thing, if that even counted as food. Standing up quickly, not wanting to waste any more of her evening, she lost her footing. Her mind fog had thickened considerably and she reached out in fear for the door handle to balance herself.

Voices could be heard outside, which suggested that the toilets had worked up quite a queue. She hoped they hadn't heard her falling about like a sad old ragdoll, too drunk to navigate even the smallest of spaces. Conjuring up even more willpower and concentration than before, George left the cubicle, walking as slowly and gracefully as she could manage. She nodded pleasantly at the gathered group of women. She turned on the oversized taps and a sudden surge of water leapt from the sink to spray her black dress indiscriminately. George let out a cry of despair as she fought to bring the unruly tap to a halt, embarrassed and upset that even when she tried to be a sophisticated adult, she was still a fool. Smiling feebly at the other women huddled in the overcrowded bathroom, it was obvious to George what they thought of her. They had knowing looks on their faces; she brought this type of attention upon herself all the time. On cue, her own inner voice made an unwelcome appearance, disgusted with her inability to show up for a hot date with a guy without being totally wankered. What did she expect?

George took a deep breath. Each step was carefully contemplated; putting one foot in front of the other took every ounce of George's concentration. The fog had infiltrated her brain and clouded her judgement. She was sure they were sat at the far side of the room, but now there was just a messy blackened table. It looked as though there had been a fire or something, and Charles was nowhere to be found.

A welcome hand slipped purposefully around her waist.

'We've had a little problem, so the sulky Chinese guy has moved us to this spot over here.' Charles carefully escorted George to the new table laid out for them; something inside made her feel that perhaps she shouldn't enquire as to why they had been relocated.

'You feeling okay?' Charles's words echoed inside her mind. She repeated them over and over, trying to make sense of them, until the words completely lost meaning and merged into one mumbled sound. George could see two of Charles; she grinned foolishly, imagining what she could do with two Charles Cunninghams. The room was a blur and try as she might to resist the urge to fall further into the fog, she was too far gone. The alcohol had taken hold and removed any trace of the sane part of George, leaving a hollow being that was undignified in every sense of the word.

What Happened?

Sunshine spilled through a crack in the curtains and teased a half-dead George to wake. She resembled a vampire more than a human. Groaning loudly, she pulled the duvet over her eyes in an attempt to block out the light, but it was futile. On waking, a low drum beat was rhythmically thumping away in her head, and the lack of moisture in her mouth meant that she would need to get up, if only to get a drink.

It took about three minutes of self-consumed assessment before the morning-after terrors forcibly kicked in.

'Oh, God.'

George remembered that last night she'd had a date with Charles. The only problem was that she couldn't actually remember the date at all. Frantically, she threw off the duvet and examined her body. She'd slept in her underwear although could not for the life of her remember going to bed or even getting in the house. Touching her most intimate areas, she assured herself that no funny business had taken place, embarrassed at having to stoop so low for verification of any sexual activities.

Recoiling into the foetal position, George gently rocked back and forth and delved deep into her mind with the hope that somewhere along the way she had managed to archive a memory from the previous evening. It was no use. Apart from arriving at the Chinese place, her mind was a complete blank. She shuddered in disgust. George could only imagine what kind of impression she'd made on Charles. It was no wonder she was single.

A hangover with memory loss, the girls classified as 'hurt locker on steds' – all the usual pain of a hangover, with the added misery of never knowing just how badly you'd behaved ('steds' meaning 'steroids', indicating a pumped-up version of hell). It was an experience that could continue to unravel for months with helpful acquaintances throwing in the odd 'Do you remember when?' knowing full well that the individual *couldn't* remember a damn thing. Bastards.

George groaned again, dug her fists firmly into the mattress and cursed repeatedly to herself. A vibrational hum signalled that her phone had amazingly survived and was somewhere in the room – a smallish victory considering the amnesia-shrouded circumstances. She heaved herself from the bed, adopted the awkward bent-over posture and scoured the floor for her phone. Perhaps there would be some hidden clues about the evening. Maybe she had been a model date? Sugar-coating her distinct lack of memory was not going to work, and dread quickly devoured any light feelings of hope.

Another vibrational hum gave away the phone's location. George had stuffed it in one of her stiletto shoes. She supposed she mistook them for a phone stand in her drunken stupor. There were several messages from Carmen, one from Debbie and one from Charles.

'Oh, God.' She placed the phone down tentatively, unsure whether opening the message was a good idea but too curious not to check it out. George mustered her courage and hastily clicked on the link. Charles had forwarded a picture of her bent over kissing an old crumpled tramp at the side of the road. Underneath the picture he had written 'Not just Chinese you like…….X'. George threw the phone across the room. She brought up her hands to cover her mouth, decidedly unsettled because of the snapshot.

'WTAF – why was I kissing a tramp?' The thought made George run to the bathroom, craving for her body to be cleansed. She briefly forgot that she had a hole where the shower used to be.

'SHIT, bastards, fucks and wankers.' George brought down her foot hard on the floor in protest. She was thoroughly annoyed that she couldn't wash away the imagined 'eau de tramp' scent after wiping out her bathroom following five years of neglect.

George retrieved her phone from across the room and took another look at the text image, one eye closed and one eye focused directly on the tramp's matted facial hair. The message didn't indicate if there had been any other issues during the evening; George wondered if she should just respond and ask. Get it out there and over with. There was an X on the message; surely this was a kiss, so that was a good sign, right? George knew with every fibre of her being that she would not be responding to Charles. She must have behaved badly, so she decided that blocking would be the only way to get through the next 24 hours.

Blocking was another technique adopted by the girls after alcohol-infused sessions. If you couldn't remember pockets of time and the evidence surrounding the situation suggested that you'd probably done something horrific, then the best thing to do was block. Take all of your energy and completely block out what might have happened. Avoid as many people as possible who might have been linked to the event, with the exception of good friends. The mind is a complicated machine and can be convinced of almost anything with enough effort, hence the infamous blocking technique, tried and tested successfully many times by them all over the years.

George flicked through the rest of her texts. It looked like Carmen had sent one on the hour every hour the previous evening. Little platitudes of encouragement, her very own cheerleader, with the occasional 'Have you shagged him yet G?' The girls had arranged to meet later at the little café on the corner, which sold the most delicious cakes and pastries. It was meant to be a kind of victory celebration and George wrestled with just how much of the truth she was willing to share. She still felt a little raw from the ordeal.

Deleting the message was an option, but if she had really pissed off Charles then most likely the image would already be all over social media.

She sighed in disbelief and accepted her defeat. George decided on a bold plan of attack. She clicked 'forward' and circulated the picture to all her friends with the witty caption 'Didn't get a shag but bagged myself a tramp Wahoo'.

George sat back and waited for the tirade of abuse to begin.

The Texts

Carmen: 'G, why is there a picture of you snogging the face off a tramp'.

George: 'Because you got me smashed drinking Rioja at your house before my date!'

Carmen: 'Oh god, what else did you do?'

George: '……………I can't remember………..'

Carmen: 'FFS G…….you okay?'

George: 'I'll survive suppose'.

The phone buzzed again – a new message from Debbie.

Debbie: 'Hurt Locker on steds! George love that picture, did you get his phone number'.

George: 'Ha ha, no I didn't'.

Debbie: 'Did he use tongue? Great beard. Love the smell of piss, me'.

George: 'Wanker'.

Debbie: 'Tramp!!!!!'

It wasn't long before Jenny joined in.

Jenny: 'I thought you were shagging Karl, who is that man?'

George: 'just some guy'

Jenny: 'See you at the coffee shop #Intrigued'.

Finally, Bella and Lucy came to the party.

Bella: 'George you know I love you right but I'm not coming to the wedding lol'.

George: 'So funny Bella'.

Bella: 'On a serious note, you do need to think about how much you are drinking G'

Really? Do I? conceded George irritably. She considered why people felt it necessary to point out really obvious stuff to her. She guessed Bella was her sister and it was in her nature to impress her moral sermons at every chance she got.

Lucy: 'Like a scene from Jeremy Kyle. Can't wait to find out all about it'.

It felt good to get the heavy burden of her failed date off her chest. George knew that the entire afternoon, if not the next six months, would be purely devoted to jokes at her expense involving tramps. Laughing a little to herself now, she had to admit it was pretty funny. Who goes out on a hot date and ends up snogging a tramp? Lucy was definitely onto something with that Jeremy Kyle comment.

The Café

George decided to walk to meet her friends at the café; she believed that the fresh air would blow away the cobwebs and ease her pounding head. Eyes like piss holes in the snow, she put on her oversized Audrey Hepburn sunglasses and enjoyed the feeling of anonymity they gave her.

The girls chose a table outside, as they often enjoyed watching the randomers bustle past on the crowded high street; no one was safe when these girls were together. George approached with caution. There were already loud barrels of laughter, and Debs was laughing so hard that she had tears trickling down the sides of her cheeks. George was already regretting her decision to be so open about her epic fail. She was acutely aware of how painful the next hour was going to be, and she was in a fragile state as well. Another round of laughter from the table and George was able to see beyond her presumption that the laugh was on her. On the near sidewalk, there was a large lump of dog poo and the girls were watching the facial expressions of the passers-by as they navigated their way around the brown mess.

George giggled. Her mother was right: it was the small things in life that brought the fun. Pulling out a chair at the table with her friends, the small group let out a hearty cheer. Debbie leant forward and deposited a fifty pence coin in front of George.

'That's for your new fella's begging cup.'

Other coins promptly followed. The girls created a small pile of change and waited for George to take the bait.

A large bottle of Prosecco was resting in a silver ice bucket on the table. George felt her body inwardly tremble – the thought of consuming more alcohol was terrifying.

The poo had gripped the girls' attention once more. One professional-looking chap stopped himself from stepping in it just in time, visibly infuriated at the close encounter. This resulted in yet another wave of hysterical laughter from the girls. A much older lady was approaching, about 4'2", wearing a grey mac and Clarks wide-fit sandals. George considered steering her to safety but didn't think her gag reflex could cope with the fumes from the poo if anything were to go wrong; she silently wished the old lady good luck.

The lady shuffled forward slowly, shaking her head. She took a tissue from her pocket and wearily bent down to remove the poo from the pavement. George borked involuntarily, sure the old girl's legs would stiffen and give way. However, upon scooping up the poo, her gnarled face was one of confusion. Debbie groaned and swiftly walked over to wrestle with the old lady for the contents of her tissue. George was unsurprisingly shocked. It was peculiar, to say the least, and she wondered if she was still under the influence from the night before, sure that the fog must be returning. George looked back inquisitively as the scene continued to unfold. She could make out the old lady exchanging a few heated words with Debs, who was casually shrugging, seemingly calm about the whole thing, with one hand resting on her hip in an 'I don't care' kind of way. The old lady scurried away, cursing under her breath, wagging a wrinkly finger in the air, evidently fuming about the altercation. Debs, on the other hand, was rather smug, tissue proudly in the palm of her hand, triumphant at seizing the poo from the old lady's grasp. Jenny, Carmen and Lucy proceeded to give Debbie a brusque round of applause and she curtsied, lapping up what George considered to be misdirected appreciation.

The poo was safely deposited onto the café table, its authenticity now obviously doubtful. Debbie had purchased a fake poo so that the girls could sit back and watch the reaction from all the people walking by. Strollers were pushed around the poo, grown men leaped, women straddled, and each showed a unique face of disgust. It was sheer comedic genius, to say the least.

'Come on, G, spill the beans.' Lucy rested her chin between both her hands, elbows propped on the table for support, hungry to hear the tale.

George rolled her eyes, the gesture lost on the girls since her eyes were hidden under the thick black lenses of her glasses.

'Okay, so I went on a date to the Chinese. Then...' She paused. The girls were hanging on every word now.

'Well, go on, what next? How come you kissed a tramp?' Jenny's tone was excitable. She was clearly thrilled to be finding out first-hand what had happened.

'Hurt locker on steds, Jen. She has no idea what happened.' Debs was grinning proudly, happy to chip in and help George with the explanation. She loved this type of inappropriately bad behaviour and was just sorry it hadn't happened on one of their nights out together.

'Jackson The Tramp Kisser. What was the gum to tooth ratio like? You know how I hate a man with too much gum.' Shaz beamed, pulling out her tongue, eyes smiling, whilst twisting her moustache at the side of her mouth between her thumb and finger.

George didn't get the chance to respond.

'So... no sex, then?' asked Lucy, who loved circling the conversation back to intercourse in general and dicks in particular. This line of questioning was thus appropriate to be coming from her.

Debbie laughed and patted George on the back.

'It was that good – she can't remember that either, Lucy. What the actual fuck, George? You make me piss. No second date, then?'

All eyes turned to George. Her cheeks flushed with embarrassment as she searched for the right words.

'Well, der, obviously not. I binned him for that tramp guy.'

Debs laughed out loud and declared a toast as a sign of respect for George.

'To tits, tinsel and tramps!' Debs' glass was high in the air and each of the girls grabbed a glass of Prosecco and chinked in unison. 'Tits, tinsel and tramps!'

'What about you, then, Lucy?' Debbie hissed. 'Heard you had a bit of a fumble yourself. Come on, let ya besties know what went on.'

All eyes shifted from George to Lucy, greedy for more girly gossip.

'Well,' said Lucy, devilish glint in her eye, 'this guy came round to fix the, erm, washing machine...'

You could've heard a pin drop. The laughter had been replaced with focused attention and wide eyes.

'Well, you know, as you'd expect, er, he fixed the bloody washing machine,' she fired off. Immediately upon finishing her sentence, Lucy quickly inhaled a large mouthful of Prosecco.

Debbie gave her a hardened dig in the arm.

'Ow, that hurt! What was that for?'

All the girls had squared in on Lucy, accusatory looks on their faces.

'Spill,' Debbie urged, supported by the others.

'Well, okay, you nosey lot, I shagged the lucky bastard, didn't I?'

Shrill laughter escaped the table. Once again, the girls held their glasses high in the air to toast their mate, who could shag literally any man that came round to her house regardless of what they were there for. Jehovah's Witnesses, be warned.

Jenny desperately wanted to know more. She shifted uncomfortably in her tight corset and continued to probe Lucy.

'So, how does it... happen? Like, how does he go from servicing your washing machine to servicing you? I just can't picture it.' Jen was beside herself with curiosity.

'Nor *should* you,' cut in Debbie, who laughed louder than ever. 'But it's a fair point, Lucy – how do you go from actual business to *business*, if you get my meaning?'

Jen nearly choked on a mouthful of Prosecco out of an eagerness to hear Lucy's tale.

'Well, first I ask him to take a seat on the couch. You know, for a break.'

The girls were gesturing wildly for her to continue.

'Alright, alright! I then make him a cup of tea, move in all close-like, laugh at everything he says, keep my eyes directly on his, pat him when he talks...'

'"Move in close"?' roared Shaz. 'No wonder I've never shagged the odd-job man. Couldn't get too close because the old bugger stinks.'

George was laughing so hard that all feelings of regret were paused.

Lucy continued on with her story in a matter-of-fact way. Well, she was, of course, a professional on the topic of sex.

'There is that chemistry and you touch by accident, all close-like. The thrill of the chase and your eyes just say to one another *should we shag*, and, of course, it's the only thing left to be done.'

She drained the rest of her glass and set it neatly back on the table. Jen's face was one of bewilderment. Surely there was more to it than that. She looked like she'd been cheated at a game of cards; she demanded to know more.

'That can't be it, Lucy. I give handymen cups of tea all the time and I don't end up shagging them.'

All eyes were now on Jen, whose quizzical expression was one of comedy.

'Well, my dear, you are married and clearly you are just not doing it right.'

More laughter spilled from the group, and before Jen could take it to heart, Lucy went on:

'While I say that I shagged him, I have to add that it was the crappiest shag I have ever had. The guy was rubbing my clitoris like it was a fucking record player. God only knows why. There was steam and everything. It's *still* aching now and his pecker was, well, it was all... snarly, and, well, it looked deformed. I had to help him push it up there and wrap it up like a little parcel.'

Jen blushed, not sure if the story had been changed for effect to save her feelings, but it certainly had struck a chord with the rest of the girls. They were all wiping away tears at the thought of such a scene. It was, of course, true, and Lucy had unexpectedly shared more with the group than she'd originally intended. Holding the title of Most Promiscuous was one thing; banging men with gnarly peckers was clearly quite another.

'Had a bit of a catastrophe last night, myself,' chimed in Bella. She swirled Prosecco around her glass. The conversation was a little like that *Mastermind* show – as soon as one of them finished sharing their misgivings under the gossip-hungry gaze of the others, it was on to the next victim.

'Well, me and Alex were having a bit last night. You know, door closed and everything so the kids couldn't hear.'

Smiles started to appear on everyone's lips as the tension slowly built.

'Well, I was on top and I was going at it when I saw the light creeping up the wall. I knew one of the kids had opened the door, but before I could move, they were shouting "Mummy!"; I froze.'

Bella continued to describe what had to be one of the most awkward situations any parent could face, and the girls eagerly waited for the tale to unfold.

'He asked me what I was doing, so I told him I was playing trains with daddy.' Even Bella laughed now. Debs was laughing so hard that there was no noise coming out, just the odd high-pitched screech and the banging of her hand on the table.

'I've not got to the best bit yet.' Bella was struggling to talk as she giggled between words. 'He only went and climbed up on Alex behind me, saying "I want to play, mummy, CHOO CHOO".'

Chairs were scraped away from the table as they all fell about in a heap. They repeated Bella's last words a little too loudly: 'CHOO CHOO'.

It was out of character for Bella to talk so plainly about one of her kids catching her having sex and George was pleased that she felt at ease enough to share her story with the girls. Perhaps she was turning a corner and starting to take life a little less seriously. The festival was definitely the first sign of this.

Ordinarily Bella's conversation centred on wonky winged Willy the Magpie and Chatty Charlie the Pidgeon, the birds from her garden. She really did have a thing for those two, and she was becoming more twitcher-like by the day. This story of misadventure was a welcome break from the spring watch rendition Bella usually performed.

A couple of older ladies sat at a table adjacent to the girls were clearly not impressed. Their faces were like those of bulldogs licking piss off a thistle. Debs was never one to let the opinions of others interfere with her fun and on recognising the looks of disgust in her café comrades, she chugged her arm up and down, bellowing 'CHOO CHOO' at the top of her lungs. Bella was never going to live this down. George's tramp escapade faded in comparison to this episode of sheer frivolity.

George was glad to have braved leaving her comfortable nest for the company of her friends, who, like her, all had stories of their own. Regretfully, pulling her thoughts inwards had her thinking of her rotten date behaviour. She knew that turning it over in her mind would not help but she also understood that her turbulent inner child would torture her for as long it could.

Carmen squeezed George's hand, having instinctively sensed her pain. She nudged her arm and gave her friend a generous smile.

'Enough talk of gnarly peckers and worn down clitorises,' shrilled Carmen. 'We've got the awards night to think about. Come on, girls, lots of champagne, handsome, eligible men...'

Lucy's eyes lit up at the 'eligible men' part but George's mind was fixated on one man. She couldn't shake last night from her mind. She fumbled about in her bag and pulled out her iPhone. Perhaps he'd called or texted and she'd missed it with all the laughter. There was nothing. Her heart sank and bitter regret pounced to the front of her mind again.

Unable to stomach any more alcohol, she made her excuses to leave. Most of the girls were half-cut and didn't protest as George kissed each of them in turn, saying her farewells and wishing them a good day.

As she walked away from her friends at the café, she braced herself, knowing that the abuse was about to begin.

'Stay away from them tramps, G. Riddled with disease, I tell you. RIDDLED.' She turned as gracefully as she could manage, a one-finger salute prepared for the girls, who applauded in response. Debbie bowed once again at the hilarity of her own comments.

Even though George's house was only a short distance from the café, it suddenly felt like a world away. The pounding in her head had increased and the feeling of failure weighed heavy on her shoulders. Forcing her posture upright she did all she could to maintain just a little dignity on her walk back. She was glad once again for the protection the sunglasses afforded her as self-indulgent tears welled up in her eyes.

Meeting Joe

A couple of days passed without any word from Charles, not even a text to say that she had been a miserable date. George had replayed the evening over and over in her mind but there was nothing more to remember, and she was sinfully breaking the girls' cardinal rule of blocking.

'Sod it.' George deleted the text from Charles and sighed loudly. There were plenty of other fuckups in her life that required her attention, and she decided that today she was going to fix at least one of them. She found Joe's details and sent him a text about the car, asking where they could meet up so she could pay him and thank him for not taking their little indiscretion through the insurance. George's phone vibrated on the coffee table and she opened up the response from Joe. He suggested a gay bar just on the outskirts of town; apparently they had a two-for-one offer on with some karaoke entertainment. George considered this for a second, not too sure about the entertainment but happy to be away from straight men. She promptly told Joe that it sounded like a great idea and that she would meet him at 1 o'clock.

Taking action always made George feel great, and a plan provided her with a huge sense of purpose. Whilst these things didn't shift the ache she felt inside for Charles, they certainly distracted her from it.

She couldn't remember the last time she'd been to a gay bar but was at least happy that she wouldn't have to make an effort. She smiled and scraped her hair back into an untidy finger-brushed bun, then threw on a pair of blue jeans and a loose shirt for the occasion. George grabbed her cash card and lipstick and forced them deep into the pockets of her jeans. It was liberating not to have a bag or spend hours getting ready, pruning and preening. She admired her scruffy self in the mirror and gave her grunge look a thumbs up. Low effort, fast-paced, no nonsense. Perhaps she should go lesbian? She immediately dismissed the thought because a) she clearly fancied men, b) it assumed that all lesbians avoided putting in any effort, which clearly wasn't the case and c) she could never lick a fanny (no offense, lesbians!).

George clocked the hole in her ceiling as she got ready to leave. As she would be paying Joe this month and she had used a couple hundred quid to drown her sorrows, the builders' fee would have to come out of next month's wages. She locked the front door behind her and waited patiently on the step for the cab to arrive. She'd considered driving but it didn't feel right given why she was going to meet Joe in the first place. Besides, she could do with a drink.

The cabbie pulled over and the text alert 'Your cab's arrived' jingled on her phone. *Not a bad service*, George thought, and scanned for a place to put her front door keys. Her jeans were tight and she almost regretted not having a bag; the bulge in her pocket made it almost painful to sit down. She carefully removed her cash card and lipstick and safely deposited them into her shirt pocket, along with her front door key now that she had removed the Disney-style keyring characters. What self-respecting women has those?

'Where to, me love?' The cabbie was in his fifties, thick Irish accent and unruly grey curly hair which looked like it hadn't seen a brush in months.

'The Jupiter Bar, please, but I need to stop at a cash machine along the way if you don't mind.'

The cabbie scratched his head.

'Did you say "The Jupiter Bar"?' His green eyes were weighing up George through the rear view mirror. He was obviously curious about her choice of destination.

'Yes, the Jupiter Bar up on Sixth Street.'

The cabbie nodded as a way of agreement and set the payment clock into motion as he slowly pulled away from the curb.

'The name's Jim. Been out all morning, I has.'

George smiled appreciatively. Not every cabbie made the effort these days, so it was nice to find one making polite conversation although he was a little difficult to understand.

'I'm George. What time do you finish, Jim?'

For a second, she had considered asking how busy his day had been, but it was so cliché that she went for one better.

'Finish at 5, then off to the local with the lads. Got a day off tomorrow. Not often that happens these days. Got to keep out here to make the money, you see.'

George nodded. She understood only too well the trappings of work and the need to top up her annual income at every opportunity.

The weather had taken a turn for the worst. The clouds were an angry black and full of rain, which threatened to come down with force. George grinned. It could rain all it liked – it wouldn't ruin her hair or make her false tan run. In fact, a little bit of rain would be quite welcome.

Sitting back comfortably in her seat, she felt entirely smug. The no-fuss, no-nonsense persona was an identity that she wore really well and one which she thoroughly enjoyed.

'Here's a cash machine, me love.' Jim had pulled the cab over and was pointing to a row of shops on the right, where George could just make out a hole in the wall. Rain had started to spot.

It was that fine rain that everyone made such a fuss about (especially Peter Kay).

'Better make a run for it, love, or you will be soaking wet.' His eyes smiled, full of tenderness, and George found herself wondering why an Irish man would be living in England. What had drawn him here? Was it work? Family? Perhaps he'd moved for love? A knot twisted in the pit of George's stomach, and she was amazed how everyday things could set her mind right back to square one thinking about Charles. Not a stranger to heartache, George knew that in a couple of weeks everything would appear much brighter. Carpe diem and all that.

Jim shrugged. He didn't understand the delayed reaction from his passenger on getting out of the taxi but his meter was running and that's all he really needed to care about. George sauntered leisurely to the cash point, rain coming down harder now, but she was not for turning this day. The rain could only upset her if she allowed it to, and she wasn't up for that. In fact, dancing in the rain was a forgotten pleasure. George looked up at the sky and strained to see as the rain found its way into her eyes. She shook her head like a wet dog, fished the card from her shirt pocket and began the process of withdrawing money. As the cash dispensed, she took a second to capture the feeling. It wasn't often she held such a large sum in her hands – and in the next ten minutes, she would be handing it over to someone else.

'You took yer time, there, love. You'll catch your death standing outside in the rain like that.' Jim looked puzzled. The youth of today, he would never understand.

George smiled. 'It's only a bit of water, Jim. Won't do me any harm.'

Jim shook his head in an overprotective, fatherly kind of way. He moved the cab back out into traffic and headed for Sixth

Street. George gingerly mopped her brow, rain dripping down the side of her face, her damp hair looking a shade darker from the rain.

'This is it, love.' Jim stopped the meter and turned to face George. His face was full of warmth.

'That'll be £5.60, pet.'

George fished in her shirt pocket for a ten pound note and handed it over. 'Take for eight, Jim.'

George smiled sweetly in return and decided she liked Jim very much. His eyes lit up like a kid's at Christmas.

'That's very kind of ya, pet.' He handed George two pound coins. 'Now, you be careful and have yourself a good time.'

'Thanks, Jim. I will.' George climbed out of the taxi into the rain, which was now a grey drizzle. A couple of guys were huddled in the smoke shelter just outside the bar. George checked her watch and wondered if Joe would already be inside. She pondered whether she would be able to make out who Joe was, given they'd never met in person before. Perhaps she should've put more thought into the practical element of meeting a stranger for the first time in a crowded bar. *Nah*. Over-planning was not her thing.

Usually entering a pub or club alone would have George feeling a little anxious and in need of some Dutch courage and reassurance, but today she felt uncharacteristically powerful and self-assured. As she nonchalantly pushed the bar door open, music and laughter flooded George's senses. She slowly surveyed the room, unsure of what she was looking for but hoping that Joe would be on the lookout, waiting for her to arrive. Pressing through the crowds she ordered herself a pint of Carling at the bar. The pub was really full considering it was one in the afternoon. Gay men and women gathered with friends. Everyone took advantage of the two-for-one happy hour. George was handed two pints. She laughed out loud, having forgot about happy hour herself, and briefly regretted her choice of drink.

A hand tapped George lightly on the shoulder from behind and a waft of masculine scent filled up her nostrils. She turned awkwardly and hoped to God that it was Joe and not a potential suitor; she wondered if her lesbian look was acting like a magnetic force for the same sex. A beautiful white smile greeted her.

'George?' a handsome young man asked.

'Yes, yes, Joe?' responded George, questioning him with her eyes.

He nodded and embraced George; he kissed her on both cheeks. Joe was Italian, with olive skin, brown eyes and slick black hair, a truly beautiful guy. It was clear from his physique that he took care of himself. George knew that if he was straight he'd be exactly the type of bloke she would be looking to snap up, but the camp voice was a less-than-subtle clue to his sexuality.

'Carling?' George held one of the pints forward to Joe and he cheerfully accepted.

'Why not? Come, come.' He linked George by the arm and directed her to a small table in the corner of the room.

George swiftly took the two hundred pounds from her shirt pocket, scared it would burn a hole if it stayed there any longer than it needed to.

'I believe this is yours.' She placed the bank notes neatly in the palm of Joe's hand, adding cheekily, 'Don't spend it all at once.'

Joe patted her hand, grinning feverishly. 'Thank you, George. Oh, I'm so happy. I am so in love; I don't know what I would be doing if I hadn't met Alfredo. He's so wonderful and it's all down to you and your car.' Joe used his hands to gush and express himself. 'That's why I really wanted to meet up and have a drink with you – really get the opportunity to tell you how truly grateful I am.'

He took a large gulp of his beer while George chugged back more than half a pint in one go. Joe's eyes widened in surprise.

'Well, aren't you quite the little beer drinker? That's so cute.'

George laughed – not a skill she'd ever been complimented on before by a man and, given that they had only just met earlier, she knew she was really going to like Joe.

'I've got just the drink. Do you like cocktails and shots, George?' Joe had a look of mischief in his eyes. He was already on his feet, pacing back and forth. She bobbed her head enthusiastically holding her hands out wide to the sides, palms up.

'I guess I do, yes. Why? What do you have in mind?'

Joe clapped his hands excitedly, eyes shining.

'Just you wait there. I'm going to get you some drinks that you will never forget.'

George found herself laughing. She enjoyed her new friend's good humour and sparkle. She wondered whether love would make *her* more sprightly and doe-eyed, as it was certainly working wonders for Joe.

Joe sang along to the music, shaking his snake hips. He carried a tray of rather unusual-looking drinks with various bits of fruit bobbing about and some of those paper umbrellas popped in. He settled the tray carefully on the table and shook his hands, jazz-style.

'Tar dar!'

George clapped. The drinks were certainly a triumph to look at, mixtures of turquoise and amber. She was unsure of the ingredients but very sure that Joe was about to get them both very drunk. She scooped up one of the little shot glasses and downed it. A thick layer of sugary film coated her teeth.

Joe quickly followed suit. He downed one of the little shots, the burning liquid causing him to cough onto the back of his hand as the fiery droplets prickled his throat. George twisted the long straw around in her rainbow-coloured cocktail. She savoured her sobriety, as she knew that once she consumed the alcohol-infused cocktail, she would probably be two brain cells lighter and just a tad drunk. Well, she had been here before, many, many times, with enough regret to fill three lifetimes.

Joe sensed George's apprehension and decided to lead the way. He picked up his cocktail glass and downed the alcohol in one. George, never one to be beaten and feeling her competitive gene kick in, picked up her glass, made a quick toast to Joe and drank the lot. The classy bird even went so far as to scoop the fruit out of the corner of the glass with her fingers before depositing it into her mouth.

He laughed hysterically and patted her on the back. 'You are hilarious. George. Another round!'

Before she could respond, he was back on his feet, making his way through the crowded pub to the bar.

George felt her shoulders relax. A mixture of the alcohol and the chilled out surroundings influenced her physicality. A lazy smile indicated that the brain fog was starting to whirl – a feeling she both loved and hated in equal amounts.

Joe skipped back towards the table, tray held high in the air with one hand; quite a skill, George duly noted, remembering her brief affair with waitressing. It was a total disaster, with five dropsies, including one bloody steak dropped on the table, still dripping. She didn't even get to finish her first shift. In fact, the concierge paid her to leave!

The tray was once again adorned with cocktails and mini shots. The colours had changed, though, and George thought it best not to ask too many questions about the ingredients.

'I'm sure that was my round,' George protested, pointing at the drinks. Joe winked.

'It's my treat. I decided that when I met you I would spend the two hundred pounds it cost to fix the car on getting you very drunk, as my way of saying thank you for introducing me to the love of my life.' Joe almost sang as he spoke, big daft grin fixed on his face, eyes bright and engaging.

'You could've just given me the money back,' George scoffed sarcastically, followed by a huge belch. Joe laughed out loud.

'Now that wouldn't have been any fun now, would it? Anyway, I insist.' He selected one of the dark green shots and handed it to George, who gratefully accepted. She wasted no time draining the contents.

The music in the bar faded and the karaoke was announced. Joe clapped eagerly in anticipation.

'Okay, which song?' He slatted down a tatty dog-eared karaoke guide in front of George covered in beer stains.

'What, sing?' She shook her head wildly from side to side. 'I sound like a dying cat. If you are trying to get me to empty the bar, then this would be the way to do it. I am NOT singing, Joe.' George spoke with fiery conviction. Singing was definitely not her thing. Joe didn't press on and simply handed George another shot, followed by a sparkly blue cocktail.

George shakily got to her feet. She wobbled, as her sense of space was totally miscalculated. She desperately needed the toilet and, doing the wee dance, she alerted Joe that she was off to find somewhere to pee.

Following the outer rim of the pub, George hoped that she would eventually stumble across the lavs. Keeping close to the edge also meant that the wall was nearby should she need the extra support.

The fog danced sweetly around her head and dulled her awareness. It felt good to let go and relax. Wearing casual clothes meant that she wasn't in stupid shoes and could lazily drag her feet along the floor.

The smell of piss meant that she was moving in the right direction, which felt like a small win. George boiled most things down into sets of challenges. Life was just more fun for her this way – a series of mini wins.

The knob was missing off the lady's door and the red paint had blistered and was peeling off. The lav door had most certainly seen better days, and George hoped that the toilets fared better. 'Fuck it.' George pushed the door ajar using her right shoulder, and the urge to piss immediately increased a thousand percent the minute a toilet came into sight.

None of the toilets had doors, which she thought was a little odd, but it didn't appear to be bothering any of the other girls who were waiting inside. Some were just pissing, and some were pissing and having conversations with people not on the toilet. (v strange.)

George bolted for a toilet and peeled down her jeans. She tried to discreetly cover her bits, but it was knowing where to look that struck George. She shifted her gaze nervously from person to person, smiling and feeling cat-lady crazy as she pissed for England. Her bladder felt like the size of a giant cow.

Rummaging around in the toilet roll dispenser, George was disturbed to find no paper, not even the bits that sometimes get stuck to the loo roll, which, in an emergency, she would've used, this very occasion being one such emergency. Dramatically, she shouted to the girls in the adjoining loos for any toilet paper that might be going spare. The chorus of no's sealed the deal, and George knew she would have to do the fanny dance to shake off the excess moisture if she wanted to leave the toilets without looking like a geriatric who'd forgotten their Tenna pad.

Gyrating back and forth George shook off as much wee as she dare given the public setting. She immediately regretted her decision not to bring out her handbag, where she always kept a mini bag of travel tissues.

The soap dispensers were also empty, and George wondered whether the two-for-one drinks offer was eating up the margin for toilet essentials.

She needed to get back to Joe. She had also acquired a taste for the shots now and, like an addict, wanted to return to the sweet heaven of drunken bliss.

There appeared to be less light in the bar as George began navigating her way back from the toilets. Afternoon was turning into evening; time was losing meaning and all George currently cared for was finding her way round the pub to where Joe would be sat, waiting for her.

'George! I've been looking for you. Come, come, we have more drinks waiting.' Joe threw a protective arm around George's waist as they pushed through the crowded bar, Joe's wideset frame creating a path between the drunken rabble. George couldn't be sure if she was walking any more, but one thing she did know was just how much she adored Joe.

'I think you are lovely.' George looked up at Joe appreciatively. The drunken lazy eye phase was in full play and it wouldn't be long before she was totally obliterated.

'Awwwww, I think you are so cute. I was worried you'd left. What were you doing in there, girl?' Joe laughed heartily and George stole the opportunity to poke him gently in the ribs.

'Not a shred of paper in them toilets, my friend, and I really don't get the no-door policy.'

'Bit prudish, are we?' Joe teased with a devilish grin.

'I am not a prude,' George insisted and went in for a second poke of the ribs. As Joe pulled his ribcage away, the karaoke man announced the next round of singers. The names sounded dangerously familiar.

Joe shrieked with delight. He clapped his hands together, then grabbed George by the arm and dragged her to the stage. Her protests were no match for Joe, who grew more confident the more the crowd cheered. In what felt like a split second, George had gone from leaving the loo to standing on stage, facing a pub full of strangers, about to embark on an activity which left her feeling cold. She still remembered the looks on her parents' faces when she enquired about how she'd performed in the school play. Her mother, never one for tact, told her quite bluntly that it was just cruel for the parents and that she should never sing in a school play again. Damn, Beryl. No need to sugar-coat it.

Joe winked excitedly as the first bars of 'I've Got You Babe' played. George was glad that the fog was stealing away her inhibitions and her fear of singing. Restrictive beliefs were never much of a match for alcohol, and she guessed that that's why she enjoyed it so much.

George winked back at Joe. She liked that he was challenging her, and she owed it to him to at least have a go. She inhaled deeply and went for it. She sang the words as they appeared on the screen which hung from the wall:

'They say our love won't pay the rent.'

The crowd in the bar laughed and clapped in equal measure as George and Joe serenaded one another. Even in song, Joe sounded unusually camp, which left George in huge fits of laughter. As the song came to an end, the pair hugged on stage and revelled in the applause, feeling most content in one another's embrace.

The stage was about eight inches from the floor. George calculated the distance as best she could. She knew that the final stage of drunkenness was just around the corner and that it wouldn't be too much longer before she arrived there. The floor was all sticky and black from the overflowing glasses and spilt beer. She focused all her effort into lifting one foot, then the other. She placed her feet where Joe's had been as he respectfully led the way back to the table.

'Joe, I think you are ad... ad... adorable.' George stumbled with her words. 'I'm very drunk and I'm probably going to need to go before I fall on my face or I'm sick or both.' George fixed her drunken, wonky-eyed gaze on Joe, who laughed heartily and held out another shot glass to George. 'I... I... I'm serious.' George announced, forcefully stepping forward, losing all balance and crashing her full weight into Joe.

'George, my darling, I will take care of you, don't worry. We are singing buddies.' Joe's doe eyes were too much to bear. She grabbed the shot glass and greedily guzzled it down. He swiftly followed. His face screwed up as the nasty aftertaste struck once more.

'Come on, then, George. Let's get you home.' Joe skilfully hoisted George from the chair, her body all limp. The fog bore down hard, and she could no longer resist the urge to let it completely wash over her. Joe giggled to himself. George was in a bit of a mess, dragging her feet sluggishly along the floor, holding onto to him as if her life depended on it.

Outside the bar, he carefully propped her up against the smoking shelter. Her face planted on the glass, feet pointed outwards, he moved away to flag down a taxi. Almost immediately, her feet began to lose their grip and she slid ungracefully to the ground.

'Aww, so sweet,' purred Joe. George was crumpled up on the ground like a rag doll. His mission now was to get her from the ground into the awaiting car. He hoped that her slight frame was not disguising a tonne of weight.

'Come on, George, time to go. That's it. You hold onto me. That's it. Come on.' Joe wrapped her arms tightly around his neck and pulled her upright into a standing position. She smiled a kind of wild-eyed crazy woman smile that left him in fits of laughter.

'You crack me up, George. Now, where do you live? Come on, now, George, tell me where you live.'

George let the question echo around her head before clumsily babbling her address: '17 Addingham Avenue.'

Joe heaved her limp but cooperative body into the taxi, chitchatting politely with the affable cabbie. They quickly discussed the address, his hand securely propping George up against the side of the door, palm stretched across her shoulder, forcing her lips to suction against the taxi window. Hideous sight! Unbeknownst to Joe, George had checked out at least 30 minutes earlier. The next morning, she would not remember having left the bar, as she ate very little that day. It hadn't taken long for the alcohol to completely steal her senses.

The cabbie pulled up against the curb and Joe admired George's little property, with its sweet little garden and a Ford on the drive. He fished the key out of George's shirt pocket, doing his best not to make contact with her breast, as the thought was more than marginally disturbing to him. He quickly weighed his options and wondered if he should ask the cabbie for support. He swiftly dismissed the idea and carefully propped George's arm behind his head and began dragging George to her front door. In the dark, it was hard to insert the key into the lock. It took a few goes before the door sprung free. Joe gently laid George on the nearest couch. Her drunkenness had caused her to become a dead weight, so his back was glad to be relieved of the heavy burden. Pleased with his handiwork, he leant over to kiss her sweetly on the forehead before he turned to leave, the cabbie patiently waiting outside.

Dry Mouth

George could feel her tongue glued tight to the roof of her mouth and a familiar dull ache in her head. She waited for the pang of regret to dutifully kick in. A couple of minutes passed and there was nothing: no remorse, no anger, no upset. She just felt hung over and was in desperate need of a drink. This was a good start, indeed. While she couldn't put her finger on the reason, she didn't feel bad, especially since she'd woke up on the couch and couldn't remember how she'd gotten there. She decided to accept that today, regret was not going to show up. Well, not yet, anyway.

Traipsing idly into the kitchen, she pulled a large tumbler from the cupboard and proceeded to fill it to the brim with organic apple juice from the fridge. The cold liquid felt good as she glugged it down. She allowed her mouth the sweet relief of moisture and provided her body with some much-needed hydration. Wiping the excess liquid from her lips on the sleeve of her top, George refilled her glass and noticed a slight chill in the air. She thought better of going back to sleep on the couch and headed for the hallway. Halfway up the stairs, George greeted the hole in her ceiling like an old friend, a quick nod and a couple of mumbled words under her breath.

She decided that she had at least another two hours in bed, judging by the darkness, and threw herself ungracefully onto the bed.

The Pictures

George had spent the weekend trying to get to grips with her to-do list. She had systematically worked through each event that required her attention. While she was still very much single, she felt an overwhelming surge of joy having tackled some of the difficult situations she had been avoiding for some time.

She was looking forward to work. She parked the Ford and walked the short distance to her building. Today more than ever she wanted to distract her mind from her failed attempts at romance by delivering a great campaign with her team. She would focus on how to help them achieve what they needed so they could progress in their careers. She did not want to selfishly indulge in her own lack of a love life.

Her colleagues politely greeted one another.

'Good morning. How are you?'

It was obvious that no one really cared for a genuine answer to the question. Greeting each other in this manner was just the thing to do. Your entire family could've been wiped out by Ebola and you would still respond in a positive manner: 'Fine, thanks, and you?'

The security guard looked up briefly at George and turned away to pretend to have some important crisis to deal with. The only crisis that that guy had was with his weight. Clearly there was no physical test when it came to hiring for security. Wishing the portly guard a good day, she strode purposefully towards the ground floor office. For some reason, this guy just seemed to get her goat.

'Have you seen it?' James the administrator was upon George the minute she walked through the large double doors, all sweaty and excited. 'Have you?' James enquired again, smiling wildly, a tall gangly guy with brown wiry hair and a bushy facial beard.

'I have no idea why you are grinning so stupidly, James. Spill.' George's response was more of a command, and James eagerly led the way to his workstation. He entered his passcode and scanned the contents of his laptop. He double-clicked an email and opened up a link that had been forwarded by several of his colleagues.

George twisted her head to the side in an attempt to make out the tangled mess of nakedness all intertwined. The image was strangely disturbing. She focused intently on the scene until she could see it, or, rather, *them*... It was Karl doing some sort of sexual act with Laverne, the large lady from the shoot.

'What the fuck,' George gasped, pulling a hand to her mouth, both a little shocked and repulsed by the image in front of her. Karl had earned himself a right reputation over the years; he was good-looking and successful, and he knew it. Every man who had ever wished for that kind of enigmatic charisma would be rubbing their hands together today. Karl, wrapped in layers of flesh, his eyes bulging, tethered with a ball strap of some sort positioned tightly between his teeth.

'Well, he is the office cat.' James laughed heartily and tapped his screensaver, which wiped the image from view. However, the photograph had already made a deep, lasting impression on George. As she was about to get up, her curiosity got the better of her when she spied another email. It was from Hilary Bloom, and George was mentioned in the subject line. She slowly turned to look up at James, eyes serious and probing, cursor hovering just over the message, ready to open.

James couldn't believe he'd been so stupid, but it was such a funny picture he hadn't gotten round to deleting it just yet. Sheepishly, he offered a feeble apology and said she shouldn't look at it. She had already double-clicked it, commanding the message to open.

The horror had George retract her face a few inches from the computer screen, her mouth wide open. She stared in disbelief at a picture of HER with shit streaked across her face, standing beside that mutt of a dog Bruno. A strange silence engulfed the cubicle. James was too scared to say a word. Not surprised that the sender was Hilary, she read the not-so-witty caption: 'George Jackson, is that really shit on your face…..LOL'. She quickly surveyed the email's recipients to see just how many people the message had been sent to. She closed her eyes and inhaled sharply. James froze, his muscles tense, and waited for her to pounce. She let out the air from her lungs and sighed in annoyance. It wasn't James's fault. Smiling wryly, she decided to let him off the hook. She patted him gently on the back and told him not to worry. It *was* a funny picture, even if it was of her.

That BITCH Hilary, fumed George. *What was her problem?* She'd never been anything but nice to her! She hoped that someone somewhere had been stupid enough to copy her in on the emails, both the one with the picture of Karl and Laverne and the one of her, although she wasn't too sure that she needed to see the latter again.

George swiftly pulled her laptop from her bag and fiddled with the power cable. She desperately hoped to get another look at Laverne exacting her revenge on a guy that had so cruelly dismissed her. Karl had really done it this time, seduced by Laverne, a woman who was very clearly scorned, waiting for the exact moment to leverage her vengeance. All of George's respect for Karl had disintegrated within seconds when he publicly shunned Laverne for being fat, yet here he was, gagged and smothered in flesh. The guy was a joke.

She breathed a sigh of relief. For months, George had wanted to shag the man's brains out. Yet, here she was, glad *not* to have succumbed to his charm. Life was going to be a little uneasy over the next few weeks for those linked to Karl, that was for sure.

'Ughhh.' The sound of someone clearing their throat had George looking up like a rabbit caught in headlights. She hadn't even found the image in her inbox, but she felt really guilty all the same. She kind of looked it, too, her cheeks flushed a little redder than usual.

'Ms Jackson.' Laverne, the large lady from the pictures, stood firm. She wore a sophisticated dress that lay heavy on her hips. *She's come a long way in the few weeks since the shoot*, George thought, and she admired the woman in front of her.

'I wanted to thank you and Charles for everything you've done for me. I've got a great offer with Miss T that's just too good to turn down. I leave tomorrow – Germany. Can't wait.'

Laverne's eyes shifted nervously as she continued.

'He was a bad sort, George. I hope I haven't offended you.'

George was a little confused. Who was a bad sort? Then the little light went on in her head.

'Oh, Karl?' George chastised herself for not catching on sooner. 'I'm not offended at all, Laverne. It was only a matter of time.'

There was an awkward silence and Laverne lunged forward. She tightly embraced George, full of gratitude for the new life that the shoot had brought her. George, on the other hand, felt dreadful. Laverne's success was more of a blunder than a planned strategy. George would bottle and remember this point in time forever – others' happiness depended on it.

'Good luck, Laverne. Well deserved.' George's tone was sincere, and she smiled intensely. She nodded ever so slightly as her way of confirming that shit really did happen for a reason, even if, at the time, you couldn't see any rhyme or reason. Laverne strolled confidently from the office and could feel a thousand eyes on her – a feeling she'd grown accustomed to over the last few weeks during her rapid rise to fame. The pictures, however, would not be damaging to her reputation. On the contrary, these were only going to help escalate her career; stitching up Karl along the way just made the experience even sweeter.

The offending sex picture came into sight as George scrolled through her long thread of unread emails, but instead of taking pleasure in another lengthy viewing, she deleted the snapshot without opening it, hoping that others had done the same when it came to the picture of her. This was definitely a turning point for George. If nothing else, she owed it to herself to take more pride in the men that she wasted so much of her energy thinking about.

A loud ringing from her laptop alerted George to the fact that it was time for the long-awaited campaign meeting. A little butterfly sparked to life inside her chest and reminded her how much she enjoyed her job – the thrill of the chase, remaining one step ahead of competitors, closing hard with manufacturers to secure the best deals for her design house. Maybe she would have another great idea that would secure her the lead role for another year. Her energy pumped. She was totally fired up and ready to go. Work was doing wonders for distracting her inner critic from chastising her failed attempts at romance.

Hilary Bloody Bloom

George was furious about the picture Hilary had sent to her colleagues around the office. She would love to give that woman a piece of her mind.

Texting frantically in the friends' WhatsApp group, George cursed, 'I've just found out that Hilary the BITCH saw me out with my mums dog when he kicked a bit of poo on my face. She's only gone and circulated a picture of me around the office'.

'POO on your face', replied Debs almost immediately.

'Yes, that little shit Bruno kicked his poo in my face as I went to bag it up'. George was already reliving the shambolic episode and involuntarily gagging.

'Funny as FUCK, firstly, you need to get me that picture and secondly give me that Hilary's phone number, I'm going to twat her'. Debs was offering support but not without wanting to get a good look at her mate covered in poo first.

'I don't have it…..bitch', responded George, wondering whether she should've texted the girls at all.

'It will all be forgotten by tomorrow, something else will happen, you know how quickly stuff blows over' Carmen offered. At least she wasn't teasing her about the poo.

'I don't know what to say George, I've walked mum's dog a million times and that's never happened to me' broke in Bella.

'How about say nothing if you can't be sympathetic Bella.' She could just picture Bella all high and mighty, stood in her ivory tower. It made her blood boil.

'Keep your hair on, just saying… Love you x'. Bella put some thought into what she said last because she knew how George would brood. Better to add some sisterly sweetness.

'Yeah, love you too…..I suppose x'. George didn't have the picture, so fuck it, she would just forget about it. In any case, she needed to get to the meeting. She was already a couple of minutes late and she knew how much tardiness irritated Hugh.

A Delightful Surprise

Hugh enthusiastically greeted colleagues as they entered the large boardroom. He handed out official strap packs which contained company context and a steer from the senior team. George rolled her eyes. The senior team were not creative, hated risks and stifled the team into delivering very safe campaigns that only just made the margin. The latest shoot, even without the Laverne piece, had been a phenomenal success and inspired women worldwide. Business profits had hiked by a staggering 15%, year-on-year.

Hugh lightly tapped George on the shoulder.

'Perhaps you should take a look inside the pack before you roll your eyes.'

Hugh and his bloody 90-page presentation packs, George thought sarcastically. She considerately turned to the first page, where the brand vision was decoratively printed, followed by a short note from the Director. George read the patter and skipped entire lines at a time. She wanted to see what was different about this edition of the management bumf. The first page eluded her; same old, same old. She turned to the second page of the glossy pack, and George discovered a new presentation slide, one that talked about the rise of the latest bold campaign and that on the back of this new tried and tested approach, a new position as head of campaigns had been created that would report straight to the Director.

Hugh looked at George. His eyes beamed over the brim of his glasses, a smile just visible on the thin line of his lips. It was peculiar because right now George was really unsure of how to take this news. She'd run a successful campaign that had worked. She'd been thanked by the Director in person, and here was a new role being described in black and white that, apparently, she was going to have to put in for against other colleagues, who were no doubt better educated and had a natural flair for interviews, even if they couldn't pull a unique campaign idea out of their arses! George slatted the pack shut on the table in disgust and Hugh physically recoiled. He turned to face the rest of the room, somewhat shocked at George's reaction to the news.

The fire in her belly that had burned so brightly just seconds earlier was now a dampened mush of emotions. She understood HR and the way that policies had to show fairness in recruiting, but this felt just a little below the belt. How many burning hoops of fire would she have to jump through to demonstrate that she was the one that could ignite positive change in both her colleagues and the numbers?

On top of everything else, she hated to be the one looking at the world through a glass-half-empty point of view. She knew that her inner voice would ramble at a speed of knots during the meeting to sarcastically throw every discussed idea under the bus. Thank God no one could hear that mad little child inside. George was sure that she'd be locked up for good if any of that nonsense was to ever creep out.

As the team worked through the pack together, other colleagues in the room remarked on what a great job George had done this year. They commented that they hoped she would be the one to get the new head of campaigns role. This little spatter of support had George's heart melting, and once again, she found herself back in the fight. It was good of people to speak out for her and recognise her efforts. The truth was that she was a great boss, easygoing, approachable, kind, full of praise and brilliant at developing others so they reach their full potential. She sensed a little gratitude in the room from colleagues whom she'd supported with their careers in the past.

Hugh giddily nodded along with the group, winking at George. Poor old sod. She didn't half give him a hard time, and it was evident that he clearly supported the view that she should be the one to get the job.

'You will go for it, won't you, George?' Sue, a colleague for several years, was scanning George's face for a reaction. Sue was a hard-working sort and with a little direction could deliver at lightning speed. She was a good person to have on the team and a great laugh to boot.

George struggled to find the right words. Her throat was suddenly dry and she was acutely aware of the silence in the room as colleagues waited to find out whether she would be going for the role. A jingle from her mobile phone broke the tension. She was on her feet, leaving the room like a scared teenager to read her text without so much as a backwards glance. Her heartbeat rapidly accelerated. The text was from Charles; she'd heard nothing from him following the disastrous date and the tramp text, and here he was, two weeks later, dropping her a note.

'I'm back'.

"I'm back"? What's that supposed to mean? Maybe he's got me mixed up with someone else. I'm going to ignore it... No, I'm not. I'm going to text back and tell him he must've got the wrong number. Of all the cheek. And two weeks later, too.

'Think you are texting the wrong person'. George pressed send immediately, quite impressed with her defiant attitude given how much she'd wanted to hear from Charles.

Charles wasted no time in responding:

'Er nope, I'm definitely trying to text you George'. Butterflies circled in her stomach and a hopeful smile escaped before her mad inner child could stop it. She looked up at the ceiling and wondered what could be going on. Why was he texting her now? Why torture her for so long if he meant to get in touch? Her phone buzzed again. Another text.

'Remember, you told me not to text while I was out of the country on a shoot? In fact you were quite insistent'.

George read the text aloud. It didn't make any sense and she couldn't remember the conversation no matter how hard she tried.

Another buzz.

'You don't remember……do you?'

George started to piece the jigsaw together in her mind. It sounded like Charles had let her know on their first date that he would be out of the country, and she'd told him not to contact her! Oh, FFS. What a bloody shambles. George typed as quickly as her fingers would let her.

'Nope, I don't remember much…..classy lady, thought you'd seen sense and scarpered'. George gritted her teeth and prayed that there was still a chance for her and Charles.

'I like a challenge and besides never been on a date before where the table has been set on fire by a hot lady'.

George brought the phone up to her chest and covered it with both hands. She slowly took in the words.

'Hot lady'. *He thinks I'm hot. OMG he thinks I'm hot.* George bounced a couple inches off the floor just as Hugh was exiting the conference room.

'Knew you'd be excited with the update. I take it that means you are putting in for the job?' Hugh took George's newfound enthusiasm as a sign that she was interested in the role. He tapped his nose.

'Between you and me, George, I get you not wanting to tell everyone in there.' Hugh patted George on the arm sweetly before turning on his heel for the conference room, ill-fitting tweed trousers hugging his hips a little too tightly.

'George, you are coming back in, aren't you?' Hugh's tone had swiftly moved from supportive to commanding.

'I just need a minute.' George smiled and wished she had superpowers that could push Hugh back into the conference room, quick and sharp so she could get back to swooning over Charles.

Her phone buzzed again.

'How about I come round yours tonight'.

George could not believe the turn of events... Here was Charles, proposing another date, and at her house, of all places.

'Okay, do you need my address?' George held her breath and impatiently waited for a response.

'I remember from when we went out last time. I will be round about 7, and just one other thing………..'

Maybe Charles was going to request that she dress up in a kinky outfit? She immediately dismissed her ludicrous thoughts – she had, she recalled, made a total mess of the last date.

'No drinking until I get there……..promise'.

This text had George taken aback; however, she guessed it was fair. Hadn't he just mentioned something about her setting a table on fire? WTF.

'PROMISE' George wrote in all caps as a way to prove that she had no intention of getting shitfaced again before their second date. She closed the message app on her iPhone and made her way back into the meeting, where Hugh was in full presentation mode. They'd already made it to slide 7, so only another 90 pages of blurb to digest before the creative fun could begin. George's head was in the clouds. She thought about her bikini line, her hairy legs and her gnarly toenails and, to top it all off, the hole in her ceiling. She would have to be quite an engaging host to distract him from that horrendous sight all night.

The meeting was gathering momentum. Colleagues offered their perspectives on certain strategy points; Hugh patiently captured their thoughts on a flipchart; and then there was the thing that George loved most: the banter, the fun that colleagues injected to keep work in perspective and bearable.

The meeting continued for another two hours. George was amazed that she was able to make any valuable contributions with so many other things whirling around in her head. They discussed the latest trends, colours, fabrics, up-and-coming designers, shoot locations, themes, the best models, catwalks and magazines you'd want to be included in.

The team agreed on three key themes, all of which would require more thought before they could be worked into recommendations for the senior team. This was a good, solid base for the group to work from, and the meeting had been extremely productive, with everyone leaving in high spirits, both engaged with and inspired by the output.

George skimmed a few more emails before she headed home and attended to herself. She was curious how she would calm her nerves, since she had promised not to touch a drop of alcohol. Today was turning out to be a pretty good day: first, Laverne, off on a new and exciting career, then Charles, texting out of the blue, and, finally, the campaign meeting being a huge success. George grinned. She was pleased with her lot and convinced that karma had become somewhat distracted with some other poor chap and was finally cutting her a well-earned break.

The Second Date

George flung open her closet and filed through her clothes. She duly noted that there were some pretty ugly garments in there, probably impulse purchases from when she went drunk shopping. These trips were meant to be for clothes shopping, but it always turned out to be more about the Prosecco and the lunch – Shaz would buy the first drink, then they'd go a shop; George would buy the second drink, then they'd go another shop, etc. Waking up the next morning to check out their purchases was always hysterical. Over video call they would take it in turns to closely watch the other's expression as they pulled from their bags the garments they'd bought the day before. Some awful pieces which also cost a fortune illustrated the levels of drunkenness they'd achieved. The rule was that you couldn't return any of the clothes so the memory could always be cherished.

'Shit.' George's mind raced. Time was quickly catching up with her, and she fought the impulse to pour herself a little wine to dull the edges.

Charles would be coming to hers, so it wasn't like he would expect her to be dressed up or anything... but at the same time, she wanted to make a good impression and needed something that would shout *SEXY* without also screaming *I HAVEN'T HAD A SHAG IN EIGHT MONTHS*. George decided on a black silk blouse and tight-fitting jeans. She knew she had a great arse and hoped that if things progressed later on with Charles that she would be able to get the darn jeans off again without performing the shuffle dance. The thought of Charles having to wrestle them off her legs filled her with dread.

'Fuck, fuck, no shower, SHIT.' George turned on the basin taps and filled the sink to the top. She reached for anything that looked like shower gel and added it to the water to create a foamy explosion in the sink. Pulling off her work dress and underwear, she walked over to the bathroom mirror and reflected on her appearance. Her crazy little inner voice was having a word with her, pointing out all of her minor imperfections. George sensed that she was stalling before the laborious process of sink washing. She would have to get that hole in the ceiling moved up her priority list. She wasn't sure how much longer she could go on this way. It had been two weeks since she'd fell through the ceiling and the purple cloth-washing had lost all of its appeal.

The foamy liquid smelled good – lemons and honey. Her whole body received an ample scrub and dab down with a towel. Job number one, although a bit of a ball-ache, was done. Selecting underwear for the occasion was job number two. If she went all-out with something outrageously sexy then he might think she was a bit tarty, but if she went for staple whites, he might not be turned on at all. What was she thinking? He was coming around for a drink, but already she had advanced the session in her mind to full-on sex. George grabbed a matching pink bra and thong from Marks & Spencer – not too trashy but just cute enough should he decide to take a look.

As she got dressed, she felt a rush of adrenalin from all the excitement. It had been ages since she'd felt anything like it, and normally to calm her nerves she would have a couple alcoholic beverages. George inhaled deeply. She needed very much to calm her nerves.

It was 6.30 p.m., and so far, she'd accomplished getting ready. Downstairs was already fairly tidy but her bedroom looked like a vile 14-year-old girl had been waging war with her makeup and clothes for the last year. George pulled the mess into a tight little pile and began the process of shoving it under her bed, using all her strength to get every last bit of mess out of sight.

Rising to her feet, she purposefully brushed her hands together. A deep film of dust from under the bed had caked her fingers.

'Erghh disgusting.' Yet another job to be added to her long list of things that needed to be mended or cleaned. It was time to go downstairs and act casual. She wanted to choose a TV show that would accentuate her knowledge of all things cultural. *Bollocks*. What did she know of culture?

Her heart started to race. She was extremely nervous, having messed up her last date so badly.

George switched on the TV and impatiently flicked through the channels, eager to find something tasteful but bearable to watch. She perched on the edge of the sofa in an attempt to avoid getting knees in her jeans and creasing her blouse. She knew the next 10 minutes would be an agonising wait.

Homes Under the Hammer was a little dull, with some absolute shitholes for houses up for sale at auction. The state of some of the properties filled George with a small sense of gratitude for her humble abode, hole in the ceiling or not. This programme would do. It was not sleazy, alcohol-related, a depressing soap or one of those reality TV shows full of self-absorbed knobheads – it was a plain old house show. Who could argue, right?

A series of knocks on the front door snapped George out of her fleeting mind babbling, that energy-sucking ritual she spent far too much time on. Standing quickly, she smoothed out the crumples of her blouse. Her eyes darted around the room to perform a final quality check. It was at times like these that she wished she listened more to her mother... Well, either that or invested in a domestic cleaner. (#delegate!)

George opened the door.

She was greeted with a pleasant masculine aroma and sexy smile. Charles was dressed casually in a pair of jeans and a blue t-shirt that offered a little look at his toned body.

'Come in.' George's eyes sparkled and her heart accelerated a few beats, so much so that she was sure he would be able to hear it. Charles stepped forward before George had the chance to turn on her heel. Their eyes became locked and for a few awkward seconds they were face to face, just inches apart. Sensing that this could be her first blunder of the evening, George ducked a little before she turned and made polite conversation.

'I'm just watching *Homes Under the Hammer*. Great programme, you know.'

Her little internal voice offered some unhelpful notes: Homes Under the Hammer? *What are you talking about? And what was that at the door, you idiot?*

Her back still to Charles, she rolled her eyes and clenched her fingers tightly into balls. How she would make it through the evening without just a little wine, she didn't know. God, this was going to be hard.

Charles reached for George's hand and slowly turned her around to face him.

'I wanted to call you so much when I was away, but you were so insistent. I should've known you were too drunk to remember.'

As he spoke, he continued to pull George closer, studying her face for a response.

She still felt humiliated about the date. The word *drunk* cut sharply through her sense of dignity like a knife.

'I'm so sorry, Charles. I can't believe I made such a fool of myself. I got carried away getting ready and I didn't realise just how much I'd drunk.'

Charles smiled evenly and raised his hand to gently cup the left side of her face. The warmth of his touch sent rippling sensations through her body. Even if she didn't want to be a slut tonight, there was not much hope of her pulling back now. A shiver of anticipation ran down her spine.

Tracing the bottom line of her lip with his thumb, he never took his eyes off hers for a second. The sexual tension was crazy. Charles expertly leaned in and kissed George, softly teasing her lips apart with his tongue. She lustfully responded and offered no resistance. The intensity of the kiss increased and he eagerly moved his hands to feel the curve of her breasts. Her inner critic congratulated her on her choice of underwear – the off-whites never would have done.

George asserted herself and broke free from Charles's accomplished embrace. Knowing what they both wanted, she confidently reached for his hand and turned to make for the stairs. She hoped to God that he wouldn't look up at the hole in the ceiling… not that she would be able to keep it a secret or anything.

They stood together in George's bedroom, just inches from one another. Charles, no longer able to contain his lust, reached forwards and hungrily kissed George. His powerful arms skilfully pulled away her clothes while simultaneously removing his own. George's breathing revealed her excitement, her longing to be touched, and she needed him now to satisfy her needs. He watched playfully as George fumbled through her bedside draw for a condom, finding only spare buttons and cotton (very rock 'n' roll). Smiling deviously, he removed a small foil packet from his wallet and gathered her back up into his arms.

George could feel his desire. She lowered her hands to circle his generous penis, and Charles groaned in appreciation. He lowered his head to take one of her pert nipples into his mouth, his skilful tongue licking at the bud before gently biting her. His fingers searched for a way into the folds of her flesh, so she opened her legs, hungry for him to touch her there. A small gasp escaped her throat as he pushed his fingers inside her and rhythmically gyrated them. She could feel the first wave of an orgasm building, and she groaned in ecstasy as the delicious ripples shook through her body.

Charles got to his feet and gently pushed George back onto the bed. He pulled her arms above her head and held them there, then teased his penis against the entrance of her vagina. George tried to break her arm free from his grasp so she could pull at his buttocks to guide him into her but he was too strong. Charles was pleased to feel how her body responded to his touch and how much she wanted him. Eager now to satisfy his own longing, he pushed his penis deep inside her, never taking his eyes from hers. The intensity of his stare intoxicated George, who was on the brink of another orgasm. She shamelessly cried out as Charles expertly brought her to climax again.

The sex was amazing. George couldn't work out for the life of her why she'd never thought of Charles romantically before. He was handsome, kind and had a good career. Plus, under the sheets, well, he certainly knew what he was doing.

'Do you have any idea how long I've been thinking about doing that to you?' Charles grinned like a cat that had gotten the cream. She propped herself up on his chest, intrigued by the question that hung in the air.

'I have no idea, Mr Cunningham. How long have you been thinking about doing that?'

They were both smiling now; they looked at one another intently, an invisible chemistry connecting them. Charles swept George's hair behind her ears.

'Well, Miss Jackson, I've been thinking about doing, er, THAT, since the day we met. You remember that shoot in Scotland? You were wearing a short red dress, had some sort of hair clippy thing in?'

George roared with laughter as she recalled the day they'd met two years ago. Scotland, not known for its great weather, especially in February, was having a rather turbulent wind storm. Needing to tame her wild frizzy locks, she'd tried to apply a new hair contraption that was meant to gather her hair in a glamorous up-do. Having absolutely no skill whatsoever when it came to hair, George failed abysmally in trying to create a thing of beauty and instead walked around looking like a hanging basket-head straight out of the '80s.

'What's so funny?'

Charles held George's hands and slipped his fingers between hers. As she attempted to speak, more laughter bubbled over – so much so that she was partially grunting like a pig and fighting hard not to snot through her nose.

'I looked a mess that day! What were you thinking?' George laughed again and brought up her hand to partially cover her mouth; she hoped it would camouflage the grunts she was unwittingly giving rise to.

'Now you come to mention it, your hair was a bit of a mess.' Charles moved his head to dodge a pillow bash from George, who, still laughing, was looking to make him pay for his derogatory comment, as true as it was. Struggling to keep charge of the pink beaded pillow, Charles wrestled George onto her back and pinned her arms and legs with his masculine frame, which sparked an electrifying desire. They hungrily eyed up one another. Their faces, just inches apart, generated a sexual intensity that neither of them had experienced before.

Charles closed the gap between them and passionately kissed George, who was thoroughly enjoying being dominated and made no attempt to struggle free. It was their second date, and George could not recall any other dates going so well – they'd had sex twice and she'd orgasmed three times, which was unheard of, and to top it off, while the physical stuff was exciting, here was a man who was genuinely nice and thought of others before himself. She wanted to pinch herself to make sure she wasn't dreaming.

Charles rolled over onto his back, out of breath. It made her feel good to think she'd gotten him so worked up. He carefully rolled away the condom, knotted it and walked to the bathroom. She quickly ducked under the covers, ashamed of what was about to ensue.

'What the hell?' Charles popped his head around the side of the door. 'Are you aware that you have a GIANT hole in your ceiling?' He emphasised the word *giant* using his hands to illustrate the point. She heard the flip top of her bin, then running water as Charles washed his hands. Still submerged in the depths of her duvet, she considered whether the truth would be a good tale to tell or whether she should fabricate some lie to cover up her lack of diligence with the leaky shower (leaked every day for five years!) and the fact that her pervy postman had seen her naked.

Charles smiled at the duvet mountain before him, but he wasn't about to let her get away without telling him the story simply because she had buried herself deep in the sheets. He yanked hard on the corner of the duvet, taking George by surprise. Her hiding place was tugged away as quick as a flash. Charles climbed on top of her, their naked flesh connecting once again, and George was quickly thanking her lucky stars for what was about to become her third successive shag of the day.

Talking softly, with a tender look in his eye, Charles stroked the side of George's face.

'I liked you that first day because you made no attempt to hide who you really were. You made me laugh and you really are beautiful. That hole in your ceiling has just sealed the deal.'

George giggled, both flattered and content. She was getting the best shag of her life from a bloke who, by all accounts, was not offended by her lack of prioritisation and common sense.

With increased confidence, she decided to ask a little more about their previous date.

'Erm, I wasn't going to bring this up, but you mentioned something about a fire in your text... At the Chinese?' She screwed up her face, now uncertain if she really wanted to know but equally unable to gamble with avoidance tactics since she frequented the Chinese as often as she did. The tramp question could wait until another day.

He tugged away the sheet she'd pulled over her eyes. Her face was already crimson with embarrassment.

'Well, now, *that* is quite a story. Never happened to me before on a first date, I can tell you that much.' His eyes were playful and she could tell that he was enjoying her agony a little too much. 'I actually think you are barred from the place.'

With those words, George turned in disgust to face the opposite wall. She huffed ever so slightly for effect, and her childish reaction only served to encourage his vexatious behaviour.

'You should've seen that poor man, his hand all burnt and *weeping*.' The exaggeration had killed his lie, and George scoffed superiorly.

'I know I would never harm another person, drunk off my face or not.'

Charles couldn't help but laugh and sensed that he might as well come clean. He didn't wish to push his luck with a woman who had occupied his dreams for so many years.

'Okay, this is the truth: you got up to go the toilet, and as you turned to walk away, you threw your serviette over your shoulder… Only thing is, it landed on the candles and kind of started a mini fire.'

She brought up both hands to cover her face. She nervously bit her lip. She now questioned why she had decided to go there. Blocking out the ugly truth was always the most appropriate option.

'I stood up and threw my glass of wine on it, only it had caught the paper tablecloth… hundreds of waiters crowded around and other diners were looking to see what was going on… All in all, a very unusual experience.' He looked rather pleased with himself and reached over to gently stroke her back. His taste for teasing her had been replaced with a strong desire to comfort and protect her instead.

George turned to face him. She lifted her shoulders apologetically, and, instinctively, he leaned forward and placed a firm kiss on her forehead. He whispered in a low, sexy voice,

'It was the best date ever.' They both laughed. She was mortified, but at least it was out there. One less cloud hanging over her head.

She thought now about the festival and the girl with whom he had appeared so intimate with. She desperately wanted to know who she was but fought the urge to ask. Perhaps that girl was his real girlfriend and George was just some side entertainment, which would be why he didn't judge her behaviours.

Already her inner ramblings were turning towards the negative and offered nothing but bleak forecasts. She snapped out of it; she was determined to enjoy whatever time she had left with Charles, having him all to herself in her bed.

Success at Last

Carmen, eager to find out how her friend had fared on her second date, sent the first message: 'How did it go?'

The girls had set up a WhatsApp group to track the success of her date with Charles.

'It was terrible. He told me how disgusting I was and then was on his way. By all accounts, the worst date ever.' George chuckled as she typed and steadied herself for the string of text abuse which was sure to follow from the girls who were so used to her unfortunate love life.

Debbie was the first to respond.

'PIG, should've pushed him through that hole in your ceiling, no one would ever suspect murder'. George shuddered, a little disturbed. That probably wouldn't have been exactly what she would've had in mind had the date been a total disaster.

Debs' response was quickly followed by Jen's.

'There's always Rob from my place, got a right thing for you George, handsome devil and all'. Again, not very encouraging. Rob was a comics nerd whose only sense of purpose was all things Marvel. Having another conversation about Thor didn't really light her fire, and she guessed that his boxer shorts would be comic-themed, which was an absolute no-no.

A little light-hearted interjection from Lucy: 'Oh well he wasn't all that anyway George, thought he looked a bit of a snob, bet he has a teeny weeny little pecker'.

This last comment made George laugh out loud. He had a great pecker, and 'snob' he definitely wasn't! It was time to put the girls out of their misery and come clean about the most fantastic three-shag date she'd ever had in her life.

Before she could, Carmen promptly joined the conversation.

'Aww well it's better to find out now than later on down the line. If anything the lesson here is don't get smashed and kiss tramps when you are trying to make a good impression'.

George's face flashed red and frustration bubbled beneath the surface.

'Oh and don't put on that Ryan Reynolds DVD you sad old sack. Get yourself down to the wine bar, there's plenty of real men down there'.

This last comment struck a nerve. She loved Mr Reynolds. Not only was she going to type back how amazing the date was, she was going to exaggerate the size of his pecker by at least two inches. Not like they'd ever find out!

'ACTUALLY campers today was the best day of my life! I'm sat here having had a whopping great big penis satisfy me three times in succession. Charles has the body of a god, he's got a great personality and he actually doesn't care that I'm a little bit of a fuckup………..so screw you all'.

There. George felt a lot better having told her friends that she'd finally gotten laid. It had been quite the dry spell, and the girls were getting used to the fact that George inadvertently messed up most of the time when it came to men.

WhatsApp jingled. Debs had posted a gruesome picture of a battered vagina.

'Dirty bitch George, wouldn't want yours'.

The rest of the girls joined in, adding their thoughts on the vile picture. They warned George that three times a day really wasn't good for the health of her vagina.

'You cock hungry whore' chimed in Lucy.

'Apparently I set the table on fire on our first date'. George grimaced as she wrote the words. Not exactly classy cool.

'FIRE?! WTAF G' was Carmen's first attempt at a response, quickly followed by Jen's:

'That's hilarious how the hell did you do that'.

'Well as I walked away from the table I'm told that I threw my napkin over my shoulder and it just so happened to land on the candle and……..BOOM'. George did recollect moving tables that evening, despite the alcohol fog being thick by that point. She smiled wickedly at the thought of Charles dealing with the mini fire on the table. She wondered if she was actually barred from the Chinese, since she had lacked the courage to ask Charles outright if it was true.

'Legend George, can you please do more of this on our nights out?' Debbie, as always, was only disappointed at not having been there to see the carnage unravel in person.

There was one final person to tell. George flicked from WhatsApp to her texting app. She coolly typed: 'I finally did it, I shagged him'. It was satisfying to be sharing some good news. She'd actually not trashed the date, and she hadn't drunk even one glass of wine – maybe the hidden message was to stop drinking so much!

Joe replied, and even by text, he was larger than life and as camp as they come.

'DARLING! That's amazing, great to get that dusty old fanny back into action! Good for you, and what a gorgeous man darling, pass him over when you're done won't you!'

Her phone buzzed again, but it wasn't Joe this time: it was Charles. Her body tingled with euphoric excitement and she opened his text with enthusiasm, keen to read his message.

'How about round two tonight at yours, say about seven?' Without a single consideration, George replied with a resounding 'Yes'. Who cared for playing it cool anyway?

The Job Interview

Getting up for a work was a doddle. Amazing how a new love interest or even just a decent shag could add a spring to one's step. George duly noted the change in her behaviour and vowed that she would do whatever it took to keep feeling this way.

Not only would she be applying for the new head of campaign role today but she was actually looking forward to it. She had started preparing an hour earlier. For the occasion, she had bought herself a new fitted suit from Karen Millen in dark blue; the pants clung perfectly to her bottom while the jacket accentuated her tiny waist. She knew that not only would they be judging the answers she gave to the questions they asked, it would also be about how she presented herself; in other words, her style had to illustrate that she had the taste to lead such demanding and important campaigns.

It only boosted her confidence even more to talk about the role with Charles. He truly believed that the last three campaigns were successful primarily because of her input. He went on to say that if she didn't get the job then she truly needed to consider where her loyalties lay and whether it was time to move on. Charles was a freelance photographer, so he had many contacts in the business and was extremely good at his job. He was in high demand. The way he saw it, if this didn't work out, he could introduce George to some of the other designer houses, where she could potentially get a new, more lucrative, position.

There it was again: that feeling of butterflies whirling around her tummy. A sensation which had escaped her for so long was now here by the bucketload and she relished the feeling of exhilaration. For the first time in her life, she really felt on the cusp of something quite exceptional and in all areas of her life, too.

Adding the final touches to her makeup, George went for a subtle, yet sophisticated, look. Her hair was perfectly sculpted into a tidy up-do (no signs of hair clippy things hanging out, which would not have been a winning look today and would have certainly detracted from her score). *Ms King would be lucky to have me*, she told herself in the mirror. She relayed positive affirmation after positive affirmation and her stance grew in both boldness and determination. This fluffy self-help stuff actually seemed to be doing the trick – Carmen had been onto something all along. Well, you lived and learned, and now it was her turn to show the world what she was made of.

The morning was clear and crisp. As she locked the front door, she inhaled deeply. The Ford Escort stood loyally on the drive. It occurred to her that her car didn't really align with her current belief status. Here she was, standing tall in a beautiful tailored suit about to drive something that sucked her entire will to live. She made up her mind: Once the ceiling was fixed, that car would be toast! Whenever that might mean. The engine roared to life but, strangely, there was no screeching. It was as if the cosmos were colluding on her behalf to ensure that everything went off without a hitch.

To build on this already freakishly great day, George decided that whatever song came onto the radio, she would sit and hear it through to take it as a means of direction or encouragement. Her mother, who appeared to be on the payroll for the grim reaper, often talked about her own mum Nanna Jackson playing her songs through the radio whenever she wanted to get her attention. *Radio heaven or something*, she would say. Not usually one for myth or folklore, she decided to go with it today. What could be the worst thing that could happen? To her absolute delight, the song that came on was Eminem's 'Lose Yourself'. Is any song better for getting a person pumped while simultaneously telling them to follow their dreams? She smiled a deep, smug smile that lit up her face and made her blue eyes twinkle softly. Success really did look good on her.

The interview was at 9.30 a.m. on the third floor, which was a restricted area reserved for senior management and VIPs. She wasn't even sure what the furnishings looked like up there and was pretty psyched to take a look. After checking in with the blonde-haired receptionist, she sat in one of the large red velvet chairs and surveyed the room from top to bottom. The colours were vibrant and bright – exactly what one might expect from a cutting-edge designer house. The fabric of the chairs was luxurious, and everything about this floor screamed *money*. The receptionist had flawless skin, poker-straight hair and big blue eyes which flattered the already exquisite ambience. She was a very petite and elegantly dressed young lady, and George decided that beauty was probably among the attributes that made someone qualified for this sort of job. Anyway, good on her. She seemed a nice sort, not like them bitchy models she had to spend so much time with.

Eyeing the time cautiously, she knew that in the next 15 minutes, she had the ability to dramatically change the course of her life. This was another invitation for deep breathing as opposed to wine... The wine, and hopefully sex, would come later when she met up with Charles to tell him all about the interview.

The receptionist skilfully responded to a call and within seconds was asking George to make her way through the big double doors which led to the top floor conference room. It wasn't even 9.30 yet, so this was a little surprising. George shot the young girl an appreciative nod and walked slowly towards the door. On saying a final prayer, she knocked and swaggered in, shoulders back, chest pushed out, peacocking for all she was worth.

The room was enormous and elaborately decorated with gilded mirrors and pictures which, she assumed, were of great value. A large conference table looked out onto the surrounding area, and through the large glass windows George could see for miles. At the far side of the room was a brown leather couch and a couple of armchairs. Ms King was sat, business-like, in one of the armchairs, wearing a pinstripe suit. Her ample bosom was on show. She was deep in thought as she read what appeared to be George's resume.

It was at this point that George recognised that her mouth was gaping open in awe of her splendid surroundings. Having let her mask of confidence slip ever so briefly, she quickly collected her thoughts and reminded herself that they needed her for this job. The destructive and untamed inner childlike voice reminded her that *she* needed this new job to fix her ceiling and get a new bloody car. She shooed away the thought like it was a skanky stray cat. No inner game of tennis would fuck this up for her today.

For a few awkward seconds, George stood statue-like a couple feet from Ms King, waiting for her to invite her over to take a seat. This approach didn't appear to be working, so she dialled up her belief levels, selected a brown leather chair which faced Ms King and casually announced her arrival.

Ms King immediately and apologetically looked up, oblivious that George had knocked and walked the entire length of the conference room. To be fair, the room was bloody enormous – she would have needed the hearing of a hawk. Then again, Ms King had called the receptionist to chivvy in George.

'I'm sorry, George. I was looking back through your details and got rather caught up. How are you today?'

A rather random interview opener, thought George, *but hey, at least it's a question I can actually pass. For the first time in a very long time, I'm playing from a ten.*

'I'm feeling really good. I've been waiting for a position like this to open up for a while, so yes, I'm excited.' George's tone was strong and even. She sat tall, with an open posture, and looked Ms King squarely in the eye.

'I see you have brought a portfolio with you, George. That's really great, but you won't be needing that today.'

Ms King paused and gathered her thoughts whilst George fought the urge to deflate like a popped balloon, having spent several days pulling together a detailed overview of her successes to date with raving endorsements from clients.

Ms King continued. She changed her position, which forced an even larger bosom to fight for freedom.

'You won't need the portfolio, George, because, you see, I've already made up my mind about the position.'

What a blow. Not exactly what you wanted to hear on walking into a job interview that you actually believed you had a shot at securing. George swallowed hard and listened intently.

'The job is yours, George. Every campaign you have run has been a huge success, and I notice that when we give you more freedom to do what you want, it's even better. You have grit, passion and determination. I'm sick of all of these PC competency frameworks that land you some smooth-talking incompetent shite. I'm not interviewing you today because you've already demonstrated to me that you are right for this role.'

The atmosphere was tense; George wanted to leap unladylike in the air and fist pump the world, but, instead, she clung professionally to the chair. Her mouth stayed closed, her back straight, and she waited for Ms King to elaborate.

'Of course, I have six other candidates to interview today, so it is in your best interest not to say a word. I'm already bored at the thought, so please don't break my confidence and give me a reason to pass you over.' The last few words were spoken with a harsher intensity – it was clear that Ms King would be as good as her word. 'Today, at exactly 5 p.m., I will call you to offer you the job and you will gracefully accept… Is everything quite clear?'

George's inner voice was both congratulatory and sceptical. It was hard to keep up with what had just happened, having prepped within an inch of her life for a hellish grilling. Her hard work had paid off – someone had been paying attention. It would be rude not to accept the promotion, full interview or not.

'I totally understand, Ms King. I look forward to speaking to you later.'

A large smile formed on the older lady's face. Her bosom poured over the lapels of her jacket; some form of prehistoric scaffolding held the two large boulders shakily in place.

'Okay. I will see you, then, George.' The interview had taken less than five minutes and already Ms King was visibly tired of the process. George almost felt sorry for the candidates that were to follow. Although she felt a little dismissed like a child and genuinely wanted to talk more about the role and lap up any peripheral praise along the way, she knew she had already achieved what she came here for and gracefully retreated, wishing Ms King a good day.

Closing the conference room door behind her she paused to allow a wave of relief to wash over her. The receptionist looked across and smiled an even wider smile than the one she had greeted her with earlier, and George suspected that she had already known the outcome. She guessed that it was her job to be in the know, and, feeling on top of the world, George reciprocated the gesture with a knowing smile and a wave of her hand.

As soon as George was in the lift and out of sight, she performed a victory dance, a little run on the spot with some hand grooving whilst spinning 360 degrees. Her excitement blocked her awareness of the lift having stopped and some of her colleagues pouring in. When her victory rotation had her facing fully forwards, George became mindful of her new company. She passed the dance off as best she could with a sheepish smile and avoided eye contact for the rest of the lift's descent; she bolted fiercely forward as soon as the doors slid open.

Super Victory

George pulled into her drive smiling like a crazed lunatic. What the hell had happened to her usual run of bad luck? She visualised her bad luck as a grotesque beast, being held captive by her dead ancestors, who were going all-out to protect her destiny. Saying a small prayer, she thanked the mystical beings, whomever they were, for cutting her a break and promised to do something worthwhile for someone else as a token of her appreciation.

The vans along the roadside had totally escaped her attention, and she saw now that her front door was ajar, with two people in white boiler suits stood by her living room window. She gasped. This was a scene from a horror film. No way did she have time to get murdered today – she'd just landed the job of her dreams and was about to get nailed again by a sex god!

The shrill tone of her mother's voice cut through the self-induced tension. It was the name that her mother was calling which had George like a cat on hot bricks: 'Charles'. Why would her mother and Charles be together in *her* house? They'd never even been officially introduced.

George pushed open the front door in an attempt to confront her mischievous mother, but it was jammed tight and she could see that builder's sheets had been securely taped around the skirting boards in her hall.

Having failed miserably at breaking into her own home, she called her mother's name like a petulant child.

'Beryl... BERYL, can you let me in, please?' She immediately heard tools scrape and her mother order Tim and Tod to move out of the way.

Within minutes, Beryl was all jazz hands, ushering George through the entrance of her own home.

'It was all his idea, you know. What a fine man, darling.'

George was seriously confused and irritated. She rolled her eyes for the first time that day, shattering her idea to demonstrate unshakably good humour.

'Whose idea? What man? What is going on, mother?'

George's reaction appeared to throw Beryl, who retreated like a kicked dog, her face surprisingly perplexed. Tim and Tod did their best to ignore the outburst. Their eyes were directed skyward to awkwardly survey the room.

'Didn't expect you back so soon. How did it go?'

George turned on her heel and was instantly shocked. She knew the voice but struggled to connect the dots. Charles stood grinning in the entrance to her kitchen, clearly amused by George's bewildered expression.

'I was starting to get a little bit worried that I might one day end up taking the express route out of your house – clearly, by accident – and so I decided to, er, help your mum fix the hole in your ceiling.'

George looked up. She was suddenly aware that she hadn't yet greeted the hole in her ceiling, being caught off-guard due to the unexpected visitors charging her castle; a smooth plasterboard covered the hole. Tim and Tod had begun the process of painting over it, and stacked to the side of her living room was a new shower unit… and a fairly expensive-looking one at that.

'How… What?'

George turned from Charles to her mother. She struggled to take it all in, her head bobbing like the Churchill dog from the insurance advert.

Charles placed his hands firmly on George's shoulders.

'A couple weeks ago, I called round. You were out, but the lovely Beryl here was washing your curtains. We got talking and, er, hatched a bit of a plan to fix the hole in your ceiling.'

George, who was not known for her ability to calmly reflect on circumstances, was about to blow. Her feminine independence had been crushed like a bug.

A hand reached up to tightly cover her mouth, which was broodily pouting.

'We didn't tell you because we knew how you would react. It's dangerous, George. Your mother and I were just looking out for you.'

His tone was much firmer, but he said something that struck a chord with her. The ceiling *was* dangerous and, admittedly, she'd put off a DIY in favour of girls' nights out and a disastrous fake tan!

She released the tension from her shoulders and managed an appreciative smile. This allowed Charles to slide his hand away, and his fear of a fight gradually faded. Beryl was still sulking in the shadows, close enough not to miss the drama but distant enough to avoid her daughter's fiery temper.

George frantically fought for something worthwhile to say that would break the tension, but her turbulent inner voice offered nothing but chaos and sarcasm: *So you can't look after yourself, then, George. They all talk about how stupid you are. And that's not to mention… how do you think you're going to pay for all this, hmmm?*

For once, the little voice had a valid point. She'd never liked to be beholden to anyone.

'This, erm… It's, er, really a lovely surprise, but I must see you straight with the, er, cost and everything.' Her words were directed solely at Charles. She swiftly assumed that he had orchestrated and paid for the secret building work. Tim and Tod saw their opportunity to bail and uttered something about the pie shop and 'see you in five'. The uncomfortableness of the situation was definitely not something they were paid to endure.

Beryl bustled out of the shadows, her expression sour.

'I paid for it, George. You know how daddy has banned me from the bingo since the, erm, *incident*. Well, I went anyway, and I won.' She was now within inches of George and fully confronted her with the facts.

'I had all this money just sitting there, you see, and nowhere to spend it without drawing attention to my misdemeanour. I must say that now I wish I hadn't bothered.' Beryl exaggerated these final words and adopted a power pose, her hands on her hips, which were clad in green lycra pants. She threw George a hostile glare, trying to find some semblance of gratitude.

George chuckled at the thought of her mother with a stash of money under her bed. Maybe she ran guns and drugs too or headed up a little mob of teenage hoodies around the streets. The chuckle gave way to full-blown laughter as she thought of that *Gangsta Granny* novel by David Walliams. Beryl's cheeks flushed pink, which suggested that she was not amused. George picked up on these vibes and leaned forward, throwing her arms around her mother's neck and kissing her gently on the cheek.

'I love you, mum. Thank you. This was very thoughtful of you.'

Beryl's lower jaw all but hit the floor, caught off guard by George's sudden change in mood.

'They are doing a brilliant job, darling, and so quickly, you know.'

Beryl took George's good humour as a green light to walk her through the highlights of the ceiling fix so far. It was all starting to sound rather like *60 Minute Makeover*, and at this thought, George was surprisingly happy to have only Tim and Tod invade her privacy as opposed to an army of unruly helpers painting and shifting her stuff everywhere, mindlessly skipping her most prized possessions.

'How did it go?'

George fought the urge to smile in response to Charles's question. The job was all hers, but she couldn't let the cat out of the bag until 5 o'clock. She shrugged casually and tried to pull off her best *poor me* impression as she sulkily gazed at the floor.

'How about I whisk us out for lunch, let Tim and Tod finish off here, and we'll take a walk afterwards?'

George agreed with a low sullen nod of her head. Charles politely extended the invite to Beryl who at once was blushing and touching her hair, explaining that she would never normally leave the house without full makeup and styling. *Yeah right*, thought George, but at least that meant she would be getting Charles all to herself. A slight blush now tinted her cheeks as she imagined the screams of pleasure that would be escaping the bedroom later that evening.

Tim and Tod pushed through the front door, and the smell of steak pie and chips engulfed the entrance. The tense atmosphere they had left had been replaced with a much lighter ambience. They were both visibly relieved. George pressed forward.

'Carry on, guys. We are heading out for some lunch, but don't worry, my mum will be here to make you guys as many cups of tea as you want.' Beryl's newly found smile turned into a scowl, and she fought off the urge to protest. She knew that her efforts would be futile with her daughter in such a determined frame of mind.

George winked at Charles and with a mischievous smile she gave a supportive thumbs up to Tim and Tod.

'Keep up the good work, boys.' Without a second glance, she walked the short distance to the Ford Escort. Boy, was Charles in for a surprise.

Lunch

The car sprung to life with a deafening screech; Charles was both appalled and amused. He turned to face George.

'This is a real shitty car.' They both laughed. There was no embarrassment or tension like she'd experienced with Karl when she'd given him a lift.

'I've been meaning to get it looked at, but you know how it is.' She shrugged and pulled away from the kerb.

'Get it looked at? You need to put it out of its misery, George!'

She tried her best to look offended, but he did have a point. Her car was a real shit heap and drew way too much unwanted attention from random pedestrians.

The expressway was empty. George put her foot down in an attempt to impress Charles with her driving skills and to provide the trusty Ford one last opportunity to shine. They had decided to go to the Ferry Inn for lunch, which was located at the side of a canal. The views were amazing and the food was exceptional.

A car ahead had become blocked by a rather large and slowly moving horsebox. Having suffered her own horse-related phobias, she decided to do the right thing and flash the poor guy out. She pulled what she thought was the light signals, and a jet of water sprayed across her windscreen. She tried again, but the same thing happened. Charles giggled. She quickly recovered and pulled the lever on the opposite side of the steering wheel. At last: success. But hey, at least she'd given the screen a much-needed wash in addition to being courteous to her fellow drivers. It was simple stuff like this that always baffled George. How did she manage to get it so wrong?

As the designated driver for the afternoon, alcohol was out of the question. George hoped that her dignity might be saved as a result. Charles gave her leg a squeeze.

'So it went well, then? The interview?'

She couldn't help but smile, which gave away a little more than she had intended.

'Go on, there's something you're not telling me.'

She pulled the car over into one of the parking lots at the inn, and as she turned off the ignition, he squeezed her leg again. This time he tickled her until she cried out for mercy.

'Alright, alright, stop it, I'll tell you!'

Charles pulled his hand away but remained close. He wanted her to know that he could reapply his torturous techniques without hesitation.

'I got it.'

George's voice was only just louder than a whisper, scared that if she told anyone before 5 o'clock that it would all go horribly wrong.

'YOU GOT IT; well done! What did I tell you?'

George pushed her hands over Charles's mouth, certain that anyone within a five mile radius would've been able to hear him.

'SSSSHHHHH. I'm not meant to say anything until after she's phoned me tonight at five!'

Charles drew his finger across his lips and crossed his heart. The gesture made George laugh out loud. She could remember doing that type of thing as a child.

Her stomach gurgled, a rather insidious sound which indicated that it was definitely time to eat. The frost from earlier had been replaced with a welcoming hot sun, and George was sure she'd have to pinch herself at some point to make sure she wasn't dreaming. Even the weather was somehow on her side! They casually strolled towards the inn's entrance, and Charles reached out to take George's hand in his, their eyes catching intently. No words were exchanged – they didn't need to be.

They ignored the sign that asked them to wait for the maître d' and expertly navigated the pub, choosing a table set back in the corner with a large window looking out onto the canal. Charles headed to the bar to order some drinks, and George was left with her own thoughts. Everything was going so well. Today had to be up there with one of the most amazing days of her life. Everything she had ever wanted appeared to be coming together.

Her mind quickly raced to darker thoughts. *Funny*, she thought, *how one's self is set to sabotage all things good*. The attractive girl at the festival had become a common theme of doubt. *Who was she? Where was she?* George knew that she would have to voice her concerns if she was ever to fully relax and enjoy her time with Charles.

A non-alcoholic fruit cocktail was gracefully set on the table. Charles had decided on a bottle of beer for himself and wasted no time in turning to drain the contents.

'So come on, then. More detail about the interview. We're sat out of the way of everyone here, so you've no reason to think we will be overheard.'

Charles sat on the bench next to George, his body making contact with hers, which, on her part, was a little distracting, to say the least. Overcome by the intensity of his gaze, she leaned in for a kiss, wanting to cash in on the success the universe had afforded her so far today.

Feeling slightly foolish by her impulsive decision to kiss so publicly she began to talk at quite a speed about the interview; she left out nothing. Ms King's ample bosom was described in all its glory, as was the victory dance in the lift... perhaps not such a key point when trying to impress one's new male friend to make him like you more than the attractive girl he was with at the festival.

There it was again: the lingering doubt. It was never going to stop. She caught her breath and whipped up the courage to ask the question that had been on her mind since the first time they'd slept together.

'The girl at the festival, who was she?'

On completing her sentence, she took a large swig of the fruit cocktail, a little embarrassed about how the words had come out. She had a knack for talking rapidly when she was nervous or upset. Charles adjusted himself on the seat and created a little room between them. She swallowed anxiously. His body language suggested that something unfavourable was about to unravel.

Charles sensed her unease and smiled sincerely.

'You mean my sister?'

He took another drink of his beer and George rolled her eyes, furious with herself for not even considering the sister angle. She was such an idiot. She fiddled with the cocktail stick in her drink and felt like something out of *Fatal Attraction*. She looked awkwardly up at Charles.

'I know what you are thinking, but I'm not... I'm really not, you know.'

Charles looked confused.

'You're not, what?' he asked and light-heartedly took another swig of his beer.

'A bloody bunny boiler.' She covered her mouth, embarrassed by the drivel that escaped her almost without thinking. She was hardwired to react on autopilot. She talked first and thought later, which she knew never drove the best outcomes.

Charles looked bewildered and pulled George's slender frame closer to his. He tilted her head with the weight from his hand so that they were looking directly at one another.

He searched her eyes; it was as if he had a question to ask but was using his other senses to fathom the answer. He slid his other hand up the length of her leg and wasted no time in kissing her passionately. The intensity of his touch awakened all of George's senses.

They had attracted a couple of old-age pensioner onlookers in the pub, who leaned out of their seats to have a good look at the snogging couple. Charles grinned and released his grip of George's athletic thigh, even though his thoughts were still very much linked to having wild sex with her there on the tavern table.

He picked up his beer.

'I remember that you had some sort of problem with your teeth at the festival.'
George screwed up her face. What was he talking about? There was nothing wrong with her teeth at the festival? She had great teeth, 'a great grid', as Debbie would call it, but let's face it – she was shitfaced 80% of the time at a festival, so he could be making a fair point.

'You know... the blue stuff?'

He was laughing now, and the horror of the memory slowly dawned on George. She remembered that she had been playing in line at the food van with her friend Jenny and slushed the blue sweet all around her teeth with a little dribble on her chin for extra effect. Her embarrassment quickly turned to defensiveness and she pushed back.

'Oh, yes, I can remember that look on your face, one of snobbery and disgust. Well, mate, I know how to have a good time.' Habit had her once again reaching for the fruit cocktail with blissful ignorance of its non-alcoholic content. She greedily guzzled it and hoped for a courage hit.

'Why were you at a festival like that anyway?' George thought she would get straight to the point. Festival-goers were generally a little on the mad side, and, well, Charles? He really didn't fit that picture at all. Horse face suddenly popped into her mind and she prayed to every god she could think of that Charles had been spared the sight of her Rocky Dennis enlarged head. No one should ever have to witness a sight like that.

'What do you mean, "a festival like that"? What type of place would you expect to see me in?' He smiled and waited for George to respond. She already wished she hadn't said it but now she knew she wasn't getting off the hook. She decided to continue with what she considered to be Charles's sort of thing.

'Well I'm thinking you're more of a jazz man, all that posh, hoity toity palaver.'

'Hoity toity.' He swigged his beer and his eyes narrowed. He knew that if he remained silent, George would want to fill in the gaps for fear of having offended him.

'Well, you are a professional man, you like nice things, fine wines and nice toilets, I bet? Well, the festival don't really have any of that… that's all I'm… saying.'

She opened up the menu and flicked through the pages. She hoped that Charles would do the same and that they could talk about something else, something less contentious and embarrassing on her part.

'Mmmmm, the ribs sound amazing. I'm definitely having those.'

George closed the menu with a slap of the pages. She wanted to pull off an air of cool decisiveness – she wanted to be seen to be a woman who knew what she wanted.

'Well, I hope you're getting a starter as well because... later... I am going to work you REAL hard.'

His words were deliberately slow and intentional. George gulped and instinctively reopened the menu to search for a calorific hit while Charles politely excused himself to go and get more drinks from the bar.

Pursing her lips, George exhaled loudly. She tried to instil some calm amongst the stunning jelly-like feeling coursing through her body. Distraction was required. She rummaged in her handbag for her phone. She saw that it was 1 o'clock, so there would be some time yet until Ms King's life-changing call. She flicked through her contacts and selected Carmen's number. She carefully started to type her a message to let her know how everything was going. Carmen could be the sole voice of discretion when she needed to be, so she decided to tell her the good news about the promotion too. Charles was inching his way back from the bar, and since George believed that mobile phones on tables in restaurants was bad manners, she slid the phone into one of the side pockets of her specially-purchased-for-interviews Michael Kors handbag.
'Know what you're having? I've asked the waitress to come over and take our order. I was thinking once we finish here we could

head off back to my place? I've got some champagne... so everything we need to celebrate your new job.'

Charles settled the drinks on the table and she nodded in agreement. While she knew where he lived, she hadn't been inside, and her curiosity was piqued. His place it was.

'So, George, I've got this friend. He owns the BMW garage out on the Trafford high street. He owes me a couple favours and I'm thinking I could get you a new car at a snip of the full price. Maybe Sunday we could head out there if you've got nothing on?'

George wasn't sure if her funds could stretch to a new car, discount or not. She still had a lot of things that needed fixing in the house. A new car was, perhaps, an extravagance she could do without.

'What's there to think about? I'm taking you. It's settled.'

He threw George a sexy wink and patted her cheekily on the hand. For a moment, she felt like an obedient child with a parent but quickly decided that he just wanted to help. It felt kind of good.

The waitress approached to take their orders. She was in her early twenties, with silky red hair and a svelte figure. George groaned and remembered a time when staying in shape hadn't taken so much effort on her part. How she yearned for those years of her life again, the body without the pain. Charles quickly turned his attention towards ordering their food and took the waitress through the different options on the menu. It appeared that Eileen (according to her uniform's name tag) enjoyed taking the order from Charles just a little too much. It was almost humorous to watch and George wasn't sure that Charles even knew the effect he had on women, which was just as well. Eileen, who'd walked over with an air of boredom and an 'I hate my job' attitude was now full of light. She played with the ends of her hair and peacocked her tits, all smiles and giggles.

George decided to break up the little flirting party; today was her day.

'Er, Eileen, how long do you think the order will take?'

Eileen turned on her heel to face George, visibly annoyed at the interruption.

'I'll go check, but about twenty minutes, usually.'

Eileen looked over at Charles and fluttered her long lashes before she returned her cool gaze to George. A party of customers had gathered at the maître d' booth and Eileen took this as her que to leave.

'I'm so happy for you, George. That Ms King needs to look after you. Other businesses would snap you up.'

He'd said this before. It was nice that someone with Charles's professional background could see how hard she worked. Although she knew she was good, self-assurance was not an attribute that she had in buckets, which is probably why up until this point she hadn't really flown from a career perspective. Now, don't get me wrong – her job was entirely decent, but she was capable of so much more.

The food arrived and with it a wonderful aroma that had them both salivating. Hungry beyond reason, George was glad to see that Charles didn't waste a lot of time with etiquette. He picked up his ribs like a caveman biting off big chunks of meat. Taking his lead, she did the same and devoured each rib at speed, hoping that the barbeque sauce wasn't all around her mouth.

She already had rib meat wedged between most of her teeth (a very special look, indeed).

It felt good not to overthink every step with Charles. She'd ordered the food she'd wanted. On plenty of other dates, she would've avoided anything that could get messy. Spaghetti bolognaise was a definite no-no, as were so many other dishes. In fact, if she was honest with herself, the karma trap she found herself in meant that she could order even the most basic of dishes and still manage to make a complete arse of herself.

She licked her lips triumphantly, the sticky sauce all over her fingers. Charles had demolished the monstrous plate of food that had been served and burped unapologetically.

'Shall we go?' Charles was already scraping back his chair, eyes darting toward the door. It was getting close to 3 o'clock, and a new wave of excitement bubbled through George. The 5 o'clock deadline was quickly materialising. Charles reached for her hand and she gladly accepted. A not-too-happy Eileen looked on; the green-eyed monster of jealousy lurked just below the surface. George grinned and flashed the sultry Eileen a look that said 'and yes, I will be shagging this very fine man later... at least twice'.

The Home

George gasped as she walked into Charles's house. The property was amazing, built to his own design some six years ago – a project he had really enjoyed from the sounds of it. The décor was tasteful and screamed class. His prized photographs hung elegantly around the rooms. George closed her mouth, trying to savour a little dignity. She didn't want to come off like an uncultured idiot, but the truth was, she didn't know anyone with such a magnificent home or so many elegant possessions. In terms of culture, George could name every shot that any respectable bartender would stock, but she knew nothing of art or sculptures.

They sauntered into the kitchen, a great, expansive room with sliding glass doors which looked out over the surrounding countryside. His fridge was one of those great big American things, all shiny, with lots of buttons and a control screen on the front. He retrieved the champagne, skilfully popped the cork and poured the contents into two champagne flutes. George thought of all the times she had attempted to pop a cork and the carnage that followed. Once, she'd nearly taken out poor Shaz's eye… what a great night that was. Charles offered her a glass and she mindfully took a little sip. While she did want to drain the entire contents in one swig, she decided against it; in fact, abstaining from alcohol seemed to have greatly enhanced their second date in comparison to the drunken catastrophe of their first date. She set her flute on the kitchen counter and walked inquisitively towards the huge sliding doors to get a better look at the view. It was totally breath-taking and she could easily understand why Charles had fought so hard to build his house on this exact spot.

She placed her hands on the large sliding doors, feeling the cool glass on the palms of her hands. Straining her eyes, she could just make out the remains of an old church to the left on the hill. Her inner voice hissed a very true remark about needing Specsavers, which she shrugged off. She wasn't ready for eye surgery, glasses or poking herself in the eyes every day with contact lenses. She would endure her lack of long distance sight with grace.

As usual, her mind ramblings had distracted her attention from Charles, who had made his way over to the doors and stood just a few inches behind her. He reached out and circled her waist with his arm, drawing her body tightly against his. George grinned. He certainly wasn't wasting any time, and she was good with that. This evening's celebratory shag was all she'd been thinking about.

She quickly surveyed her surroundings. As elegant as the kitchen was, she wasn't sure if cold marble slapping her bare arse would be the best end to her evening. Charles must have read her mind. He held out his hand and escorted her to the stylish staircase, where he swept her off her feet like she was the lightest feather in the world. She couldn't for the life of her ever remember anyone having literally swept her from her feet before... Except for when she was eight by some awful kid named Rupert, and it wasn't so much *sweeping* but a rugby tackle/collision which had propelled her into the air over the fat kid's shoulder.

She decided she could roll with this show of masculinity and strength. Charles really did have a great body. The butterflies were back dancing around her tummy and she decided to take advantage of her position; she fiercely kissed Charles, pulling boldly at his shirt.

The celebratory sex was even better than she'd been imagining. He really did have an elite box of tricks, a box which she hoped was like Mary Poppins's bag – a magical, never-ending buffet of surprises.

Sliding under the covers, he kissed her body, aligning himself with her nether-region.

'Jesus, George, did someone charge you for this Brazilian?'

She threw her hands over her face and closed her eyes. Her shaving expedition hadn't quite gone to plan. After the disastrous tanning affair, George had opted to try some of the more intimate beauty treatments on herself, a decision she now deeply regretted.

Charles surfaced with a big grin on his face and she kept her hands firmly in place, embarrassed beyond belief. She knew that he wouldn't give up, so she started to explain.

'Well, I've kind of had a few bad runs at the salon, you know.' She let out a low groan.

Charles laughed and continued to tease her.

'Well, I didn't fancy having my vagina butchered by one of them pruned and preened women who look down on the rest of us for not having the time to keep up with torturous beauty regimes.' She sullenly spat out the last words, obviously a little intimidated by the typical beauty professional.

'So you, er, decided to butcher it yourself?' he asked playfully. George saw her opportunity to strike. She reached for a pillow and brought it crashing down on his head, her poor feminine pride in tatters.

George had tried to perfect the landing strip in her bedroom the night before. It had seemed like such a simple task that she didn't even refer to the internet or any books for useful advice and tips. Layering on a heavy dose of hair removal cream as directed by the pamphlet, she sat back and waited for the five minutes to be up. Unfortunately, a burning sensation kicked in around the two-minute-twenty mark, which called for some serious reversal action. Hopping from one leg to the other, she scraped off the cream using anything at hand and shouted profanities at the top of her voice. Holy fuck, who made this stuff? Having failed to remove much hair with the cream but now sporting a light burn mark around her vagina, she opted for the good old razor. How hard could it possibly be?

Legs akimbo for the second time, she dragged the razor down each side of her bush and rinsed the excess hair in the sink. Pubic hair was so wiry and unattractive. She needed very much to see how the landing strip was taking shape, so she reached for the bathroom mirror and held it steady so she could decide whether the strip was symmetrical. She felt that the right-hand side seemed a little bushier, so she dragged the razor through the hair once again, satisfied that it would be the finishing stroke. On second inspection, she had taken too much hair from the right-hand side and now needed to level off on the left. With caution, she proceeded to drag the razor down the left-hand side. She understood that this could be a catastrophic move. Her only saving grace was that her vagina didn't get too much public air-time.

The result was that of a pubescent 12-year-old. The bush was now more of an unruly strip of hair, not symmetrical and quite long… not at all the picture of beauty that she had envisaged. This wasn't a triumph, but at least she wasn't sat on a beauty therapist's bed feeling like her vagina could somehow be winning awards for 'freakiest vag' of the year or wondering if her vag would be the topic of conversation during the therapist's coffee break. Oh, the humiliation! She could imagine bumping into the girls on a night out and them all giving each other knowing looks, sly like a pack of hyenas. No, that could never happen. She would have to be happy with her handiwork. Novice or not, she had minimised the risk of him ungracefully choking on pubic hair and that would have to do.

Charles ducked back under the covers for a second look, pinning her down to restrict her movement. The familiar ring of her mobile phone could be heard coming from the kitchen and George screamed out, 'Holy fuck, what time is it?!'

Charles emerged from the covers and looked cautiously at the clock on his bedside table.

'It's 5 o'clock.' He understood the ramifications of the time and the importance of this for George.

She leapt from the bed with absolutely no regard for her nakedness and ran as quickly as she could down Charles's stairs; the big open windows offered very little cover during the early hours of the evening.

Panting heavily, she swiped the screen on her iPhone to accept the call. A very bemused Ms King was evidently aware that everything wasn't quite as it should be.

'Everything okay there, George? You sound like you've just done 10 rounds with Mike Tyson.'

The cold from the marble tiles was sinking into George's bones and her nipples stood at attention. In her best telephone voice, she quickly responded, 'All okay. I'm training for the London Marathon. Takes a lot out of you, you know.'

The lie was regretted the moment it left her mouth, but at such short notice, she needed to get the thought out of her mind that Ms King could somehow telepathically see her stood naked in a kitchen, having just had sex.

'Well, get you, George. Not exactly my cup of tea but certainly a big goal. Getting down to business, then: as discussed, the job is yours. You start Monday, and I will have the contract drawn up for you. How does that sound?' Ms King, as always, was to the point. George, now aching from the cold, with goose-bumps blanketing her body, wanted to bring the conversation to an end.

'Sounds great. Can't wait. And thank you for the opportunity.'

George sincerely hoped that she was giving Ms King the right impression: This really was the job of her dreams, and she knew she would be really good at it.

'Well, all good then, George. See you later.'

For once, George appreciated Ms King's lack of conversational grace. Once the call had ended, she flew up the staircase and into the bedroom, determinedly dive-bombing under the duvet, eager to seek out some warmth and shelter her nakedness.

Charles pulled her closer, transferring the heat from his body to hers. The strength of his arms provided a protective barrier. Her shaking limbs grew quiet as his warmth emanated through her body. Charles gently rolled her over onto her back.

'All sorted, then?' he asked, hair all ruffled, looking as sexy as ever. George nodded and appreciatively smiled, drinking in his masculinity. She felt like she'd grown more in these last few weeks than she had in the last few years, and Charles had everything to do with it.

'Well, I hope my neighbour Bertrand didn't cop an eyeful as you sprinted down the stairs. I can imagine him being the stalker type.' He pulled a scared face. He knew that George would take the bait and fight back in order to protect her honour. He knew he could win a play fight, and he knew that that's where the fight would end and the sex would start. They had such astounding chemistry; he wondered how he'd managed to keep his hands off her all these years, and right now he was simply glad he didn't have to.

Telling the Mates

George fired up WhatsApp and decided it was about time to let her friends know that she had been successful in getting the job. It was great to have some positive news to share instead of the hideous regretful stories she so often had to recall. The painful, embarrassing stories would haunt her for life. Social media was always at hand to capture the incidents.

'Great news, not only am I now shagging a very fit bloke EVERY DAY but I just landed a promotion at work running all of the designer campaigns! Anyone fancy a celebration?'
A couple of minutes passed before the first response arrived with a series of vibrations.

'Great news babe, drinks on you then with a fancy new promotion. Big office, car even?'

Jen was after the detail, which triggered a *D'OH* reaction from George. She was so caught up in the success of it all that George realised she hadn't asked even the most basic of questions at the interview in relation to her job offer package.

'I guess so… :)'.

George loved emojis. What was it that her history teacher used to say? Ahh, that's right: *a picture says a thousand words*. And when you haven't got the words, a smiley face with its tongue out would suffice for all the words one ever really needed.

'Not gonna go all posh on us now are you George? I wanted to get you wankered next weekend, chat up a couple of tramps, pass one over for me'. Debbie lived for the chaos. It's like the madness gave her energy and an unbreakable optimism for life. George's run of good luck was never going to be very popular with Debs, not because she wanted bad things to happen to her friends, but because, in general, the less-settled that people were, the more they liked to party, and partying meant getting fucked up, which just so happened to be Debbie's favourite pastime.

'Huge congrats, love you to the moon big G, always knew you could do it'. Carmen could always be relied on to inject a little class into the occasion.

'Celebration? I'm in, well done sis, where we going?' Just as Bella's message arrived, Lucy and Shaz joined the conversation.

'Whoop whoop, let's go Beat Bar Saturday Jackson, well done hunny x'. George considered Shaz's proposal of the Beat Bar. Not exactly classy, but now that she wasn't on the prowl for eligible bachelors anymore, cheap drinks had their own appeal.

'Sounds great George, didn't even know you were going for another job you sneaky devil! Well done babe'.

George laughed to herself while reading Lucy's message. She was probably just rolling off the gardener, having somehow managed to have sex with him, to send her this text. Yet, here was Lucy calling *George* the sneaky one!

'Thanks ladies, lets meet at the Beat Bar Saturday at 7, we can always go on from there xx'.

George's last text was met with a string of smiley faces and kisses, then one final piece of input from Debs.

'George, can you bring that gay mate of yours out? I'd really like to have a crack at him, fine arse on that lad'.

George belly laughed. What was Debs like, trying to turn a homosexual man? But Joe could look after himself and she knew it would be nice to have everyone there together.

'I'll see what I can do xx'.

George placed her phone on the bedside table and went to appreciate Tim and Tod's handiwork in the bathroom. The shower had been fitted, so once again she could bathe like a grownup, which brought a huge smile to her face. She bit her lip and looked closely at the various dials and shower jets running up and down the body of the fitting. She just hoped all of this new-fangled technology wasn't a new disaster waiting to happen.

She uttered a few positive affirmations to herself and blessed the new shower by half-whispering a few babbled words. She hadn't quite got the hang of this affirmation stuff from Carmen but wanted to cling onto the success she had experienced over the last few days.

Looking around her bedroom she could see that everything looked a little crisper. She definitely sensed that the room had been polished, and on looking under her bed, the pile of rubbish she'd gathered was no longer there. A chilling thought crossed her mind, and with the delicacy of a bomb disposal expert, she opened the door of her bedside cabinet, where she immediately gasped in horror.

Jesus Christ. There, in all their glory, was her collection of vibrators. From the looks of things, Beryl had polished these too and arranged them by height. George brought her hands up to cover her face. The scene was strangely unnerving… nobody's mother ever needs to see their daughter's collection of sex toys, EVER.

Sensing the irony of it all, George reached for her iPhone and snapped a picture of the neatly stacked sex kit. She laughed to herself and loaded the image to the WhatsApp group with the caption 'Mother for hire, will clean and stack sex toys'.

God bless Beryl, but arranging sex toys? Really?

George pulled a face. What if her mother brought up the dildos in conversation? It all felt a bit weird and dirty. She leaned forward and pushed the neatly stacked vibrators over. Only the rabbit deluxe remained standing, which George respected. That vibrator had it going on.

Stripping off her clothes, she instinctively knew that it was time to test the shower. She would wash away some of the images she had of her and Beryl discussing which dildos were best. Charles would be eager to find out whether she liked the shower unit he'd picked out for her, so in the spirit of *out with the old and in with the new*, she took a leap of faith and, without referring to the instruction manual (I mean, who does that?), pressed the On button. Jets of water fired like bullets from up and down the body of the unit. One jet was strategically placed at head height and very nearly took out her right eye. The temperature of the water was ice cold, and she fiddled with the dial and performed what looked like an Irish jig, ducking and diving out of the fire of the jets. It was clear that on this first attempt, eyes half-shut, she wasn't going to work out how to work the damn thing. Now that her body felt like it had just been pounded by a very angry rhinoceros, George decided that enough was enough for one day.

Stumbling from the shower like a wounded animal, George gathered a fluffy pink towel around her and dabbed away at her trembling body. The shower carnage was an instance where she would usually curse and blame the thing for her so-called bad luck, but, inhaling deeply, she could picture Carmen in her mind wishing for her to be grateful. George had experienced first-hand what a positive mind-set could do for her, even if sometimes she felt like a babbling spiritual idiot. She equally felt that some situations were a stretch too far. Having thanked the shower in her mind for a lesson she was certain she didn't need to be taught, she turned on her heel and flipped it the bird. *Get fucked*. There. Normality had resumed and she instantly felt better. A little cursing was her way, and it meant that lying later to Charles about the shower would be that much easier.

New Car

George had made the most of her weekend lie-in, so she had briefly forgotten that Charles was coming around to take her to the BMW garage to look at cars.

His horn sounded outside, which signalled a growing impatience. She pulled on a casual hooded top that her mother had neatly hung in her wardrobe (it was like being twelve again, but unlike the dildo arranging, she could find no awkward downside to this show of support).

Hair unbrushed and gathered back by her fingers into a makeshift bun and sporting obvious bed marks on her face, she ran down the stairs, desperate to bring the car's beeping to a halt. Charles smiled. He found it endearing that George wasn't one of those women that couldn't leave the house unless they were under fourteen tonnes of foundation and mascara. Feeling somewhat dishevelled, George smoothed her top, tucked stray hairs behind her ears and patted her cheeks to encourage her circulation to provide a natural glow (and disguise the pillow imprints on the sides of her face).

'Morning,' George offered as cheerfully as she could once she had opened the car door and got inside.

Charles grinned. She wished now that she had set her alarm. It would've been nice to turn up just a little bit more glam and prepared.

'You just got up?' Charles enquired sarcastically, already aware of the answer but loving how teasing George always lead to a play fight and then a show of affection. George dug him squarely in the arm, not wanting to disappoint, and he let out a squeal. Her bony fingers hurt more than expected. Charles pulled her free from her seatbelt and kissed her softly.

'Good morning, George.'

Damn, this man was good. Just one kiss and she was putty in his hands. Charles sat back in his seat, fired up the ignition and pulled away from the kerb. They were off to his mate's garage and George still wasn't sure how she felt about it or what she could reasonably afford without having to apply for some sort of credit.

Not for the first time, it was as if Charles could read her mind and, to be honest, she was glad of it.

'So this mate of mine is going to give you the car for free.'

He looked gingerly at George. He knew that she wouldn't take too kindly to being seen as a charity case, so before she could refuse, he continued to explain.

'I did an advertising campaign for him a couple of years back. Business was really bad and because I knew him, I did it for free.'

George looked a little less tense but it was clear he needed to continue.

'The campaign paid off… Well, it more than paid off. Profits went up more than 35% and a couple clients I knew bought some cars, so, you see, he's wanted to give me a car for ages and I just haven't needed one… until now.'

He could see from the look in George's eyes that she still wasn't sure. He'd only just got away with fixing her ceiling so he was aware that he might not actually pull this off despite the fact that George needed a new car, even if she hadn't quite worked it out for herself yet.

'Okay, so there's this thing called paying it forward.'

George turned to meet his gaze, intrigued by what he'd said.

'You do something nice for someone and all they've got to do when they find the right time is pay it forward to someone else. It causes some sort of positive ripple effect. Oh, and the thing is, it has to be kind of big.'

George could see that Charles genuinely wanted nothing more than to help her out. He was such a kind soul and she felt bad for feeling uneasy about accepting his gesture. Her dad had always told her growing up that nothing came for free, and a dose of that and a strong independent will of her own had made her wary of men who offered gifts with no strings attached. In her experience, there were always strings.

Repeating one of Carmen's positive mantras in her mind, she shook off her inner cynic and turned to face Charles.

'I really appreciate you doing this for me. Thank you.'

The words hadn't come out quite the way she had expected, but at least she had swallowed her pride and was about to allow Charles the rare privilege of giving her something really expensive for nothing in return.

The garage was just ahead and, for the first time, George felt a little excited to be going to buy a new car. She'd never owned a real *brand new* car before. Over the years, she'd had many new second-hand cars, but now that it came time to own a *really* new car, she started to think about the things that really mattered, like what colour would suit her best. Obviously not the most important aspect of purchasing a car from a man's perspective, but from George's, colour was about the only thing she felt qualified to judge.

The forecourt was filled with lots of new shiny, sophisticated BMWs, and Charles encouraged George to take a look around while he caught up with his friend, a thin, balding man with a bright red face and friendly eyes. Unable to contain her enthusiasm much longer, she did as she was instructed. George found herself drawn to all of the cars that were shiny and red. A bold colour, indeed, and one she felt would sit nicely with the new image she would like to portray... except she'd just noticed a bean stain down the front of her top. Her mother, trying to be helpful, had hung up all of her dirty clothes from underneath the bed. *FFS*. George folded her arms to disguise the crusty orange dinner badge.

'Take a look inside; she's a real beauty.'

Charles's friend was behind her now. He opened the door and gently ushered her inside. The new car smell instantly made an impression. The seats were leather and the dashboard practically sparkled with numerous dials and indicators.

'A real popular motor, this one, I tell you. Would you like to take her for a drive?'

George was caught a little off-guard, overwhelmed by all of the modern technology. Of course she wanted to take the car out, but she was also concerned that somehow she would press the wrong button or dial and write the car off.

'Automatic or manual?' asked the dealership guy. George had no idea and, to her relief, Charles had joined them to answer what had seemed to her to be quite a technical question. 'Automatic for this one, I think.' He winked at George and she smiled weakly, trying to conceal her very limited knowledge of cars.

Charles climbed into the backseat while George was presented with the keys, an action that shouldn't've had her heart accelerating at a speed of knots, but the old fight or flight mechanism was alarmingly present. George fumbled with the keys and located the ignition. She was relieved that she could at

least perform this one simple task. The car, however, didn't start as she expected, and the dealership guy leaned over to offer his hand and formally introduce himself.
'It's Dan, by the way, and if you just press this button here while holding down the brake, that should get her going.'

George's hands were sweating; her heart was pounding. She held down the brake and pressed the button, which brought the car to life with a low purr. It was quite a satisfying sound when your current ride easily breaks all official noise legislations.

Dan fastened his seatbelt.

'Let's take her around the block; see what you think.'

He pointed in the direction of the forecourt exit and George reached down to put the car in first gear. There was no gear stick and a distinct lack of pedals... The car was now moving but it was clear to both passengers that George had never driven an automatic before.

There was no oncoming traffic at the forecourt exit, so George veered the car onto the main road. She tried desperately to work out the operating rhythm. The lights ahead were red, and with an increased amount of adrenalin coursing through her veins, George accidentally performed an emergency stop which forced everyone to lunge forwards, caught completely unawares. Dan gulped and turned to George. She muttered profanities under her breath and eagerly reviewed all the dials and pressed each of the pedals. The lights turned to green and the cars behind started to beep in protest as George's car remained stationery. Only slug-like progress was made. She used both feet to manipulate the pedals but only inched forward a little before the car stalled.

'*Mother of fucks*, alright, I'm trying to go.'

George was now completely oblivious to her passengers. She allowed the gravity of the situation to throw her into a terminal downward spiral. Dan, although on heightened alert, remained calm and slowly started to talk George through the mechanics of the car. He apologised and blamed himself for not having shown her the differences between a manual and an automatic, then gave her the most important piece of advice, which was to lose one of her feet from the pedals. Automatics were like go carts: they needed very little intervention from people with the exception of accelerating and stopping. A substantial queue of cars had now built up behind George and she knew that with very little patience of her own when it came to driving, she needed to get her shit together.

Dan's soft tone and assurance gave George the confidence she needed to have another go and it wasn't long before she mastered the rhythm of the car. She drove the block not once but three times. They returned to the forecourt and George felt both embarrassed and accomplished in equal measures – a rare blend of emotions. The car was amazing. It even held on hills with no effort from her whatsoever. Even though Dan had assured her that the car wouldn't roll, George had needed to experience a few steep inclines before she was able to fully believe it.

Charles squeezed her bum and nuzzled her neck softy.
'So, is this the one?'

It was kind of nice that he wasn't teasing her for her earlier driving display, poor as it was. George turned to face him and agreed that this car was definitely the one. Dan looked over the moon, which surprised George because, all things taken into account, here was a guy who made a living out of selling cars who was about to give one away for free.

The closeness between Charles and Dan was obvious. They signed some papers, shook hands and embraced; the latter told a story of a deep friendship. George tried her best to make her signature look grown-up and professional, but try as she might, handwriting was not a skill that she had ever acquired, even though she had been practising her signature since she was eleven (signing herself as Mrs Michael, wife to George, obviously, from Wham!).

George got back into Charles's car. She was glad to kick back and relax. Today was Sunday, and raising one's BP on God's good day of rest was fairly unacceptable by anyone's standards.

It was a few seconds before George realised that everything was not quite in order. The car was silent and Charles had made no attempt to pull out of the forecourt.

'You do want the car, don't you, George?'

Charles was dangling her new BMW keys in the air inquisitively, and it suddenly dawned on her that she was meant to be driving her new car home.

'Oh, I see, sorry, on autopilot, its Sunday and everything, you know?' She stopped babbling. It was adding no value and Charles's stern expression appeared unshakable. Irritably, she snatched the keys from his hand and huffed, seeming distinctly like a teenager; the show of temper was more for her own stupidity than anything else.

'Meet you at Starbucks on the corner of Duke Street? I'll buy you a coffee,' George shouted as she skipped cheerfully over to her new prized possession.

She recognised that her behaviour did not scream that of an appreciative girlfriend and was hoping that by the time they'd got to Duke Street she would be able to find the right words to thank Charles for everything that he had done for her.

Her inner voice activated like a shark that could smell blood in the water some five miles away. *This guy isn't going to want to stay with you. Your hair's a mess, you can't drive for shit and there is bean juice at least two weeks old down the front of your top. And, if that wasn't bad enough, you are a right stroppy cow.*

George thanked her mad little voice – another technique Carmen had shared with her. Christ, she even thanked her toothpaste when it fell over her suit before work the other day. This practise was either really working or she was slowly turning into a batty, middle-aged, tree-hugging hippie.

George waved goodbye to Dan and quickly got into the car before he could change his mind – not that he had any intentions of doing so, but having grown so accustomed to the darker side of karma, George decided that she wasn't taking any chances.

The drive to Starbucks was incredibly liberating: there was no noise, no embarrassment and having mastered the automatic, she was driving for the first time with very little effort indeed. The new car stereo had her squealing with delight; little round buttons along the rim of the steering wheel let her alter the music channel and turn up the volume.
She bobbed her head up and down to 'Black Skinhead' by Kanye West which blasted out at full volume. It was probably not the coolest thing she could've done as she pulled into Starbucks. It was Sunday and folk were just trying to have pleasant conversations with one another. They made no attempt to hide their annoyance at George as she got out of the car. Luckily, Charles had already made his way inside and was sitting in one of the narrow booths in the centre of the coffee shop.

'I've ordered us two iced mochas – hope that's okay. How was your drive?' Charles was either really good at hiding his feelings or he didn't pick up on the small stuff. Perhaps she just overthought everything and made mountains out of molehills. Her rudeness went unchecked back at the garage, and she had promised herself that she would find a way to tell Charles just how much she appreciated his help.

'I am really grateful, you know.'

George spoke in a low, serious tone and fidgeted with the sugar sachets on the table. She did not fully understand why she struggled so much with verbalising her emotions. Charles was now the most important thing in her life and she wasn't going to let her own fear of looking stupid ruin it for her. She dug deep, mustered her courage and lifted her head to look Charles squarely in the eye.

'I've never met anyone like you before. You don't criticise me for getting things wrong, you don't judge me and you are always trying to help.'

Charles went to cut in but she pushed on, determined to finish what she had to say.

'I really, really like you and I can't thank you enough for helping me find the courage to go for my new job, fixing the ceiling and now the car. You are a great guy.'
Charles scooped both of George's hands into his and brought them towards his mouth, where he kissed them more than once.

'Can't say I think too much of that top, George.' Evidently, Charles was not one for highly charged scenes either, and by deflecting the conversation he was lightening the mood, although it was clear that her good intentions were not lost on him.

The iced mocha gave George brain freeze. She cradled her head and rocked back and forth as she waited for the intensity of the pain to ease. This was a sight that obviously tickled Charles, who was doing his best not to double over in laughter. She stuck her hand high in the air and caught the waitress's attention, beckoning her over so she could settle their bill. She wanted to pay for coffee... not that it in any way equalled the generosity of receiving a car.

The waitress came quickly. She held one of those Switch card payment machines.

'You want to pay contactless?'

George hadn't registered for the contactless application on her card and proceeded to tell the waitress all about it.

'Let me see your card, darling.' The waitress efficiently removed the card from George's grasp. She identified the contactless symbol, turned the card around to George and walked her through how to use her debit card. Turns out that if a person's card has a contactless symbol on it, that person can use it without signing up for anything additional at the bank. George smiled half-heartedly at the waitress. She held her card over the payment machine and the transaction completed in seconds, which would have been rather impressive had she not made such an idiot of herself.
'Fancy coming back to mine? I could help wash that top.'

Charles looked super hot and George admired the way he cut to the chase when there was something that he wanted. When it came to her, she was all his.

First Day of the New Job

After her unsuccessful debut of the shower, George read the manual not once but three times, ducking in and out whilst practising with the dials. It turns out that reading instruction manuals can be quite enlightening when you own a new gadget. Pushing through the boredom threshold of reading said guides would need to become another one of George's new habits.

As with every important milestone in her life, George had purchased the perfect outfit for day number one of her new job. This time, she had gone for a tailored skirt suit with a white silk top and a pair of black stilettoes. She didn't really appreciate flats or those shoes with a stumpy little heel – she liked the feeling of height and how it intimidated the snarky little men at work, men consumed by their own egos and angry because their DNA did not afford them the one quality that hugely appealed to women.

Collecting her BMW keys from the kitchen table, George felt thoroughly excited. She was up earlier in the morning these days and was lighter on her feet. Moving forwards had never been easier. Her mind wandered back to the afternoon she'd spent having sex with Charles and enjoying one another's company. For the first time, George considered herself to be truly happy.

It was important for her to get an early start today, not just to avoid pervy Jarvis but to exercise her professional motivation. Come to think of it, she hadn't seen Jarvis for ages; perhaps he was on holiday. George was completely aware that one of her biggest strengths was her drive. Plenty of her colleagues at work had more skill than her, but none could match her levels of determination. Today, she would start working on her strategy for the year ahead and she had some amazingly creative ideas.

Charles had shown her how to pair her iPhone to the car stereo so she could listen to her own music. This was killer for passers-by but amazing for boosting her energy levels. She was able to tune into her favourite songs, which anchored her with feelings of joy and success.

As she pressed the pedals of her BMW, George felt a tight snip from her new shoes; the discomfort was expected but still unpleasant. Driving to work was a satisfying experience now, especially when she thought of how her trusty Ford had screeched like a wild animal. The scrap man gave her a paltry £50 for a car she'd owned for more than seven years. At another time in her life, she would've seen the scrap man's offer as an insult, but since she had her new BMW, the £50 was graciously accepted.

Walking towards the fashion house, she was aware that her new shoes were a huge mistake. Her walk, although seemingly dignified, was painful, and she winced every time the shoes bit the soft skin around her ankles. Pushing through was the only option in her mind, even if that meant going home with the trotters of a homeless tramp. She would not allow a small thing like poorly manufactured shoes get in the way of her big day.

The security guard greeted her with a welcome fit for a queen. He relayed instructions that Ms King had left for her to move to the second floor, where there was an open office ready for George to make her own. The experience was kind of surreal. Never had the security guard been so cheerful and polite. *Funny*, she thought, *what a job title can do for a person.* But hey, she wanted in. The life of easy was much more up her street.

The office offered some exceptional views of the town. Beyond the industrial buildings, George could see the hills that led up to the lakes, a place that she and the girls often liked to escape to. As if on cue, her mad little voice interjected. *You are an imposter. What are you doing with an office like this? They will find out, you know. They will find out and then what will you do?* She felt a small pang of anxiety because she knew that she would have to prove herself to the other executives. Ms King's word would only stand the test of time if others could see the value of having George around.

Picturing a childish cartoon version of her turbulent inner child and a sawn-off shotgun, she did the decent thing and relived herself of the negativity. With one shot fired in her head, she blew away the unhelpful thoughts as far as she could. Who needed a judging panel with such an intense inner critic?

Ms King had organised a 9.30 meeting where George would be introduced to other members of the executive team. It was an occasion she had always dreamt she would relish but now felt familiar bouts of self-doubt.

Preparing to impress everyone at the office meant she had missed her morning coffee and usual affirmation routine, a deliberate attempt for her to generate positivity and calm. She did whatever she could to distract her mind from her insane inner ramblings and to avoid cruising on autopilot. She could not risk another mistake like the one with Laverne. God, where was the coffee machine? She surveyed the floor and identified what looked to be a kitchen. *Crisis averted*, she thought cheerfully, making mental notes of her new surroundings and all the key facilities. A lofty *hello* from the mail guy cruising from the lift and a fresh cup of Starbucks coffee planted squarely on her desk had her grinning like a Cheshire cat. She knew she was going to love the mail guy. This was already so much better than the ground floor, where she used to sit.

The night before, Carmen had dropped off a beautiful pink Swarovski crystal pen and a card to wish her luck in her new role. George loved how thoughtful her best friend was and pridefully deposited the pen in place on her new desk. A medium-sized brown package with her name on it was already waiting for her and like a kid at Christmas she wasted no time in peeling back the layers to reveal the contents. Shaz had found a rather unflattering picture of her on the company website; it looked exactly like her ID door pass. Shaz had made up a mug, mouse mat and keyring with the distasteful image on each one, along with the caption 'Congratulations, Jackson'. Only Shaz. Still, she loved the lengths she went to try and wind her up. She greedily guzzled her coffee and pushed Shaz's gifts to the side of her desk.

So far, she wasn't aware if any of the resources from her old department would be assigned along with the role change and carefully she considered who would be up for the task. For her strategy to fly, she would need to surround herself with all of her best people, who so deserved it. The thought made George tingle with motherly affection. Su was a kindred spirit; they had both worked tirelessly on the last campaign, so George would make sure to do everything in her power to get Su the recognition she deserved. *Best impress first*, she thought, *and then get the dream team stood up.*

She considerately pulled together some initial ideas on her laptop in case the introductions turned into a cross-examination. Her confidence grew a little. Innovation was her thing, and the ideas came thick and fast. George organised them into a logical sequence of events.

The meeting was in Ms King's office and, eager to arrive on time looking polished and in control, she headed for the elevator. Thankfully, there were no other people in the lift, which allowed her to exhale loudly, practising her breathing techniques which were designed to slow the beating of her heart and restore her inner calm (thank you, Carmen).

Ms King's assistant smiled gracefully and looked as beautiful as ever. George slowed her step; the piercing from her shoes nipped fiercely at her feet. With her next step, George lost her balance completely. One foot landed on the floor without any additional height whatsoever, whereas the other foot remained four inches in the air, supported by the heel of her shoe. She didn't expect £105 shoes to last forever, but what she did expect at the very least was to be able to get through one very important day. Her heel hung limply at the side of her foot. A single thread prevented it from being completely cut off. She was going to have to find a way through, with the 9.30 about to start.

She balanced her weight on one foot and used her tiptoes on the other. She hobbled into Ms King's office, where, to her surprise, the execs were already seated since they had had an earlier pre-meet to discuss the yearly budgets. Thankfully, a seat was available right at the end of the table, which provided her with a relatively small chance of not drawing attention to herself. As she tiptoed forwards, she said 'hello' politely and greeted everyone with a big smile. She hoped that it would be enough to keep them distracted from her feet.

Ms King narrowed her eyes suspiciously as George took her seat. Nothing got past this woman – she was as shrewd as they came. There were six senior people sat around the table who tapped away at their laptops. The four men were surprisingly old, at least sixty-five or so, and the two women were in their late fifties, faces thick with makeup, Botox built up around their mouths and eyes.
The pressure of the heel incident caused George's core temperature to rapidly increase, so to prevent flushing red, she removed her tailored jacket and hung it casually on the back of her chair. She instantly felt relived as the cool air wrapped around her arms and face. Ms King invited her to speak and she confidently introduced herself. She spoke passionately about successful campaigns and ideas that would have the fashion house go from good to great by capitalising on all available opportunities.

It was a fantastic meet and greet. George had said all the right things. The execs nodded in agreement and were engaged by her enthusiastic delivery. Ms King thanked George and swiftly moved the conversation onto the next agenda point. All attendees looked in the direction of the presentation boards, which had come alive with graphs and numbers.

An uncomfortable itch had taken hold of George's throat. The silk material around her neck was proving to be really agitating; she fumbled with her top and rubbed furiously. A square object could be felt through the fabric. She cringed as she realised that she had her top on back to front. The spiky little plastic clips that held the label in place scratching away at her skin.

Ms King masterfully summarised the last slide and pointed out important numbers and links with the overall strategy. The execs continued to tap away on their laptops in response, heads down, zombie-like behaviour. This provided George with an excellent opportunity to tear away at her throat. The itch had evolved into a maddening sensation which she struggled to contain.

Finally, Ms King looked over at George and excused her from the meeting. She politely thanked George for her contribution. The execs succinctly looked up and nodded at George. Their attention from the task at hand was distracted for less than a second, then they were immediately back to mechanically beavering away.

George collected her jacket from the back of her chair and recognised that exiting the room with her heel-less shoe would be far more difficult than entering it. There was really only one thing for it: speed. She just needed to move as fast as she could. In zombie movies, the undead were generally really slow-moving creatures, and based on this hypothesis, she stood a really good chance of escaping without anyone discovering her secret.

She counted down from three in her head, then legged it. Ms King looked a little baffled as George darted from the office. With the exception of Ms King's PA, the third floor was empty. Unable to conceal her agitation any longer, George removed her top and bit off the plastic hooks, then put it back on the right way round. Her shoes were next to go. She angrily snapped off both heels and deposited them in the bin just outside the elevator. Ms King's PA smiled sweetly, having witnessed the wardrobe malfunction; George laughed and presented her with a thumbs up. At least she could see the funny side.

The safety of her office was a welcoming refuge and George pulled together a contingency list; spare shoes took pride in first place. Never again would she be caught off guard, and with the space she had available to her, she could also keep a couple of spare outfits on standby too. Meetings with dinner badges would become a thing of the past.

Feeling somewhat overwhelmed by the generosity of her friends and family over the last few weeks George knew that it was time to restore some balance. Beryl had gotten the hole in the ceiling fixed and Charles had ensured that he called in an old favour to get her a new car. Whilst she was certain she wouldn't be able to match the cash value of the offerings, she was pretty sure that her pay raise would allow her to show her thanks in at least small ways.

The last time she was in Charles's kitchen, she had snuck a photograph of some of the bottles of champagne. She quickly searched Google for 'Champagne Dom Pérignon': £140 a bottle. *Eeek.* Her eyes widened. She'd never spent this much on plonk before. She selected a quantity of two from the scroll bar, ordering one for Charles, writing a sexy little thank-you note, and one for Dan the car dealership guy, keeping this note as succinct and professional as possible.

Now for her mother. What would Beryl like? Hmmmm. She sighed considerately before embarking on a Google search for a weekend vacation with activities. Her mother loved to Salsa; the mere thought made George retch, the idea of Beryl steaming about the place in her ill-fitting spandex pants, looking all hot and bothered. 'Oooooh.' She shuddered involuntarily, but given that she wouldn't have to witness the atrocity, she booked without concern.

There. All arranged. She wrote a little email to her mum with the booking details attached, then she sat back and admired her handiwork. It felt good to be giving and she gushed with delight, satisfied that the sentiment would land well with all three of them.

In her inbox were a number of emails from Ms King. One detailed her budget and what resources she could tap into. George thought about the team she could create and what this would mean for Su, which brought a smile to her face. She felt a little like a shoeless hobo but set to work on her vision. She knew she wouldn't be moving very far in her bare feet. Getting to her car would be problematic, but, hey, she worked for a designer house. There was bound to be something she could improvise with, and all things said and done, she had been in tougher pickles than this.

The Bombshell

Charles seemed distracted. The sex was as good as ever, but he was quiet. His mind was obviously brooding on something. George didn't like to intrude; people often shared their thoughts when they were ready, but something was definitely off and she guessed that it wouldn't hurt to ask.

'Penny for them?'

Charles turned to look at her. He went to speak and caught himself. His reaction unnerved George, who could now sense that something big was about to happen.

'I need to talk to you about something.' He straightened himself in the bed and propped a pillow up behind him. George scooped the duvet around her and sat up, mirroring his posture. Her face was now one of concern.

'I've been offered a job in California. It's a job I've wanted for many years and it turns out that the head guy that was running things out there has decided to pack it all in. The job is mine if I want it.'

Charles looked down and paid attention to his fingers as he talked. His lack of eye contact said many things in George's mind.

An awkward tension cloaked George's shoulders. What was she meant to do – jump for joy, pat him on the back and congratulate him? Or ask him what that meant for them? His inability to connect at this time suggested that it meant the end of the road for them. She picked up on this cue; George got up from the bed and started to get dressed.

'What are you doing, George?'

Charles was at least now making eye contact, but there was no fight from him. It was obvious that he had already made up his mind to go and live and work in California. Their two-month fling was hardly a contest for him landing his dream job.

'I can see that you need some time to think and so it's probably best if I went.'

As the words left her mouth they triggered a deep emotion within her, and she fought back the urge to cry. Her perfect little world was crumbling right before her eyes. She wanted Charles to leap from the bed and tell her that he didn't intend to take the job, that he wanted to be with her, but he just sat there. It was all the confirmation she needed. Without a backwards glance, she picked up her bag and left the room. A tear broke free and slowly rolled down the side of her cheek. A feeling of worthlessness washed over her; a life without Charles now seemed very likely.

Fumbling with the radio buttons in her car, she started to search for a song. She wanted something slow and melancholy. 'Creep' by Radiohead was playing on Rock FM. *Suitable*, she thought. She turned up the volume.

For a split second, she considered getting out of the car and demanding for Charles to talk her through what he intended to do. Her current state was delicate, though, and she wasn't sure a face-to-face standoff, which ended with him telling her that it was over, would be the best ending to her day.

She wiped her tear-stained face and started up the car. She slowly reversed out of the drive and wondered if she would ever find herself at his place again.

George hadn't banked on spending the evening alone and, feeling less than okay, she took a detour to Beer Bellies. This shop served every alcoholic beverage known to man. George was unsure of what tipple would get her started, so she ordered many different wines and alcopops, including a bottle of vodka, from the old lady trapped behind the glass. Everything in this shop was nailed down behind a glass screen. There had been two armed robberies so she understood the precaution, but she also felt a little sadder knowing that there were men like

Charles in the world who were kind and caring, and then there was this robbing scumbag sort.

She paid contactless for the second time, the novelty already wearing thin, and attempted to smile at the old lady. She realised that it probably came off as a look of trapped wind, what with her heart feeling like it had been mashed in a blender at full speed.

Her carrier bag clanked as she left the shop; the various glass bottles in her bag crashed into one another. *Classy*, hissed her inner critic.

'Get fucked,' George said by accident. She allowed the sharpness of her tongue to bring her mind to a complete halt.

George fired up the WhatsApp group and sent an SOS to her friends. Replies came back almost instantly but she had forgotten how she forfeited her place on the road trip to Snowdon in favour of being with Charles. She groaned.

'Fuck, wanker, shit and tits.' She rested the bag on the floor of her passenger seat and texted Joe in one last desperate attempt not to be home alone, feeling as dreadful as she did.

'You free tonight? Like right now, I could do with a mate'.

George wasn't ready to share the whole story yet and didn't want Joe running for the hills. Sadness was such a soul-sucking experience.

'Darling, I'm free as a bird, give me 5 x'.

Joe's quick response lifted George's spirits. At least if she was going to get completely shitfaced and rage at the world, then she would be doing it in great company.

On the drive home, she thought about smashing up her new shower to spite Charles given that he'd picked it out but considered the point that he wouldn't even know and, as ever, how she would come off in the worst possible way. What a ridiculous thought. She chastised herself for even thinking such a thing.

She searched for some glasses in her cupboard which weren't cracked, dusty or cloudy. She poured herself a generous amount of vodka and knocked it back in one go. The taste of the alcohol made her screw up her face like a gurner. True to his word, Joe knocked on the door, anxious to find out what was going on with his friend. George appeared, glass in hand, looking like a wrung-out sponge: no energy and completely sparkle-less.

'You better have one of those for me, darling.'

He brushed past George and headed straight for the kitchen. He poured himself a vodka and refilled George's glass. He decided that the more pissed she was, the sooner she would spill.

'So are you going to tell me what's going on?' Joe narrowed his eyes inquisitively.

'Can't we just get smashed?' responded George. She knew that saying the words out loud only made it more real.

'Darling, at some point tonight, you are going to tell me, so do it now and then we can get shitfaced and put the world to rights.'

She loved Joe and, not needing much convincing, she replayed the scene which had taken place earlier that evening between her and Charles.

'You telling me that he didn't look at you when he was telling you this?' Joe was seriously annoyed.

George shrugged in response.

'What a coward. What a terrible little TWAT.' Joe covered his mouth with his hand – he hated the word *twat*, and the shock on his face made George laugh. The pair of them giggled like schoolkids. He fished around in George's carrier bag to inspect the alcohol purchase as well as old bottles of gin and Warninks George had stashed away in the cupboard.
'Let's make an African monkey,' said Joe, visibly excited. He started mixing alcohols that clearly had no business being together. He used a cappuccino spoon to stir the concoction. George looked a little pale; she knew she had work tomorrow, and those drinks looked lethal.

'Once we've had these, I was thinking a little Cards Against Humanity, *Just Dance* and, yes, you guessed it – some karaoke.' Joe clapped his hands, delighted with his own suggestions, and pulled George by the arm to the living room, deadly drinks in hand. He provided George with a '1, 2, 3' and they both drained their glasses, then slammed them on the floor, eager to see who had finished the lethal liquid first.

The alcohol fog wrapped around George like a warm blanket and she laughed away with Joe. His company provided the much-needed distraction her mind desired.

'Okay, so, first card: "The young boy smiled because X had played with his X"'. Joe stifled a giggle and waited for George to feed in her hand. Her first card was 'Rolf Harris' and her second, would you believe it, was 'naked bum'. It was obviously very wrong, but perhaps that was why this game was so hilariously funny. They fell about, laughing and impressed with themselves for having cards that contextually worked together. They played a couple more rounds before Joe decided that he'd had enough. George was barely capable of reading; she chewed her words as they came out.

Joe expertly hooked up the Nintendo Wii and handed George a controller. He selected Michael Jackson's 'Beat It', which seemed appropriate for the occasion. He could see that George wasn't far from falling over from being completely wasted. He encouraged her to think of the words and dance as if telling Charles to beat it; he wanted her to feel the emotion. The characters on screen began to move. Joe mimicked them with exact timing and precision and his score increased as he minced about in time with the directions. George flung the controller to the floor, opting instead for her own uncharted 'Beat It' moves. She threw out wide arms and gestured wildly with her thumbs. The pair were drunk beyond belief. Their inhibitions drowned, they danced around, oblivious to the world, as if taking part in some Neolithic ritual, making offerings to the gods.

George seemed to be suddenly struck by paralysis. She stood, motionless, in front of the TV, her face ashen as if she'd just seen a ghost.

'What's wrong, George?' Joe continued to dance as he spoke, his face one of concern and empathy.

'What if he texts me? Where's my phone – I need to find my phone.'

George was a panic-stricken mess. She leapt about the place trying to find her handbag. Hurdling into the kitchen, her expression sour, she located her bag and dumped its contents aggressively onto the floor. Her phone was the first thing to fall from her bag, making a clattering sound as it made contact with the floor. It suggested that the whole mess could've been avoided had she just taken a little more care and time to pick it out.

Joe rushed in to see what the commotion was and found George whimpering, sat back against the kitchen units on the floor amongst the stuff she had strewn from her bag, her iPhone in hand. The fight had completely gone out of her. She dropped her phone to the floor and a small pitiful sob escaped her throat. It was evident that whatever she had been looking for – or, rather, *hoping* for – she hadn't found.

'He doesn't want me anymore... There's no texts and he hasn't called.'

George struggled to speak. Her breath was ragged; eyes red and puffy, she seemed like a small child. Joe hated to see George this way and decided that if he ever crossed paths with Charles Cunningham, he would give him a piece of his mind (after pinching his bum, of course – the guy was an absolute dish).

Joe anchored in on what made his and George's relationship so special: humour. Now seemed like a good a time as any to turn the tears into laugher.

'Darling, I did tell you about having a soggy tutu.' He released his grip around George's shoulders and sat back, a mischievous grin on his face. She looked up quizzically.

'A soggy tutu?' She sniffed and used her arm to wipe away the excess snot.

'You know, darling – down there.' Joe pointed towards George's private bits, and she slapped him playfully across the arm.

'I do not have a soggy tutu, you cheeky beggar.' A small trace of a smile formed across her lips.

'Well, darling, there can't be another reason for that man not to want all of this.' He used both his hands to emphasise George's frame. She sniffed again, exhausted now. Her eyes dropped as she leaned against Joe.

'Come on, then, George, let's get you to bed.'

Joe used his masculine frame to bring George to her feet and guide her into the living room, where he made her comfortable on the couch, propping a pillow under her head. He draped a soft grey blanket over her, downed the rest of his drink and curled up on the adjacent sofa. He felt bad for George and was glad that fate had brought them together. He had Alfredo and although he hadn't told George yet, they were about to take their relationship to the next level and move in together. He would tell her, though. He just had to find the right time.

The Day after Drinking on a School Night

George could hear the melodic bird song outside, something she usually relished. She cautiously opened her eyes. Her head throbbed and she saw that she was in her living room with Joe asleep on the other couch, purring with the rise and fall of his chest. She stretched out her limbs, feeling somewhat less than human. It looked like today would be a write off…

'Holy fuck.' She jumped up from the couch. It was 08.50 – she was meant to be in work for 9.00 and in a meeting at 9.30. There was no way she could phone in sick, not after horse face. Besides, she had just started a new job a week ago. She shouted, 'Joe, Joe, I'm a fucking mess and I've got to go to work.'

'SSSSSsssssssss.' Joe managed some irritation in his tone, having just been woken up. 'I'll help you, just stop screaming, you banshee.' Joe ruffled the back of his head with his hand.

'You brush your hair with a banger, love?' Joe laughed, amused with his own joke. She pulled her face like an angry teen sticking out her tongue and rubbed away at her eyes, yawning loudly.

'Holy fuck, George. Now you look like bloody Alice Cooper.'

George had managed to rub yesterday's eye makeup all down the sides of her face. She looked hideous; looking like Alice Coper would've been an improvement.

How come Joe got to remain gorgeous despite having drunk as much as her? Life was a total bitch. She had eyes like piss holes in snow, skin like a raging cokehead's and she was sure she could feel her internal organs aching from the alcohol rot. Joe pulled himself to his feet and dusted down his top where some crumbs remained from his nocturnal snack.

'I'll go make you an alcohol cure.' He headed for the kitchen and George climbed the stairs to her room. There was no time for a shower. She sprayed her hair with some dry shampoo and reapplied deodorant on top of the deodorant from the night before. The thought was kind of grim, but this was a DEFCON 1 situation. She stooped her posture and felt slight relief from the nausea. She hastily pulled clothes from her wardrobe; she needed to look smart, but she was desperate for comfort.

George decided that a dress would probably be the safest option and selected a light weight, dark navy peplum design from her wardrobe – great for camouflaging inflated beer bellies. She tugged the zip at the side and managed to catch an ounce of her flesh; her face contorted in pain. Crying out in discomfort, a little over-exaggerated, she spoke her favourite words, 'for fuck's sake', followed by a roll of her eyes. Barefoot, agitated and weary, she ran down the stairs to where the attractive Joe (attractive even without sleep despite having consumed litres of vodka) was calling her to come and drink up his alcohol rescue remedy.

Just one swig of the concoction was enough to convince George that if any more of the drink's contents made it into her stomach, she would almost certainly be sick for life. Thrusting the glass back into Joe's hands disapprovingly she suppressed a retch. Her kitchen floor was still covered with the contents of her bag. Gulping in some air to try and alleviate the sickly feeling, she began the task of scooping up her tissues, tampons (Christ, hundreds of tampons – it was like her trademark!), then her purse and mints back into her bag. What had she been thinking? It was 9 o'clock. She reached for her car keys, but Joe shouted in protest. He insisted that she needed to take a taxi since she was probably still under the influence. She rolled her eyes, but he did have a point. She lashed her car keys sulkily onto the couch and urged Joe to get on with it.

'Right, then,' remarked Joe dramatically, one hand on his hip. He pulled his phone out of the front pocket of his jeans and started to dial one of his friends that worked down the local taxi rank.

George paced back and forth, muttering profanities under her breath. Her head was pounding. She had very little patience to wait for a taxi. Joe, on the other hand, was cool as a cucumber. He went back into the kitchen to look for something nutritious for George to snack on. He knew that the hangover hunger pangs would kick in soon and then she would turn into a real piece of work. Every minute that passed was an agonising wait. George pulled off her best foetal position whilst standing – a very odd sight, indeed, but very much required. She couldn't remember having ever felt so vile.

The familiar honk of a cab sounded outside and she removed her hand from the wall using all of her strength to straighten her posture without activating her gag reflex. The thought of wearing vomit badges all day was an unbearable notion.

'Lock up behind you,' she managed. She squinted like a vampire as the morning sun caught her eyes. The cab door was like a *Krypton Factor* challenge; each attempt increased her frustration. She dropped F bombs like an immature teenager, face scrunched up tightly, posture bent to aid with the nausea. If it ruffled her feathers to open a cab door, then today was going to be a very long day indeed.

Eventually the door handle clicked open. It was a small win but a win all the same. She bundled herself inside, fastened her seatbelt and adjusted her dress in an attempt to restore some dignity. The taxi driver enquired about her destination, and she was sure he rolled his eyes when she told him how her work was only a short distance from where she lived. She had a good mind to scold him given that she was the customer, but in all honesty, she lacked the motivation and considered that in his position she would've probably done the same.

Joe ran from the house and motioned for George to open her window. It was like playing a rubbish game of charades. She struggled to hear the frenzied Joe and needed very much to be on her way, so she opened the window, visibly annoyed, to figure out what he was saying. An extra tall Bombay Bad Boy pot noodle was thrust into her hands, and before she could protest, Joe was on his way, whistling to himself. The taxi driver revved the engine and pulled away. George nursed the pot noodle like a newborn baby, scared of noodle spillage in her already delicate condition. She wondered what the hell went through her friend's mind. Under what conditions would a Bombay Bad Boy ever be the answer?

The taxi pulled up abruptly and she cupped the side of her pot noodle. Some of the scalding liquid spilled onto her fingers and prompted what had to be her hundredth F bomb of the day.

The cabbie took her money and impatiently handed back the stray tampon which had accompanied the small pile of loose change. He eyed her handling of the pot noodle suspiciously and she knew that one false move meant he would charge her extra. Food contraband was clearly labelled on the taxi window as a no-go.

Shuffling towards the entrance, she looked like a pensioner trying to jog; there was something awkward and unrhythmic about her moves. Her throat was dry, the handbag felt like a giant 50 kg suitcase and the pot noodle was making just about everything she tried to do impossible. Sparing no thought for the cleaners, she rammed the offending pot noodle into the foyer bin. The statuesque contraption had probably never sampled a Bombay Bad Boy before.

She had ten minutes to spare before the 09.30 meeting which, indeed, in itself was another mini victory, but as she sat at her desk, the first wave of sadness swept over her. The reason for her ridiculous hungover state was that she and Charles were no longer a thing. She checked her phone just in case he'd changed his mind but there were no texts and no calls.

Ms King charged into the office. Her boobs, as always, splashed over the side of her blouse. She held a piece of paper and what looked like some tickets. George pulled herself into the straightest, most alert position she could muster and tightly pursed her lips shut. She appreciated that her boss would not want a whiff of last night's alcoholic beverages.

'I need you to fly to Germany, then we've hired you a car to drive to the hotel. Bit of a mess, I'm afraid, and I'm sorry about the short notice, but I need you to meet Hans and sign the new contract tomorrow first thing. Flight doesn't leave until 5, so go home and pack your things; it's only the one night.'

The piece of paper and accompanying tickets were slatted on George's desk dictatorially. Ms King didn't wait for replies – she gave orders and knew that her instructions would be followed.

George's inner voice buzzed in. *Oh, how are you, George, how was your evening? Have you got any plans? Only I need your help – would you be able to go to Germany for me?* Her inner child mimicked Ms King's voice inside her head. She was a woman with very little time for personal chitchat and focused only on the task rather than the person. She collected the tickets and thoughtfully read the airport destinations and times; she wasn't sure if she should laugh or cry. On one hand, she got some time to recover at home before she had to catch her flight. On the other, she knew that the creeping hangover tiredness would only increase as the day went on. Feeling well and truly back on the menu for bad karma to attack, she decided that losing her job and her man in the same week was probably not a great idea. She tucked the tickets into a deep pocket inside her handbag and dialled for another cabbie, hoping that this one wouldn't disapprove so openly given that her home was only five minutes away. Wasn't a fare still a fare?

Her phone vibrated. George quickly pressed her fingerprint to force it open and prayed that Charles had decided that he could work out a way to have the job in California and her as well. Her heart sank. It was a text from her mum.

'Old man Bates has kicked the bucket, can't believe the old bugger lasted this long, thought you should know'.

George deleted the text. She was furious with herself for having gotten her hopes up. Her mother was batshit crazy; why did she have to be a messenger for the dead? It truly was a morbid pastime, and one of these days, she would have to tell her.

The Airport

Under normal circumstances, George would've been excited by the opportunity to travel. Flying out to a new destination was always thrilling, what with the chances to meet new people and experience their culture. Today though was different – her usual anticipation was replaced with dread. Her run of good luck was well and truly over. The lyrics of Alanis Morissette's song 'Ironic' bounced around her head: 'He waited his whole darn life to take that flight, and as the plane crashed down, he thought, *well isn't this right?*'

The airport bustled with people, reminding George of the London Underground, everyone just looking out for themselves, pushing and shoving to get to where they needed to be. A tap on the shoulder from behind made her aware that she was next in line for the check-in desk. Her bleak reflections broke and her dark mood thickened by the second.
George hadn't been able to find her overnight suitcase. Bloody Beryl must've moved it somewhere thinking she was doing George a favour. Furious, she had been forced to opt instead for a case that made her look like she was going on holiday for a week. The whole checking in thing, especially alone, was chronic, so not being able to skip this part of the process was profoundly irritating. She cursed herself for not being more aware of where she kept her things. That postage stamp-sized suitcase had to be somewhere; she vowed that when she found it, she would kick the shit out of it or her mum. The blame today would be projected on all other people and inanimate objects. Accountability for herself was swiftly determined not to be an option.

George was happy to be free from the burden of her large, unruly, blue fabric suitcase, which was something even the Clampetts would've been ashamed to be seen with. Coffee needed to be next. She required a caffeine injection and a little word with herself, so she promptly sat herself in a corner booth at the nearest coffee shop, back to the world. She briefly pondered the difficulties she would face when driving at night on the other side of the road in Germany and concluded that death would be a very real possibility for her given her current frame of mind. George thought about when she left her handbrake off and how her car rolled into Joe's car. She thought about how she always managed to spray water on her windscreen when she was, in fact, trying to flash other drivers out. Yes, the next 12 hours did look very bleak indeed.

That was it. She was driving herself crazy with her critical inner self-talk. She wasn't sure she should be left alone with her own derogatory thoughts for such a long time. George made a pit stop at WHSmith to buy a few magazines and some books to distract herself from the intolerable chatter.

Not one for science fiction or self-help books, she picked up autobiographies of Sue Perkins and Miranda Hart followed by a few scrappy magazines displaying inflated arses and wobbly bellies on the front. It was sad, the lengths that photographers would go to in order to find celebrities looking their worst, but she took comfort in the knowledge that there were other unfortunate misfits out there who were getting a much harder time than she was. At least her misdemeanours were not splashed on the front pages of a magazine for all to laugh at and ridicule.

Her plane was ready to board, and she thanked God for small mercies. At least she wouldn't have to endure a long delay in possibly one of the busiest places she could be. She felt very small and very alone.

On the plane, she was seated next to an older gentleman and his wife. She was pleased about this because there was something about the way older people interacted with her that made her feel instantly safe and less on-edge. They exchanged names and a few polite questions. George learned that the couple had been married for more than 35 years. The old man's eyes lit up as he shared this proud fact and lovingly squeezed his wife's hand. George's heart sank – 35 years of marriage and here she was struggling to maintain a relationship that lasted longer than two months. Once again her mind had turned to Charles and a sickly feeling formed at the pit of her stomach.

The air hostesses launched into their usual routine. They pointed out the nearest exits and illustrated how to fasten the air masks around one's face. George felt under her seat for her life belt and, satisfied it was there, studied the safety card. She considered thoughtfully whether she would, in fact, remove her stud earrings and stiletto heels during an emergency as suggested on the card, or whether she would just panic because she knew that the most likely outcome of plane failure was death. The safety card was nonsense. It even had a picture of false teeth. *FFS, at least let the poor bastards die with some dignity,* thought George. Who in their right mind would think, 'Shit, the plane is crashing' and whip out their false teeth? Very bizarre.

George held onto the armrest and closed her eyes as the engine boomed. The initial take-off always sparked a little fear in George, who would usually muck about with her mates having been at the airport bar leading up to take off. Her knuckles were white as she tightly gripped the arms the same way she would on a roller coaster ride. Gulping hard, she muttered a few Hail Mary's and hoped that none of the other passengers could detect her fear, terrified now that she might yet still be sick and part with last night's alcoholic beverages.

As the plane started to lift, water cascaded from the seat in front of her. The bottom of her legs and shoes were sprayed with a warm liquid. Alarmed, she called out to the passenger so that they might pick up the drink she assumed they were so clumsily spilling.

'Excuse me,' she said tapping the chair. 'Excuse me, you are spilling a drink. I'm getting soaking wet here.'

The passenger directly in front did not budge, but the guy in front and to the left of the suspect passenger turned to look at George coyly.

'I'm really sorry, love... She feels terrible... But the thing is... You see, she's terrified of flying.'

Slowly, the guy's words began to register. There was no drink to be picked up – the woman in front was so terrified that she'd pissed herself. The steep angle of the plane's ascent had resulted in George taking a full-on splattering of piss all over her suede loafers.

She tried to comprehend how such unique blessings were bestowed upon her. The poor little 'Why me' voice was in full theatrical swing. She pressed the call button above her head, removed her soggy loafers and asked if the hostess could bring her some paper towels. George explained that there had been an unfortunate accident from the seat in front. She tried her utmost not to sound annoyed. Rummaging through her handbag, she tried to find some antibacterial gel. She was sure that she had a little tube somewhere, but all she could find were several pound coins, chewing gum and 16 tampons.

Had she not been sat on a plane, she would've screamed out loud. How the fuck could one person be dealt so much bad shit? Why was she sat behind the camel pissing passenger that was afraid to fly... Why? Why did she have fourteen million tampons in every bag that she owned? Why did Charles have to get a new job so far away... Why? Why always her?

It was as if the older lady beside her could sense her despair and thickening bad mood. She leaned over to fold some antibacterial gel into her hands. She smiled softly and spoke in a low melodic whisper.

'Don't you worry, dear. We will get you all cleaned up; you'll see.' The old lady patted George's hand gently and then turned to face her husband, who kissed her appreciatively on the top of her head. Without words, her husband rose to his feet and opened the locker above his head. He retrieved a silver backpack that looked too bulky and heavy for an older guy. He instinctively pulled at one of the side zips and took out some baby wipes, then offered them reassuringly to George. She graciously accepted them and wiped down her feet first, then her shoes.

'Thank you. That was really kind of you.' George beamed and handed back the packet of wipes to the couple, who cuddled again, their genuine affection sparking a longing in George's soul.

She needed some air and gently asked the couple if she could squeeze past to use the toilet. George was glad to steal a few seconds alone, and tears pricked at the backs of her eyes. Her feelings of self-loathing were swiftly cut short as an immediate cloud of unbearable fanny mist bombarded her senses. She retched, covering her mouth, eyes wide with disbelief. She did her best not to breathe in. Whomever had beaten her to the toilets had not washed their bits in a very long time, and she feared the reaction of the next passenger who would mistakenly think that the fanny whiff belonged to her. As she left the toilets, she wanted to tactfully explain to the next woman in line, a blonde woman in her early twenties with heavy makeup, but she couldn't find the words. What exactly do you to say to someone? 'Er, excuse me, but that fanny aroma in the toilets, well, it doesn't belong to me.'

Sitting back down, George smiled affectionately at the old couple, who nodded politely, then tightly closed her eyes. She was tired and beaten. She prayed for the relief of sleep but decided that if sleep didn't come, she would practise tightening her pelvic floor, just in case Joe was onto something with that soggy tutu thing. Sure enough, though, she was out as soon as she rested her head.

Suitcase Hell

George woke up feeling marginally better. Her neck ached from her cramped sleeping position and her mouth was once again as dry as the Arabian desert. It was like the gift that kept on giving – the hangover from hell.

She joined the old couple at the carousel and waited patiently for her blue fabric suitcase to make an appearance. She duly noted that all the other passengers now also looked like they had lost the will to live. Each was ready to pounce like a savage beast to retrieve their belongings. Screaming kids, tired and hungry, clung to their mothers whilst couples argued over how to stack the luggage onto the trolley. She wondered if any of them needed a drink of water quite as badly as her. A thick film coated the inside of her lips from lack of hydration.

An official Tannoy message reverberated around the airport that called out her details and asked her to make her way to the information desk. George looked around, a little unnerved. As much as she had laughed when asked who had packed her suitcase, she was now wondering if she had managed to turn into a Columbian drug smuggler without even knowing it. The thoughts were unhelpful. Of course she wasn't being singled out for being a drug baron… She didn't even know what most drugs were called, let alone what they looked like.

Rolling her eyes, she mumbled a 'FFS' and wished the old couple a safe journey, then started dragging her heels in the direction of the information desk. She considered what the problem might be. For what possible reason might she be needed to talk to someone else? Her lips started to stick to her gums from the lack of moisture.

The desk was manned by two beautifully made-up assistants, both in their early twenties. One was blonde with petite mouse-like features and the other had dark hair elegantly pinned to the top of her head. She rather admired the ladies for being able to pull this off. Having only ever worked a couple of night shifts herself, and quitting that job a few days later, George knew it took a special kind of person to be able to work through the misery of being awake at all hours and having customers shout at you while knowing that everyone else was safely tucked in bed. Nope, a night-time worker, she was not.

She provided Ingrid the blonde assistant with her name and passport details and was told to wait whilst Ingrid efficiently disappeared through a door that led into an adjoining room. George looked at her watch, tutted and then scanned the airport for the car hire desk. She needed her luggage and then to pick up her car for the dreaded road trip. Ingrid was back and was sheepishly wheeling George's blue fabric suitcase behind her. It was now battered and open despite having been wrapped a million times in some cling film type of material.

Ingrid, in her best English, attempted to explain that her suitcase had become damaged. She did her best to look remorseful on behalf of the travel company. George thanked her and accepted the tiny receipt she was being offered; at best, from what she could make out, George was being offered a voucher that would have another suitcase sent directly to her hotel for the journey home. Tired and in desperate need of a drink, George dragged what was left of her blue suitcase over to the car hire.

The Clampetts had absolutely nothing on her now. Some clothes spilled out of her case while other clothes were held in place by the see-through cling film. A bright pink thong stretched across the top of her case... Accident from the people pulling her case back together? She thought not. She counted on her fingers how many misdemeanours she had encountered since Charles had dropped the bombshell of his new job. She bought into the magic number three for disasters (urban myth from her mother backed up by the De La Soul tune). Travelling to Germany in the first place had to be number one; being pissed on during take-off was absolutely number two; and then, finally, her case being cracked open for all and sundry to see her knickers was, without doubt, number three. She collected her car keys and hoped that she had appeased the law of karma enough for one day. Mumbling a little prayer she asked to be carried safely through the next two hours of driving.

The Hotel

The car journey largely went without issue. There was only one dodgy left turn to speak of where she miscalculated the side of the road she was meant to be on and nearly ploughed directly into an oncoming van. Near-death experience averted, she was actually quite proud of herself. Who would've thought: George, a legend at driving in foreign countries. She could be Judith Chalmers and travel the world, sharing her stories of culture and delight with the world. No, she'd gone too far; it was definitely an achievement but it didn't make her a travel programme presenter. *FFS*. At all times, her mind had to be either attacking her or rambling with ridiculous fantasies.

The Sat Nav was brilliant and announced in an authoritarian robotic male voice that she had reached her destination. Her eyes were starting to droop and her back ached from sitting bolt upright, giving as much attention as she could to the task of night driving on the wrong side of the road (well, to George, it was the wrong side). Driving anywhere unfamiliar could be daunting so this was truly next-level stuff. The car park was eerily silent. She rubbed her eyes and for the first time was aware of her accommodation. Drab exterior, handmade posters in the reception window written in crayon and curtains that looked like they had seen better days. She put her initial impression down to the fact that it was night-time. Perhaps she was missing out on some splendour that only the daylight hours could afford.

Fighting off her fear of the dark, she mustered up the energy to get out of the car and retrieve her luggage from the boot. She considered what the hoteliers might think of her, with her blue fabric suitcase like a street hobo's, pink thong strapped across the front. She accepted that she probably didn't have any room to judge the hotel and was sure that Ms King's PA would've booked somewhere appropriate.

The foyer was dimly lit. There were no receptionists and, to her dismay, the door was locked. She reached inside her pocket for the tickets and pieces of paper Ms King had handed over back in the UK. There was a number on the hotel paper circled in red. She dialled impatiently and realised now how badly she needed to pee. From the dry mouth to the intense burning of her bladder, she marvelled at how delightful the human body was.

A half-awake lady's voice greeted her at the other end of the line in German. *Not a great start*, thought George, but at this point, she was running out of options. Like most British people in foreign countries, George spoke more slowly and pointed out her predicament, stuck outside the hotel. While she talked more slowly, she added a twang as her attempt at not appearing lazy or uneducated. At least this way she would appear to be making an effort. It was idiotic, really, because she couldn't speak a word of German and the person at the other end of the phone damn well knew it. Her phony twang hindered instead of helped.

'Meet me round the side of the hotel, Ms Jackson. There is a red light above the door. I will come and meet you and give you a key; we can do proper check-in first thing in the morning.' The lady at the other end of the phone, to George's delight, spoke perfect English. As instructed, she heaved her case around to the side entrance and looked for the red light. The door was actually pretty hard to miss – a bright red light flashed above. Either it was broken or it was meant to flash, and there was something a little sinister about that.

An older lady who wore a brown heavy-checked dressing gown, peep toe slippers and hair wrapped in some sort of blue cloth, her rollers just visible, appeared at the door and held out a key. George couldn't help but take another look at the trotters that splayed out of the peepy-toed slippers like fat restricted sausages, nails all coarse and yellowing.

'Welcome, dear. We don't have all night.' The key was thrust into George's hand and she was instructed to take Room 232. She repeated the number a couple times in her mind, as the key had no identifying marks.

'You are up the stairs and to the left. Good evening.' Her thick German accent reminded George of some of the old spy films she used to love watching with her dad. But this was no film that she could just escape from. The lady looked George up and down like she was a piece of meat and eyed the blue fabric suitcase disdainfully before she shuffled away, her bulbous toes clinging onto the peepy-toe monstrosities.

George had no intention of dragging her dilapidated suitcase up any flights of stairs.

'Would I be able to take the lift?'

She hopefully looked in the direction of the lift and the hotelier. Her need for a pee was now quite urgent.
'Oh no, lift is out of order. You take the stairs.' George was sure that the old lady had smirked spitefully before peeling off down the corridor. She guessed that a helping hand with her luggage and room service was totally out of the question.

Feeling somewhat cheated and just a tad cross she decided that in the morning, she would be having words. What a completely shambolic hotel. Beaten and without options she bent down and began the process of hauling her not-so-splendid suitcase up the stairs. Perhaps it was a saving grace that she had arrived later in the evening, when the hotel was quiet. The thought of all the other guests looking on as she struggled to drag her suitcase was not a good one, and George was sure that her feet still stank of piss.

The corridors were dark and the strip lighting offered only a little assistance. She could barely make out the way she needed to head for Room 233. George was suddenly panic-stricken. It was Room 233, wasn't it? Her annoyance with the lady and the trashy little hotel took up too much of her brainpower, and the one key fact that she needed to remember now suddenly eluded her.

The piss-stained loafers were starting to chafe, and her irritation built as she recalled the take-off episode. And now, here she was, trying to remember what room she was in and dragging her broken-arse suitcase all over the maze-like corridors of the hotel. George held onto her crotch, her pee now threatening to release at any moment, and headed for Room 233. It looked like she'd stuck her finger in an electrical mains socket, jittering from side to side, the wee dance ungracefully unleashed. Room 233 was finally in sight. She exhaled with relief and used the hand that had been holding on to her crotch to carefully unlock the door. Why did this hotel still have keys, FFS?

A small click signalled the door coming free; however, the small euphoric feeling was not to last. She entered the room and it became quite clear that George was not alone. On the bed, a woman was splayed on all fours, male friend behind her, having sex. And if that wasn't enough to deal with, the guy had hold of a rather large pineapple, which he was using to rhythmically slap the woman's arse. She was either squealing with pure delight or she was in some considerable pain.

The woman's face turned white as she realised that George was observing their pineapple sex scene from the foot of the bed. Their eyes locked for a few awkward seconds and George backed out of the room as quickly as she could manage. Feeling just a little violated, warm pee now trickled freely down her leg. The weird sex scene had caused her mind and bladder to disengage from one another.

Holy. Fuck. She patted her forehead with her hand. *Think, George – what room?* She dragged her case to Room 232. It was obvious that she had some kind of master key. She decided that kinky sex or not, in the next room, she would have to use the bathroom to remove her sodden, piss-stained clothes. *FFS. Could this day get any worse?*

Without hesitation, she tried the key with Room 232. She lacked the luxury of time. One eye closed, she tentatively made her way inside. The lights were off, which she considered a good sign, but on second thought, she decided that anything could be going down in this creepy hotel.

An unflattering u-shaped pee stain now covered her pants. She was beyond angry. She flicked on the lights like she was performing a magic trick. *Ta da!* The room was clear. She breathed a sigh of relief and swiftly made her way into the faintly lit bathroom. Repulsed by her wet clothes, she stripped quickly, kicking off her loafers against the side of the bath. She couldn't believe that she'd actually pissed herself in front of a pair of strangers. What had she been thinking? But, of course, she *hadn't* been thinking. Escaping the pineapple sex show at that point was the only thing that had been on her mind. The peeing herself bit was more of an involuntary reaction.

The large double bed was adorned with a brown patchwork quilt. The decor was like something out of the 1950s. Lilac flowery wallpaper and a blue carpet? WTAF. Tormented beyond belief she sat wearily on the bed and an excruciating creak broke free as her weight made contact. A small sob gave way to bigger sobs, then a full-on wailing, snotty cry. George let the reality of the last few days spill out unrestrained. She stripped off her underwear, too tired to wash away the grime of the day, climbed under the covers and turned out the lights.

Night-time Trouble

A loud crashing woke George abruptly. She surveyed the room, scared and acutely aware that there was something or someone else now in the room with her. She was absolutely terrified and her body went completely rigid under the duvet as she froze, scared for her life... and naked.

There was definitely more than one person. The sucking noises sounded like they were kissing, and the fear that George felt now turned to dread as she figured that for the second time that evening she would be witnessing some sort of seedy sexual act.

She courageously jumped up from the bed and shouted in her best batshit crazy voice for whomever it was to get the fuck out. The lights were now on and George stood by the bedside table, one arm covering her crotch, the other covering her boobs, makeup from her eyes all over her face from her earlier crying episode. She looked absolutely fucking mental. (On the upside, she had nailed her second Alice Cooper impression in the last 24 hours.)

An old, unattractive fat man stood with his mouth gaped open, his trousers loose and shirt unbuttoned. He clearly did not expect to see someone in the room. A younger, more attractive lady stood to the side of him. She wore what can only be described as black fuck-me boots and a pink velvet leotard; she also brandished some sort of leather whip.

George searched for the words to verbalise her distress, but it seemed that the fat guy knew he needed to make a hasty retreat.

'Es tut uns leid.' He spoke in a nervous German accent and used his hands to suggest that George should could keep calm, as he would be leaving. You could tell from the younger lady's face that this shit happened to her all the time. Unconcerned, she threw George a look of *so what* and left without a fuss.

Her heart was racing. Misunderstanding or not, random people entering her room scared the shit out of her and she was totally freaked. The incident left her feeling wired. She caught a glimpse of her appearance in the dresser mirror – she did a great job pulling off a crazed crack whore junkie kind of look.

There wasn't much in the room by way of furniture, but she moved whatever she could find in front of her door to build a barricade which would protect her from the seedy randomers of the night. She was in a knocking shop for sure. Potentially she would not be able to bank on those two being the last intruders of the night. She rolled her eyes habitually with a 'FFS' thrown in for good measure.

The strange events had kept her alert and awake. She checked her watch: 3.32 a.m.... or was it? She could never be sure of the time abroad. She always checked a variety of sources: phone, watch, TV... She drove herself mad. Try as she might, she couldn't get back to sleep. Every noise had her sat bolt upright as she stared in the direction of the door and waited for something to happen.

If she stared at the barricade of furniture for long enough, she could actually convince herself that it was moving and that, indeed, someone from outside was trying to get in. Her mind was almost certainly playing tricks on her now – alone, shattered and feeling lower than ever. She recalculated the number of misdemeanours she'd encountered since her split with Charles and wondered if this was going to be a taste of things to come. The magic three had turned into the magic six:

1. Being sent to Germany out of the blue, with a hangover from hell.
2. Getting pissed on by a stranger during take-off.
3. Her suitcase getting damaged and wrapped in film.

4. Observing a sinister sexual act involving a pineapple.
5. Pissing herself upon observing said sinister sex act.
6. And, finally, having strangers wake her up in the middle of the night in her bedroom about to have kinky sex… FFS!

Morning has Broken

George rubbed at her face and groaned loudly. She actually felt worse today than she had felt yesterday on waking up with her hangover, except the nausea was replaced by hunger. She was ravenous.

She considered herself to be made of tough stuff, but without any sleep, she was either a whining baby or a psychotic madwoman. She rehearsed all the things she would say to the receptionist at the check-in desk and made a mental list of them. She screwed up her face when it came to the arse-slapping pineapple sex scene. She had it all perfectly planned in her mind. By the time she finished with this hotel, they would be begging her to take some form of compensation or she would ruin their reputation on Tripadvisor.

The bathroom had ugly orange tiles with a Poundland shower curtain and a toilet that Aggie and Maggie would've loved to have gotten their hands on.

Ordinarily, she might've opted to refuse to shower on being greeted with such an offensive bathroom but like it or not she needed to shower. She stank. She stank really bad. She reached up and cautiously twisted the knobs on the shower unit, standing back just in case. To her relief the shower worked just fine and at least she would be able to replace her Alice Cooper face with a fresher, cleaner one, although her eyes were still like piss holes in snow. The shower obviously did not match the state-of-the-art contraption she'd just had installed; she smiled when she thought about the hole in her ceiling, then frowned as her thoughts turned to Charles. It would be so easy to cry today. The lack of sleep took her to the brink. But she was determined to tap into the uglier side of sleep deprivation and, once again, went through the conversation she would be having with the receptionist at the check-in desk.

The silver lining for the day was that all she had to do was meet this German guy Hans – or was he Austrian? – sign a contract, have a look around the building and board a plane home. Surely, she would be able to do this.

There was a refreshment tray in the corner of the room. A small, portable kettle with sachets of coffee, tea and sugar were neatly stacked. The biscuit was some sort of rich tea with raisins pressed in for good measure... Why would anyone ruin a biscuit this way? Raisins were for babies with nubbins for teeth. She did not indulge in the room's coffee cart. Once, she had gone to Blackpool with a gang of friends from work and one of them had shit in the kettle. Like, really, who does that? But the memory had made a lasting impression and she guessed that there were hotel-kettle-shitting freaks all over the world.

Surprisingly, the shower had managed to wash away a few of the cobwebs and she did actually feel more human, although her eye bags were still puffy and black. She prodded them in turn with her finger and hoped that they might deflate. She decided that a strong concealer needed to be applied if she wanted Hans to take her seriously.

The room was dim, so it was hard to see if her efforts were really paying off or if, in fact, in the harsh light of day, her makeup would be overkill. Either way, a trowel might be required to remove the layers of foundation and liquid concealer. *Fuck it.* If Yves Saint Laurent was selling it, then it had it to be good shit.

There was no way she could eat breakfast at this hotel. That was, if the seedy knocking shop with the flashing red light even served breakfast. Perhaps there was a menu for the special kind of room service that you could order here. She thought of the fat German man and a cold shiver ran up her spine, the hairs on her arms abruptly standing on end.

Her suit wasn't too crumpled. The cracked-open suitcase had served its purpose well and she was actually rather pleased with the image she would be presenting today, all things said and done.

She weaved the cling film back around her case and chuckled a little to herself. Staggering how eventful her life was; her time for sharing her experiences was long overdue. She flipped on her iPhone and fired up the WhatsApp group, where Joe was now an honorary member. It was time to tell her story, from the pissing lady on the plane to the arse-slapping pineapple sex scene, to pissing herself and the knocking shop antics.

It wasn't long before the girls chimed in.

'A fucking pineapple..........WTAF'. Even Lucy was astounded by that part of the story, even though she would no doubt at some point be trying it for herself.

'They came into your room, that's terrible George'. Bella was probably already Googling complaint links.

'Again, why do you have soooo much fun without me, why couldn't she piss on you while I was there? FFS George......Timing!' Once again, Debs was just hacked off because she missed the whole debacle.

'LMAO XX'. Short and sweet message from Jen, probably stressed to the max getting the baby ready for nursery.

'Sounds disgusting. I'd have charged her for some new shoes'. A true Carmen response if ever there was one. Image and reputation always came first.

'You okay G, Charles been in touch'. Joe's response was off kilter compared to the others; George hadn't shared her ugly news with the world yet, but here it was, large as life.

'What's this about Charles?' Carmen had obviously read between the lines.

'He's moving to California……but all good, look at me the jet setter'. George tried to put a positive spin on it. She didn't want everyone to know how terrible she felt inside, but it was genuinely hard.

'Fuck a German, hung like horses?' Lucy quickly responded, as always, taking the conversation back to sex. Surprisingly, she continued: 'I need to tell you all something.'

'Come on then, spit it out', Shaz chimed in, thinking Lucy might've caught the clap or something from all the shagging.

'Well you know how you haven't seen that Jarvis bloke for a while…….' Lucy was treading cautiously, which aroused suspicion amongst the girls.

'You bloody didn't. Did you???" George was quickly onto her and couldn't quite believe what she imagined Lucy was about to say.

'Of course I did G. I'm a woman with needs, he's a young lad, plenty of stamina, in fact we do it TWICE when we meet up, he got put onto my round a couple of weeks ago'. Lucy was completely unashamed. 'He's like my Monday morning working from home SHAG, sets you up for the day you know girls, you should try it'.

'I'd rather stick a fork in my eye Lucy'. George screwed up her face in disgust, wincing at the thought of Jarvis so much as stroking her arm.

'I've got some news too', added Joe with a couple of heart emojis.

'Come on then lad spill, we've all got to get off to work in a minute'. Debs was never one for mincing her words.

'I'm moving in with Alfredo, he asked me the other night, I'm so excited'. Another couple of star emojis, followed by some hearts. Joe was obviously ecstatic and George was happy that at least one of them was proving lucky in love.

'Amazing Joe, great news'. George really was pleased for her friend even though it poked at the sickly feeling in her stomach, a feeling of disappointment which rattled her torturous inner voice into flight.

'Thanks G, love ya, drinks when you get home, Joe X'.

The rest of the girls rushed to congratulate their new friend on his blossoming romance with Alfredo.

'Congrats Joe X', offered Carmen, who was surely already thinking about what sophisticated gift she could buy them both.

'Nice one lad, sounds like we need to have a drink to toast your news'. Good old Debs, loving anything that got the group thinking about a pissed-up celebration.

'Bless ya Joe, I'm made up for you X'. Shaz was the last one to offer Joe some good cheer. Jen was probably already tucking the baby into the back seat of her car, ready for nursery. Anything to avoid nappies and baby poop all day.

'Hope you are okay G, phone me later'. Carmen knew George better than she knew herself. She wouldn't fall for her lousy attempt at positivity and Carmen must have understood why George didn't want to share how she truly felt with the others.

George locked her phone screen.

It was time to show these hotel motherfuckers exactly who they had messed with.

Cat Got Your Tongue?

George waited her turn at the shoddily decorated reception desk. It appeared that the old lady from the previous evening was not working this morning, which was a shame, as George was surely going to recount the seedy back door entrance, with its flashing red light and lack of assistance with her luggage. (Roxanne, eat your heart out.)

Her body language told its own story: arms folded, foot out in front, toe tapping impatiently, with the occasional eye roll thrown in to emphasise her annoyance.

Finally, it was her turn. She would get to regurgitate the story she had been practising since 4.00 that morning. Suzie was another old dear who worked at the hotel, with twinkling blue eyes, false teeth, weathered skin and a small tuft of yellowish hair worn in a bun on her head. *Packet dye*, thought George. It was unevenly distributed along the strands of her hair and big blocks of grey roots were on display. Suzie politely called George forwards and complimented her on her fine suit and pretty eyes.

The compliment felt good and disarmed George of her intention to attack. Suzie enthusiastically informed George that the hotelier had purchased her a new suitcase – one which was just the type that busy professionals like herself would own.

Opening the little hatch which separated the reception desk from the front of the hotel, Suzie wheeled in, to George's delight, what had to be the most elegant Calvin Klein suitcase she'd ever laid her eyes on.

George found herself grinning appreciatively but recalled that she did indeed have some topical business that she needed to discuss with the receptionist, as amazing as Suzie was.

'Last night,' George began shakily, 'I, er... I had a bit of a fright.' As she spoke, the lady that had been having her arse slapped with a pineapple the previous evening pulled up beside her, elbows propped idly on the reception desk, a look of boredom etched across her face. George did a double take. Now she was too embarrassed to vocalise her discontent and wondered if the fat German dude was also in the queue to speak to the receptionist.

Suzie dutifully took charge.

'There's no formal check-in necessary, Ms Jackson. It's all been sorted by your company. I do hope the new suitcase is to your satisfaction.'

George briefly froze and looked from Suzie to pineapple girl, then back to Suzie, as if in a trance. She collected her new suitcase, all thoughts now of kicking off evaporating like hot steam from a kettle.

Back in her room, perched on the end of her bed, George replayed what had just happened. She had gone to the reception desk with such great intentions and had left without saying a single word, although now she did own some designer luggage. She smiled as the penny dropped. She'd just been duped by a sweet little old woman who cashed in on the laws of psychology, social reciprocation and flattery. *Why, that old dog,* thought George. But, to be fair, it had totally worked.

She chalked the experience up as the tide turning in her favour. The magic three count was back on, but this time it was the first of three good things that would happen to her.

Sweaty Lips

The designer house was a charming 18th century building which boasted an elaborate exterior and intricate designs carved deep into the stone. George smiled. It felt good to be a part of something that felt so sophisticated and grown up. The sliding doors opened as the detector sensed her presence.

Hiring assistants in Germany clearly came with the same specifications as they had back in the UK. The tall brunette with flawless skin and full red lips welcomed her with a generous smile and showed her to a seat. She informed George that Hans would be down to collect her in about five minutes.
Her mind ramblings were off. What she noticed about her company's beautiful PAs was that they all came with a healthy dose of good looks and personal charisma – a great mix, to be sure. She congratulated her company's winning recruitment formula. Along the years, attractiveness had subconsciously entrapped even the smartest of people at one time or another.

Hans appeared and enthusiastically clapped his hands. He made no attempt to hide his appreciation for the tall assistant's bum; he smacked it hard as she leaned over the counter to retrieve a pen. He practically salivated like a dog.

Hans was a fleshy chap, about 5'4", with shoulder-length, dodgy, permed brown hair. He wore a tight-fitting navy suit. His most distinguishing feature was his big lips, exactly like those of a giant Gourami fish, pouty and sweaty. George recalled a bloke that Bella had kissed when they were kids. She'd never gotten over it. His lips had been like inflatable dinghies and Bella'd had spit all over her face from a snog that had lasted less than 15 seconds.

George hoped that their encounter would be brief. There was something about Hans that she found completely intolerable given that they hadn't yet exchanged a single word.

She stood to receive his hand and shook it firmly, aware of how his eyes took in every inch of her body. His facial expression suggested that he was less than pleased with what he was being presented with.

Charming, thought George. Some fat guy was publicly appraising her assets with his eyes as if he were some sort of demigod. Perhaps she was missing something.

'Ah, George, delighted, I'm sure. You're so much shorter than I imagined! Come, come, follow me to the office.' Hans spoke quickly. His impeccable English was cloaked in an authoritarian German accent.

She rolled her eyes. Her inner voice chimed in bitterly. *And you're a lot fatter than I expected, dude with huge, sweaty lips. But hey – DNA is a game of Russian roulette.*

She followed Hans, as instructed, and she was taken aback as every bum pinch or obvious tit ogle was met with gratitude from the beautiful ladies adorning his office. George was baffled. Just the sight of those enormous lips had her completely on edge and she backed away for fear of drowning in the sweat that dripped from his chops. Bella's experience had been enough for the both of them.

Hans had a large office on the first floor. Everything was white and spread out; her sitting on the chair made the place look messy, and she thought she caught a look from Hans which implied that he thought exactly the same thing.

'Okay, so this shouldn't take long. I have the contract somewhere. Let me find it, I just need you to read it through and sign it. Ms King always insists on having someone come over – won't let me send it via mail. Very strange.' Hans leafed through a number of papers scattered across his desk, and his eyes lit up as he identified the correct one.

'Here we are,' he exclaimed excitedly and shook the papers in the air. George was convinced that if he bent over, his trousers would rip. The gusset was practically eaten by his left arse cheek.

He confidently placed the papers in George's lap and rested one Jeremy Beadle-sized hand on her knee for a rather unpleasant few seconds.

'Time for coffee,' he announced merrily. 'Let's give you a moment alone to review without any interruptions.'

Hans swished his permed hair from side to side, parting his fringe with his fingers. George resisted the urge to laugh. She had at least another two hours with this egomaniac. The plan was to read the contract quickly, look for anything that appeared to be out of line, question as needed, sign, then get the fuck out of there.

The first few paragraphs were pretty standard, but as she got to some of the smaller print, there were a number of penalties weaved in that felt more than just a little OTT. *Shit*. On second thought, she would take the contract with her and give it some deep thought on the journey home before she signed up for anything. What was this fat little man up to? From the fabric acquisition to the carrier costs, she would be agreeing to some pretty excessive penalties if a single detail was out of line.

'Ta da.' Hans was back with two coffees. Evidence from his office whoring was on his right cheek in the form of a red lipstick mark. He set the cups down on the clinical white coffee table and pulled out a tube of lip balm from his inner jacket pocket. With precision, he applied a liberal layer. His lips became larger than life and glistened as he rubbed them together for maximum effect.

He looked at George pitifully and offered her the lip balm, which she politely refused. The very thought caused a small amount of vomit to rise up at the back of her throat. She swallowed hard.

Her phone vibrated. It was a much-needed distraction. She apologised to Hans and took out her phone. It was her mum, who was, once again, bringing greetings from the grave.

'Hello darling, Bob from number 52 is dead, he had terrible bunions you know, oh and the smell from that ulcer on his leg… it's a blessing for us all you know. I should help clean up his house but I can't face it darling'.

In normal circumstances, George would mumble a 'FFS', roll her eyes and delete the message without a second thought… but this was no normal situation. She decided to use her mum's death calling to her advantage.

George skilfully applied her best resting bitch face and turned to Hans, who was immediately aware of the change in energy. She told him of the bad news she had just received about Uncle Bob and how she needed to get back to the UK, quick smart. She would not be able to sign the contract right now, but she would have them back to him at the earliest opportunity.

It appeared that even demigods like Hans had a heart when it came to death. He ushered her busily towards the door. Unfortunately for George, she never banked on the long lingering kiss he left on her forehead as he said goodbye.

Outside in the fresh air, she dug deep in her handbag and rifled amongst the tampons until she found a tissue. The repulsive spit spot was already air-drying on her forehead. Bella was not wrong when she said that men with big sweaty lips were to be avoided at all costs. Hans was such a dick splash.

Airport Purchase

Entirely satisfied with dodging the Hans bullet, George decided to spoil herself. The airport was full of overpriced tat, but she didn't care. She would indulge regardless. She settled on a small brown leather handbag from a boutique the size of her en-suite. Tassels hung from the fringe and whilst she wasn't quite sure about her new purchase, she knew she could always palm it off on her mother as a prezzie should she change her mind at a later date. Her mother would be thankful to not be on the receiving end of a half-eaten airport Toblerone, which had become her staple holiday present... not that this trip could be classified as a holiday.

The shop assistant made polite conversation and congratulated George on such a great choice. Her exaggerated flamboyance was completely lost on George, who nodded weakly in response. The smugness she felt having escaped a day with Hans was quickly replaced with the dull ache of detachment which hurt far worse than any physical pain she had ever endured. She thought about Charles and wondered what he might be up to and if he'd thought of her at all. Scrolling to the notes section of her iPhone she began to list her favourite Ryan Reynolds movies. She had a huge hole to fill, and past experience had taught her well. If you wanted to get over a bloke then this was the only way to do it.

On a more positive note George's new salary meant that she could save 10% of her wages in an ISA like a real grownup. In addition to this, she had set up the Moneybox app on her phone which would deduct £100 a month from her wages, and she could contribute an additional £20 per week if she was feeling flush.

Withdrawing money via the app took three weeks, so she knew that she wouldn't be able to make any rash decisions or blow her money on extravagances she could do without. Firing up the app and watching her money grow gave George a sense of self-worth. From here on out, she would most certainly be taking care of everything in her life by herself. Recognising that her alone time would increase since she was not seeing Charles anymore, she also enrolled in some Spanish classes at the local college. George had always fantasised about living in Spain so this was the first step in making her dreams a reality. Taking small steps towards her goals didn't remove the ache for Charles, but the precise feeling of gratification was a good one. *Fuck men*, she thought dryly. She would become successful and happy without one. The rabbit deluxe vibrator was definitely coming back onto the pitch.

Next stop was the wine and cheese shop since she had skim-read the Sue Perkins autobiography. She intended to buy some of the smelliest cheese she could find. Her intention was to adopt the Perkins family tradition of hiding said cheese in an unusual place in a friend's house. The very thought brought a devious smile to her lips.

All shopped out after one boutique purchase and one very smelly cheese transaction, it was time to scrutinise the contract handed to her by the womaniser Hans. The airport had many restaurants and coffee shops, so she carefully selected one where she felt she would go relatively undisturbed. There was no way that she would let sweaty-lipped Hans the Dick Splash get one over on her. It was a shame that the pong from the cheese was making her eyes water. The trip home sat next to some randomers would be very interesting indeed. She considered if she should share that the odour wasn't actually coming from her body. Then she remembered the fanny mist on the way there and she thought, *To hell with it – best to keep them guessing.*

Hope

It was one of the longest weeks of her life. Never ever would she get shitfaced on a school night again. Her head pounded incessantly. She grumpily turned off her alarm and dragged her bones into the shower, which made her think of Charles. Damn that fine man. Without thought, she collected her dirty laundry from her new designer suitcase, deposited the lot into her washing machine and twisted away at a few knobs. She never really understood what any of it meant. Her iron also escaped her, the maddest thing, with various cloud symbols and dials. It was all way too complicated.

The contract had tuned out to have a number of penalty clauses embedded in the small print, none of which George felt inclined to sign up for. She would point out these details to Ms King first thing. After work, she intended to lock the doors and spend the weekend on the couch in her onesie and watch endless movies of Ryan Reynolds. She could hear Carmen's jeering voice in her head but she didn't care. She was well and truly beyond convincing that there was any other way.

Her usual quick pace to the office was replaced with a more subdued shuffle, her energy quickly fading. Her face said it all. She wore a mask of misery, her hair was greasy and she sported a rather unflattering dress with geometric prints (probably a drunk shopping purchase with Shaz).

Bumping into Hilary Bloom was the absolute last thing she needed as she entered the foyer. George lowered her eyes and hoped to escape her gaze. She wasn't in the mood for a fight today. Besides, she hadn't rehearsed what she would say about the photo incident, that bloody witch. Hilary was all sing-songy and shouted 'Darling!' before she insisted that George come over and give her a kiss.

How dare this woman so blatantly call out to her as if they were friends after sharing such a vile picture of her round the office? Bloody models. Again she considered dodging but knew all too well that it was in her best interest to avoid negative feedback from top sought-after models. Since she was not doing too well with karma these days, she wasn't going to leave anything to chance.

Hilary looked amazing, as usual, in a floaty summer skirt, pleated perfection with a soft pink satin blouse. Her makeup and hair were impeccable, as usual, and George inwardly groaned as Hilary pecked her on the cheek. Her teeth reflected the light as she smiled broadly.

'Well, hello, George. Looking slightly better than the other week – where were you running with some pooch? And was it, er, *poo* on your face?' Hilary enjoyed George's pained expression and considered how far to push her.

George seethed inside.

'Pooch? Poo on my face?' was all George could muster. She wanted to scream at Hilary. Why was she such a bitch? She knew that if she caused any offense to Hilary she could end up in some serious trouble and so decided to style it out.

'I took the dog out, went to pick up his poo and he kicked it at me. That's all there is to it, really.' The words fell out of her mouth in a matter-of-fact, cheery, not-arsed kind of way. She enjoyed the fact that Hilary wasn't expecting her to be so transparent with the truth.

'Great picture of me going around the office. Had me laughing for ages.' Her tone was one of gaiety. George was thinking fast on her feet and the twisted Hilary was almost lost for words.

Hilary shook her head.

'Oh, right. Anyway, half-expected to see you at Charles Cunningham's leaving party last night.'

There it was, another low blow. This woman knew exactly how to get at George's very core. The news cruelly slapped her in the face.

'Oh, Charles's party. I, er, don't think I was invited.'

George tried her best to hide the hurt from her voice. She felt both annoyed and betrayed. They had worked together professionally all these years. At the very least, he owed her an air of civility.

'Well, that's not what he said, darling. In fact, I'm sure he asked me at least twice if I'd seen you. Poured his heart out to me over some woman. Said he'd sent her a big text saying he'd made a big mistake and that he loved her and that she hadn't even bothered to text back, blah blah blah. Dreadful bore, you know. He's rolling out on the tenth at 2.'

Hilary wafted her arm and narrowed her beady eyes to make her point. George was caught off guard. She hadn't received a text from him. Maybe he had some other woman, like she'd always expected. Either way, she needed to find her iPhone. A glimmer of hope flickered; the mere mention of his name jolted her awake like a shot of adrenalin.

'The tenth at 2?' enquired George shyly, not wanting to be bitten by Hilary's sharp tongue for a third time.

'Yes, that's when the old bore is leaving,' Hilary dryly laughed.

Hilary was already bored of teasing her. She knew that Charles was pining over George. How utterly tedious, especially since she was hoping to get her claws into him that evening. What a dish. Why was someone like Charles besotted with a loser like George? It completely baffled Hilary and had scuppered her plans for getting her leg over and potentially earning some new introductions to the Californian circuit.

Hilary dismissively looked at George. She was pleased at having made at least a little chink in her armour and was unaware of Charles's love for her. Hilary wasn't about to let her in on that secret and knew that George would be crushed if she believed that she had not been invited to the leaving party.
Hilary spied her opportunity to leave George with the anguish of her thoughts and ran over to Karl, all teeth and smiles. The two of them kissed each other on both cheeks, laughing just a little too loudly. George was unmoved. The pair of arseholes were welcome to one another.

George locked herself in the toilet cubicle and rifled through her bag in a frenzy to find her phone. Her iPhone was nowhere in sight. She tried desperately to think about where it could be but had no memory of having left the house with it. She would have to share the contract details with Ms King and use the same excuse that she'd used on Hans to get out of work early. Her sanity and future happiness depended on it. Telling lies to get out of work, she believed, would come back to bite her on the bum, but she rationalised with herself that the death text was real, and without Charles, she already felt like a little bit of her was dying. The risk with karma was worth taking.

Ms King was impressed with George's keen eye for detail as she pointed out the specific lines in the contract associated with the heavy monetary penalties. Ms King gritted her teeth. It was obvious that she hadn't been expecting any of this to be there. Once again, George felt proud for having added some value through her new role. George continued to tell Ms King that there was a death in the family and that she needed to leave earlier, if at all possible.

Ms King, whilst a ball breaker with a rare lack of conversational skills, was still a little human, and she insisted that George leave right away.

'George!' she called as she was about to leave her office. 'What did you make of Hans?'

Eeek. What to say? Play it safe and make up some bullshit story? She had no idea what Ms King's relationship was like with the guy. However, she trusted her instincts and decided that honesty was always the best policy. She said just two words: 'Dick splash'.

Ms King was a little surprised with George's choice of language but light-heartedly laughed.

'Dick splash indeed. Well, you are a great judge of character, George. Now, go on. Get on home.'

The Phone

Her house looked as though it had been burgled by a couple of crackheads. She tossed cushions, magazines and anything else that lay around out of the way as she hunted for her iPhone. It was absolutely nowhere in sight. In fact, the last time she could remember using it was in the airport to call a cab.

She sat on the couch and sobbed with her head in her hands. Perhaps she'd left it in the cab and would never see it again. She called a timeout by putting the kettle on. A nice cup of tea was just what the doctor ordered. The kettle rattled steadily and she decided to multitask as she waited for it to boil. She dragged her wet clothes from the washing machine one by one to place them on the maiden to dry.

The mystery of the iPhone was very quickly solved, as there, under the pile of clothes, was one very wet, one very dead, iPhone. She looked on in horror. What a complete fuckup. She had lost everything – all her contacts, all her messages and now she would never know if she was the woman that Charles was talking about with Hilary.

She screamed. The neighbours would think that she was in some sort of terrible distress, but this was an emergency. She picked up two small plates that were on the dish drainer and angrily threw them to the floor. Porcelain shards scattered indiscriminately across the floor.

'Mother of fucks. You fucking twat, wanker, bastard.' The anger gave way to huge sobs. She might as well have been at a funeral. She was eaten up, a woman teetering on the edge. The pongy cheese that she'd left on the side filled her nostrils and enraged her senses. She lifted the cheese from the smooth plastic packet and beat it against the kitchen cupboards like a madwoman on meth. The cheese firmly held its own and released more toxic fumes the more it was shaken.

She fell to the floor, broken, the smelliest cheese in the world in hand. She cried a year's worth of tears while rocking back and forth. Life was really unfair.

Fuck the chimp paradox. Why did that phenomenon have to be true? Why couldn't she have her cake and eat it when there were so many woman roaming the earth with it all? Hilary Sodding Bloom with her perfect tits and perfect little life. Fucking bitch. She wailed for what felt like an hour until there were no more tears. Her face was all red and blotchy and her hair looked like she'd taken a 100-volt shock from all of the cheese banging. The plan was to draw the curtains and go on mourning as long as she had Ryan Reynolds and take-away menus. She was undeniably down, but she was most certainly not out.

Misery

George lay across her couch in an unattractive Tigger onesie. Various empty biscuit and popcorn wrappers cluttered the floor. There were half-drunk mugs of tea amongst empty wine bottles; it was like the couch was her island and the debris that floated around her were signs that she was still alive.

Having destroyed her iPhone, she had pulled the house phone over and propped it up on the end of the couch. With the exceptions of Carmen and her mum, she couldn't think of anyone else that had her number, but strangely, its presence offered a little comfort.

The curtains blocked out all natural light while she watched back-to-back films that featured Mr R. She ate and drank any calorific rubbish she could get her hands on. Without Facebook, Snapchat and WhatsApp, she felt truly detached and isolated. The world could've been falling apart for all she knew, but she was here, trapped in her own little bubble of misery. She considered herself to be quite Medusa-like in that just one look from her could attach bad karma to you for life and hit you with an instant feeling of misfortune and mayhem. Having endured so much of her own, she decided that the drawn curtains were for the safety of the world outside. She had to protect her neighbours from her run of bad luck.

She closed her eyes and drifted off. She had no idea of the time and decided that on her island all behaviour was acceptable. It was nice to stop the constant inner chatter, that voice which tortured her and scrutinised every aspect of her and Charles's relationship. She must've got something wrong in addition to the tramp kissing and table fire fiascos, she'd just not managed to work it out yet.

Her slumber was interrupted by the loud ringing of the house phone. She was surprised and a little frightened, as she had not heard the jingle for some time. Whomever it was, they were persistent. It was either the PPI people or her mother and, feeling the way she did right now, it was actually a great time to give them a piece of her mind.

It was Beryl. She rolled her eyes and smiled. At least she was right about some things. Her mum talked quickly and angrily. George pulled the phone away from her ear as her mother's pitch rose with intensity.

'Are you listening to me?'

Aware that she was only catching every other word, she brought the phone back up to her face.

'Mum, can you calm down? I'm struggling to keep up.' George smiled. Her response was tame. She could've gone all sullen and hostile on her arse but chose a more adult approach.

'That bag you gave me, George, where did you get it?'

'What, the tassley thing?'

'Yes, the tassley thing, where did you get it?'

'I bought it at the airport.' She considered her response. The airport smacked of presents bought as afterthoughts. She added '...in a very expensive boutique.'

'Huh, well, it's caused me a whole lot of bother.' George rolled her eyes again and mimicked her mother's voice.

'I was in Marks & Spencer – I'm a regular, you know – and as I was about to leave, I set off the door alarms.'

'You what?' George had no idea what her mother was rambling on about.

'Yes, dear, I set off the door alarm! Two big burly security guards marched me to the office in front of everyone to check inside my bag.'

George was now listening intently. The story caught her interest and offered a little humour – someone else's karma as always was comedy gold.

'The reason I'd set off the alarm, dear, is because of that tassley bag you got me.' Her mother's tone was now very direct and accusatory.

'How did the bag set off the door alarm, mother? It's leather with TASSLES!'

'They'd not bothered to take off the security tag hidden in the little zip pocket, had they? Terrible experience. Everyone thought I was a shoplifter. Can you believe it? Me! People thinking I'M A SHOPLIFTER.'

George was stuck for words and covered the mouth part of the phone with her hand. She held the receiver away from her face as she laughed a very wicked, very deep, laugh.

'George, are you still there? I'm furious. I've asked for a written apology and in the future I will be double-checking everything you buy me.'

George went to hang up but her mother had beaten her to it, clearly one very disgruntled old lady. Giving away the bag, however, was a success. She'd managed to avoid the ordeal that was somehow in store for her; her gut instinct appeared to be in fully working order.

Snuggling back down under the duvet on her couch, sly smile tracing her lips, she was disturbed for a second time, this time by a loud knocking at the door. She froze. There was absolutely no way she could answer it. She was in her onesie and the place looked like a bomb had hit. Carmen shouted through the letter box.

'G, it's me! Open up – I'm not leaving!'

The wind had picked up and Carmen must've been freezing. Maybe she would give up.

George buried her head underneath the duvet and looked for an escape as Carmen continued to bang away on her front door. She continued to lift the letter box to shout through her commands.

George felt dreadful. She couldn't leave her oldest and dearest friend out in the cold. Huffing like a spoiled child, she threw the duvet off the couch to expose the glory of her body wrapped in the most hideous onesie ever created by man. Burnt orange had never really done much for her complexion (or anyone else's, now she came to think of it).

She walked the short distance to her door and her limbs ached from being stationery for too long. She steadied herself and inhaled sharply before she let Carmen in, who would likely be full of advice and one-liners. 'Plenty more fish in the sea' and all that – the standard crap that friends said to one another in an attempt to cheer them up.

The second she unlocked the front door, Carmen charged through, swiftly followed by Bella, Debs, Lucy and Shaz. A full military coup had been carefully planned and was being executed. As she re-entered her living room, the toxic fog that she had been so blissfully unaware of hit her full-on.

Carmen pulled open the curtains and opened the windows to let in a little air. Bella picked up the stray packets thrown randomly around the room. Debs took charge of the TV. She shut off Ryan Reynolds and shot George a look of *what the fuck*. Her friends had seen her down before, but this was an all-time low.

Carmen patted the seat next to her on the couch and insisted that George come and sit down next to her. There was nowhere to run, so even when George thought she might bolt, her Olympian power would fail her – with five friends in the room, she didn't stand much chance of overpowering them all.

The wind blew through the window and knocked over a tall grey vase. The noise shook George awake. Carmen patted the seat again and, like a compliant puppy, George did as she was instructed.

'When does Charles leave?'

George heard the question but sat mute and unresponsive. Carmen quickly became fed up and shook her best friend by the shoulder.

'G, when does he leave?'

The girls anxiously awaited George's answer. Her face was dotted with remnants of a kebab she'd munched on earlier.

'If you must know, he leaves at 2. Leaves this godawful weather and me, his godawful girlfriend... ex-girlfriend,' she corrected herself.

Carmen rolled up her sleeve to check the time on her watch.

'We can make it. We can still make it. Up, get up!'

Carmen pushed George with all her might, who was now totally bewildered by what was going on. Debs spat on her hand and rubbed around George's mouth; she screamed out in disbelief. This type of thing hadn't happened to her since she was five in school when her mother would spit-wipe her face clean before waving goodbye.

Shaz, a distinct glint of revenge in her eyes, offered to find George some suitable clothes. She was still furious at the whole festival kidnapping fiasco, when George was responsible for packing her bag. George opened her mouth to protest, but it was too late. Carmen was barking orders for Shaz to find George's coat. Wherever they were going, she would still be wearing her onesie... nice. Shaz looked back, smiled appreciatively and winked at George.

'Don't worry, Jackson, I'll find you a nice one.'

There it was again, that *every dog has its day* signal, but since George had had more than her fair share of days. She decided that whatever the purpose of the military coup, she might as well play along.

Shaz returned with a very unflattering buffalo fur jacket, which looked like the skin had been ripped off the back of a dead animal. She'd bought the imitation coat from a second-hand shop for a fancy-dress night out and hadn't seen the damn thing in years.

Lucy covered her nose. It wasn't moth balls… the coat smelt like it had once been alive and had been rotting in the back of some cupboard for years. George wasn't sure that the coat had any saving grace, even if it was nearly floor-length and would protect her from the weather. Debs smirked and gave Carmen a thumbs-up as Shaz finished fastening the tooth-shaped buttons on George's flamboyant coat.

'Let's go, let's go!' Carmen shouted to assemble the girls by the door. She pushed them outside one by one.

'In the car, girls. Get George in the back between you.'

There was one very obvious problem: entirely more people than legal passenger seats. Debs quickly did the sums, shrugged and heaved herself into the back of the car.

There was a knock on the window. It was Joe, who was tightly holding a beautiful pink orchid. Debs opened the car door and ordered Joe to get in. He immediately obeyed, feeling somewhat threated. Given the circumstances and the already overcrowded vehicle, George could not fathom why Joe would follow such a ludicrous command. Her mates had gone barking fucking mad, crammed into a car like sardines, likely compelled to take George somewhere to make a total arse of herself.

The backseat was all moans and groans. George was perched on Lucy's knee and Joe was laid across the back of the car floor, plant held firmly in the air. Carmen ignored the fact that she was breaking about a thousand laws. She put her foot down and ordered Bella to switch on Smooth FM.

'George, I can't believe Ryan Reynolds is your go-to when you're not feeling yourself. What about The Rock or Vin Diesel... a man with some brawn.' Lucy licked her lips seductively.

The girls, plus Joe, nodded in agreement. George rolled her eyes. Apparently she made bad choices even in a depressive state. Why did Lucy get to set the tone for taste in men, having shagged the putrid Jarvis?

They were in the fast lane of the motorway. Drizzly rain showed up to accompany the blustery winds. Carmen felt that they better get George's head straight so she started walking her through the plan.

'Okay, so, George: We are going to be at the airport in five minutes. When we get there, we need you to find the check-in desk for California so you can find Charles.'

Carmen turned to face them in the back as she spoke, which sent Joe into a frenzy. He now genuinely feared for his life, as he lacked any kind of seatbelt to protect him in case of a collision.

'Arghhhhhhhhh, turn around, you silly woman!' Joe screamed like a girl. It was hilarious. He added, 'And why should George beg for this Charles? He's not exactly begged for *her*.'

Debs kicked Joe, which caused him to scream again.

'What was that for?!' The pink orchid wobbled as Joe rubbed his arm. He shot Debs a look of utter disgust, who simply smiled in response.

'Turns out he loves George. Sent a big text to explain. But dozy arse here has only gone and washed her iPhone.'

George couldn't quite believe what Carmen was saying. How could she know that he had sent her a text?

'That bitch Hilary Bloom was at an art exhibition I attended last night. She told me everything. I may have spilled a little champagne on her when it was clear that she hadn't bothered to tell you that Charles had literally spent all night moping over you, upset that you hadn't responded to his text or attended his leaving party.' The girls and Joe cheered. Carmen wasn't one for causing a scene, but nobody got away with treating her friends like shit, no matter who they were.

George's eyes lit up. She rubbed her fingers together and continued with the spit wash Debs had started earlier.

'He loves you, George,' Carmen said sweetly. The car jerked as Carmen accelerated, and the pink orchid had to be rescued for a third time, as the commotion pushed Debs forwards, which elicited some muffled Italian swear words from Joe. His arm must've been killing him, as not one of them offered to hold the pretty flower while he lay jammed, limbs all twisted on the car floor.

A chorus of 'Hungry Eyes' broke out; Smooth FM delivered a shot of enthusiasm as they made the turn for the airport. George felt her heartbeat accelerate. She needed to find Charles and tell him how she felt since her life had been a disaster since they'd not been together.

Carmen pulled the car into a space and there was a mad scramble for people to get out. Debs accidentally knocked the pink orchid to the ground and smashed the pot as she dragged her feet over Joe's head. She looked back, unfazed; apologising wasn't really her thing. The mission was to get George to the airport, so fannying about with the orchid would have only wasted time.

'Go, George! Go get him!' The girls jumped and whooped in the air as George found her strength and set off at speed towards the departure terminal.

The terminal boards flashed with various destinations and a mixture of airlines. George's eyes darted wildly from one to the next trying to find the California flight. She had decided on the journey there that she would do whatever it took to convince Charles to stay – something she should've done when he'd told her about the job. Beg, plead... her pride would be in tatters, but hey, the guy was worth it. Try as she might, George could not find the check-in desk and time was quickly running out.

George approached one of the many customer service assistants and asked about the California flights and where she could find the check-in. The guy at the counter was tall, thin and very pale. Her plea registered only a look of annoyance on the young guy's face. He clearly had better things to do, such as play Tetris on his iPhone.

As the guy tapped away at his phone screen, George noticed just how big his hands were; the keyboard took a pounding from every touch. Her mind ramblings wanted to play, but she needed to remain focused on the job at hand. Finding Charles was her number one priority. He sighed, disinterested, and told her that the desk had closed ten minutes ago.

She screamed. She completely forgot herself. The check-in desk was closed – she was too late. The young man looked horrified as random passengers stopped what they were doing to look in their direction, intrigued by the pantomime shouting.

'Sorry about that,' said George, patting down her hair in an attempt to regain some decorum.

'I need to know if my friend has checked in. It's an emergency.' George was satisfied with her pleading tone, quite sure the young man would do just about anything to get rid of her.

'What's the emergency?' he muttered snootily. Boredom was etched across his face as he looked at the time on his watch. He was somehow more disinterested than ever.

'I can't tell you that,' replied George in haste. 'I just need to know if a Charles Cunningham has checked in.'

She drummed her fingers up and down on the counter, nerves frayed, patience depleted.

'We don't give out personal details,' said the man. He didn't even bother to look in her direction.

'Get me your boss,' George demanded, furious. The thin guy was now fully tuned into the conversation. His face snarled like someone had just stuck a plump finger up his arse.

'You heard me, skinny. Get me the head honcho,' she hissed. She was quite unprepared to take any more of this unhelpful man's bollocks.

The young lad called for a Mr Grimes on his radio. George assumed that Mr Grimes would be his boss. Unfortunately for her, she was way off. Mr Grimes turned out to be security.

The young assistant sat back in his chair, smiling, fully pleased with his little plan. His eyes dared George to do something about it. She considered running for the second time that day but Mr Grimes shot her a serious look and she decided to follow him without making any more of a fuss.

The Drive Home

Her heart sank as she left the terminal. George's loyal friends were grouped together, teeth chattering with the cold, excited to see their friend leave the airport with Charles... but she was alone.

Carmen broke rank and ran to meet George. It looked as though Charles must've already checked in and here was George being escorted from the terminal by head of security for her unruly behaviour. Debs stifled a laugh. Being thrown out of an airport was right up there in her world of crazy.

The friends piled back in the car; an unhappy silence replaced the earlier eagerness. Joe respectfully laid across the floor and cursed as Debs purposely rolled her foot over his chest while smiling and licking her lips. It was a small mercy that he was gay – he did not envy the man that would have to entertain her and satisfy her needs.

Carmen was fully aware that she would be dropping off George at the disturbing Ryan Reynolds pity party they had found her at earlier. She wondered if this latest setback would push her into an even worse state.

'I'm dropping you off at home, George, so you can get cleaned up, and then we are going for tea.' Carmen did not ask George: she told her. She emphasised her instructions by nodding as she spoke.

George looked at her long buffalo coat and laughed. No wonder airport security had thrown her out. She looked completely barmy!

'Okay.' She smiled at Carmen. She was done with wallowing. She still felt like shite but the knowledge that Charles loved her lifted her spirits. It was a far superior feeling to that of feeling unwanted. The grey cloud at least had a little rainbow now.

The car stopped and the process of everyone untangling their bodies begun so that George could get out. The car came alive with groans. Joe pulled himself upright and kept his eye on Debs. He knew that she would be in for a quick feel the minute his back was turned.

As she dragged her sad, buffalo-coated existence towards her house, George's heart almost stopped. There, sat at the side of her garden with his suitcase, was Charles. He stood to attention as soon as he saw George walking hastily down the path so he could greet her.

Joe knocked on the car and urged the girls to get out so they could witness what was about to take place. Charles ran to George, now like a man possessed.

'I needed to see you – I understand why you didn't text me. I'm so sorry.' He spoke quickly as he tried to explain.

George jumped in. She was pained to see just how upset he was.

'I washed my iPhone,' she said, aware that the words sounded better in her head than they did out loud. A gust of wind swept a string of snot up the side of George's cheek, and before she could wipe it away, Charles stepped in and used the sleeve of his jacket to wipe her face while using his other arm to pull her closer.

They stood there for a few seconds, inches from one another, undeniable chemistry burning between them.

'I can't believe you washed your iPhone.' The realisation was evident in his voice as he understood why she hadn't responded to his texts.

He pulled her closer still and passionately kissed her.

George's friends had gathered at the bottom of the garden. They cheered and wolf-whistled; this was what they all had been waiting for.

'So… you're not going to California?' George finally managed as they came up for air.

'And miss you in that furry delight?' He eyed up the buffalo coat sarcastically. 'Never.'

'I don't want to stop you from taking your dream job in California; it wouldn't be fair.' George couldn't believe what she was saying, but she knew it would become the unspoken elephant in the room that would eventually eat away at their relationship.

'Turns out I can have my dream job and still live here. Best of both worlds.'

George flew into his arms and kissed him intensely, not needing to hear another word. Her heart burst with love. All fears of bad karma melted away, and her thoughts quickly turned to the excitement she could feel growing in Charles's pants.

'Er, haven't you lot got somewhere to be?' George turned to face her faithful friends, winking wickedly as she eagerly led Charles by the hand into her house and out of sight.

Printed in Great Britain
by Amazon